P

"Pandian launches a supernatural cozy series that hits high marks for a modern twist on an ancient practice. Amusing supporting characters and historical details solidify this engaging mystery."
—*Library Journal*

"Pandian sets this series apart from other paranormal mysteries with Zoe's cute nonhuman sidekick and some mouthwatering vegan recipes." —*Publishers Weekly*

"This new series is off to an excellent start with an intriguing, eccentric amateur detective... This reviewer is eagerly anticipating more from this series, and a return of a cast more fun than an episode of Portlandia." —*RT Book Reviews*

"Zoe and Dorian are my new favorite amateur-sleuth duo!"
—Victoria Laurie, *New York Times* bestselling author

"*The Accidental Alchemist* is a recipe for a great read. Gigi Pandian's pen never disappoints." —Juliet Blackwell, *New York Times* bestselling author of the Witchcraft Mystery Series

"Mysterious, captivating, and infused with the rich history of the Northwest... fantastic." —*Portland Book Review*

"Readers won't want to put this book down." —*Vegetarian Journal*

THE ALCHEMIST OF FIRE AND FORTUNE

AN ACCIDENTAL ALCHEMIST MYSTERY

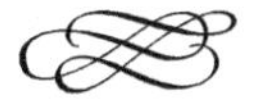

GIGI PANDIAN

GARGOYLE GIRL PRODUCTIONS

Gargoyle Girl Productions

First edition

Cover design by Gargoyle Girl Productions

Cover gargoyle illustration by Hugh D'Andrade/Jennifer Vaughn Artist Agent

Print ISBN: 978-1-938213-16-8

eBook ISBN: 978-1-938213-15-1

CHAPTER 1

The day was almost perfect enough for me to forget about the blackmail.

"Nitrogen Alchemy." Nicolas sniffed the pint glass in his hand as the wind picked up and blew his unruly hair around his face. "I don't know about this."

The crow's feet around his silver-blue eyes crinkled, so I knew he was smiling behind the murky glass. The horn-rimmed glasses with thick lenses amplified the effect. I'd been worried that today was too much for him, but he showed no signs of slowing down.

Nicolas, his wife Perenelle, and I were nestled into the far corner of one of the wooden slab tables set up for communal seating in the back garden of a new brewpub in Portland, underneath the shade of laurel trees. Snatches of sunlight filtered through the leaves onto their heads. Nicolas and Perenelle were one of those couples who had grown to look like each other. Their features were quite different, but their hair was so wild that if you saw them together you'd think they'd done it on purpose. The billowing waves of Perenelle's auburn tresses did as they pleased, and Nicolas's gray-infused curls had been known to pop a hat right off his head.

The two of them were new in town, and today was the day I'd promised them a full tour of the city. Nicolas had been ill for the past month, recovering from injuries sustained during a grievous attack. This was the first week he was deemed fit enough for a day on the town.

We started the day at Blue Sky Teas, the café run by my dear friend Blue, before walking to downtown Portland to visit Powell's Books. It was a long walk, but we had all grown up walking much longer distances than people think is normal these days. The excursion to the legendary independent bookstore had taken up far more hours than I'd planned on, as I should have known it would. Nicolas and Perenelle were endlessly curious. They always had been. It was well after lunchtime when we emerged with three bursting bags of books and had gone in search of sustenance.

I'd never been to this restaurant and brewpub before, but when Perenelle saw it was named PDX Alchemy, she'd insisted we try it. It was midafternoon and the outdoor seating area was less than half full. An assortment of people were engaged in animated conversations, from opinions on a new tract of tiny homes to speculation about a recent unsolved local museum heist at the Oregon Gold History Museum. The robbery resulted in one of the private museum's owners, Harrison Cabot, lying in a hospital bed in a coma. The heist had been carried out by a lone thief, but the spoils were immense: 20 gold nuggets, most of which were larger than anything ever seen before. Until I'd moved to Portland, I didn't know that the California Gold Rush also extended northward into Oregon, or that it had produced such fortune.

"I really don't know about this," Nicolas repeated, eyeing the dark beer and the images of a sun and moon etched into the glass.

Perenelle gave an encouraging nudge to her beloved husband.

With a look from her, he tilted the pint glass toward his lips. "*Magnifique*! Darling, have you sampled your ale yet?"

Perenelle graced him with a smile and held up her half-empty pint glass.

I needed to keep my wits about me to keep them out of trouble, so I'd ordered a glass of homemade ginger ale. Nicolas and Perenelle had each ordered beers with the word Alchemy in their titles. We were sharing a family-size basket of oven-crisped root vegetable chips while we waited for our main meals.

"You've found a wonderful home here, Zoe." Perenelle tilted her head toward the canopy of tree branches above us. It was a wistful look, the kind of smile filled with both genuine happiness and regret. With her eyes closed, perhaps she was thinking of her younger days in the French countryside.

She popped the last deep red beet chip into her mouth, then frowned. "I seem to have eaten everything myself. I didn't mean to do that. It appears I'm still making up for lost time." It was true. Perenelle had finished three quarters of the basket on her own, devouring the sweet potato, carrot, and beet slivers. I understood her impulse. After where she'd been, I'd be ravenous too.

Nicolas and Perenelle weren't my parents, but with the role they'd played when I was younger, they came close. I was thrilled to have them back in my life. They'd been through a lot, and while I wished I would have known about their peril earlier, I was glad I'd been able to help free them.

Perenelle gave a start and nearly dropped her beer as our waiter—a handsome twenty-something with tortoiseshell patterned glasses and a tattoo of an open book on his forearm—dropped off three plates of food at our table.

"Sorry to startle you." He gave her a charming smile and asked if we needed anything else.

Perenelle had been jumpy all week. I thought, at first, that she was backsliding in her adjustment to life in Portland. That the novelty had worn off, or that the worry for Nicolas was too much. I would have understood if that was the case. She was homesick for France, and her husband was recovering slowly from a near-fatal wound that affected him in unexpected ways. Some were minor, such as needing glasses for the first time. Some were more worrisome, such as how much he needed to sleep.

After the third day of hearing my floorboards creak under the weight of Perenelle's steps in the small hours of the night, I confronted her. That's when she showed me the note.

Blackmail.

She begged me not to tell Nicolas. It would stunt his recovery, she said. Even if he'd been well, I suspected she wouldn't have wanted to worry him.

"Might I trouble you for the alchemical formula for this brew?" Nicolas inquired of the waiter.

The waiter blinked at him. "You mean the recipe for the beer? I'm not sure I can give that to you…"

"Not a worry, good man." Nicolas flicked his fingers as a dismissal. "Off you go, then."

"Thank you," I added hastily, feeling my face flush. "They're visiting from abroad." Like that explained anything.

The waiter laughed before departing. I'm sure he was used to dealing with eccentric patrons.

"It's not polite," I said, "to dismiss wait staff."

"The ale," Nicolas declared as he chewed his first bite of food, "is far better than this pile of emerald and chartreuse-colored leaves."

I lifted a stainless-steel tumbler of apple cider vinaigrette and poured it over his grains and greens bowl. "Try it now."

He did so and grinned. "The ale is still better." He reached inside his jacket—one I'd obtained at a local thrift store while he was recuperating at my house—and extracted an empty glass vial with a cork stopper. He popped the cork and poured a measure of the beer inside it.

"You walk around with an empty vial in your jacket?"

"Three of them." He demonstrated the new pocket that secured two other vials. Nicolas had always been handy. "One never knows when one will discover something worth analyzing. Such as that note of yours, dear." He paused and locked eyes with Perenelle.

Perenelle's fork slipped from her grasp. "My note?"

"We've known each other for so, so many years, my love. Did you think I would not notice your distress? I know you did not wish to worry me, but in turn that worried me all the more. I hope you two did not pay this miscreant." He took another sip of beer and let out a satisfied sigh. "Yes, by the time I'm fully recovered, I'll have learned what alchemy they have used to create this delicious brew, and this blackmail nonsense will be cleared up."

"You knew." Perenelle burst out laughing and looked back and forth between me and Nicolas. "Zoe, he knew! You're truly not worried, my love?"

"There's no reason to give them any of our dwindling stores of precious gold," said Nicolas, "just because someone has discovered you're one of the greatest alchemists of all time."

CHAPTER 2

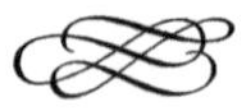

I should probably back up and explain that Nicolas and Perenelle aren't simply old friends who've been married since they were young. They've been together for more than 700 years. Nicolas was once my mentor. He was born in the early 14th century, though I didn't meet him until 1700. I was 24 years old at the time. Perenelle was never as famous as Nicolas. Yet in truth, she was more accomplished than her husband by far.

We're all alchemists. In a city like Portland, Oregon, the word "alchemy" is bantered about casually, used in the name of bars, restaurants, or herbal products. The name fits. Alchemy means transformation. Specifically, transforming the impure into the pure. That can mean different things to different people. To some, it's tangible changes to physical objects, like transmuting a dirty old piece of metal into a pristine chunk of gold. To others, it's the desire for immortality. It also applies to people seeking to elevate their consciousness.

In practice, many people practice a subtle form of alchemy without knowing it. When you take an old piece of junk found in a heap of trash and transform it into something beautiful and new, that's alchemy. It's also a transformation of the impure into the pure when you cast off a toxic way of life and heal your body and soul, perhaps by ridding your life of the people who hurt you and focusing your energy on planting a new garden.

Most people don't know that the more extreme forms of alchemy are indeed achievable. You might have heard of Nicolas in history books, as a scribe and bookseller who discovered a book of alchemy, and afterward he and his wife gave large amounts of money to charity. What you might not know is that when he and his wife's graves were exhumed after their deaths, their gravesites were empty.

They faked their deaths to change their identities and continue living on, making gold for charity and training apprentices they deemed worthy. I was one of those apprentices. My brother and I had fled our home of Salem Village as teenagers, and I was supporting us with the herbal tinctures I made. Nobody believed it was me, not my brother Thomas, with such an aptitude. Until Nicolas.

By the way, he looks absolutely nothing like the illustration of Nicolas Flamel that exists on the internet. When I showed him the illustration of a man with small eyes and a full beard covering a large chin, he laughed and laughed.

He and Perenelle do, however, look entirely human, since they are. Perenelle insists on wearing ankle-length skirts and dresses, claiming that slacks feel too confining. Otherwise, they fit in. With their bohemian hair, they *especially* fit in here.

The same couldn't be said of my housemate Dorian. Which is why he wasn't here with us today. He only explored the city under the cover of darkness.

"When did you find out about the blackmail?" Perenelle whisper-screamed at her husband. "And why didn't you ask me about it?"

"I believed you would come to me when you were ready. The night before last, you were up half the night pacing, stealing glances at a piece of paper. You dropped it in your exhaustion when you finally fell into a restless slumber at dawn. I found the note next to your skirts on the floor in our room. I understood immediately why you looked so distressed. I knew, too, why you did not come to me. You fear I'm too fragile. But my dearest, I feel better than I have in years. Now that I've demonstrated this to you today—we've walked more than 10 kilometers, have we not?—are you two ready to tell me what's going on?"

"Incorrigible man." Perenelle kissed his cheek and took his hand in hers.

"We didn't want to worry you," I said, "because we thought the same thing. There's nothing to be done. We all know that alchemy hides itself. People see what they expect to see. Even if the anonymous note-writer goes public with their video showing Perenelle performing an alchemical transformation—"

"There's a video?" Nicolas raised his bushy eyebrows. "This, I did not know."

"Not a high resolution one," I said, but their faces remained blank as I spoke. The two of them spoke near-perfect English, with only the faintest accents, but had gaps in their knowledge of the present-day world. They'd kept up with modern English and the current world in general, thanks to their inadvertent captors. But without being out in the world themselves, their knowledge was limited. I was glad the traumatic experience was already beginning to fade from their minds, but not what they'd learned from it.

"High resolution means a very good quality video," I explained. "The opposite of what they have of Perenelle." I would have worried more if there was a higher resolution video, but people knew that even that could be faked with CGI these days.

"You read the note," Perenelle said. "Did you not notice the website written at the bottom?"

"Ah!" Nicolas cried. "I assumed it was a code. I have never been the one good at ciphers."

"We weren't sure at first either." I lowered my voice. "But typing it into a browser took us right to a video showing Perenelle making gold. At the end there was a phone number to call once she'd created enough gold for a payoff."

"But as you both know," Perenelle added, "the threat of exposure isn't necessarily dire. Everyone sees only what they wish to believe. People today are as they have been throughout time: both marvelous and maddening." She sighed. "No matter. I have only managed to make one piece of gold. We couldn't pay the blackmailer at Elements Art House if we wanted to."

Nicolas grasped his fork like a dagger. "You know who it is? Tell me, who is this miscreant?"

"She doesn't know who it is," I cut in. "But we can narrow it down. They took a video from outside her rented studio at Elements Art House, through the high window, and they sent the note to her via the Elements mailing address. Which shows they know she practices art and alchemy there. But it also suggests they might not have a key to get inside when it's not open to the public for classes, because they sent the note in the mail instead of taking the risk of hand-delivering it."

Perenelle crinkled her freckled nose. The expression gave her a girlish look she had always hated. "Always wise beyond your years, Zoe."

Though all of my body except for my hair stopped aging physically when I was 28, I've been alive for 380 years. I hoped I'd gained some perspective in that time.

"Oh!" Nicolas pointed at a fried onion basket at the table across from ours. "What's that on that gentleman's plate?"

Perenelle's lips ticked up into a smile. "I shouldn't have worried about distressing him. His mind is racing from one thing to the next, as usual. And that steaming creation does look rather like a piece of art. It's shaped like a flower. Stop frowning, Zoe. Enjoy your meal."

But I was still worried. *I know what you are. I will keep your secret in exchange for 10 pieces of gold.* If a blackmailer realized what Perenelle was truly capable of, would they give up after one note?

CHAPTER 3

I awoke with the sun, as I always did.

Sitting on my back porch overlooking the thriving garden, I breathed in the comforting, earthy scent of the jasmine green tea blend that Max had made for me. I'd fixed myself a cup before stepping outside in bare feet. Taking a sip, I could feel his energy and loving intent in the mixture. Since he knew how sensitive I was to caffeine, he'd made the tea using the older, larger leaves of the *camellia sinensis* tea plants he grew in his backyard garden, and infused the hand-picked-and-dried unoxidized green tea leaves with jasmine, also from his garden.

The combination of sipping lovingly made tea and looking out over my flourishing garden filled with herbs, greens, berries, and even edible weeds like nettles, calmed my racing mind. I was in a somewhat precarious spot in Portland. Before settling down here a year ago, for decades I'd been living an itinerant existence in my Airstream trailer, because I couldn't let myself stay in any one place for too long. After a time, people would begin to notice I didn't age. But when I'd visited Portland, I'd fallen in love with the city—its laid-back people, vibrant greenery, tumultuous weather, and quirky architectural landscape. I'd also fallen in love with a remarkable man, Max Liu.

Only a few more minutes until I'd get to talk with him.

Max was in China for his grandfather's funeral. I missed having him sitting here with me. Each day we were talking at 7 a.m. my time, shortly after I got up, and 10 p.m. his time, shortly before he'd be going to sleep.

If you'd asked me about Max last month, I would have told you he was my boyfriend. A serious one. I even had a key to his house. But now? I was no longer certain what we were. He had finally seen what it meant that I was an alchemist. When I first told Max I was an alchemist, once I trusted him enough to do so, he thought I meant it in the free-spirit Portland kind of way, like being a plant-whispering herbalist who's great at working in nature. When I tried again, more explicitly, to explain just how old I was, he became concerned that I believed what I was telling him. He didn't think it could be true—not until he and his sister had seen what happened when I rescued the Flamels. He'd been the one I confided in to help me get Nicolas and Perenelle unquestioning medical attention shortly after I rescued them, and he was still processing what he'd learned.* (**The Alchemist's Illusion*.)

It was probably for the best that we had this break from each other, but I missed him more than I imagined I would.

On our daily phone calls, we still had the easy rapport we always did. But I could tell Max was holding something back. It wasn't only the fact that he expressed his desire to speak without video. There was something in his voice. It didn't sound like he had a cold, but rather there was something stilted in his phrasing. That wasn't quite the right description either, but it was the closest I could articulate to what I felt when we spoke from afar.

I'd offered to go with him to his grandfather's funeral, but he said it would be easier with family on his own. I didn't fight him. He was right. I didn't want to insert our own drama into this time for his family to come together.

My pulse quickened as my phone rang a few seconds after the clock clicked over to 7 o'clock.

"Max."

"Even with one word, your voice is a tonic for my soul."

"Rough day?"

"How's Nicolas after that day out yesterday?"

Families and funerals could be difficult, so I didn't press. I answered his question instead. "He did far better than I expected him to." I told him about how long we spent at Powell's Books and the brewpub we discovered. I refrained from mentioning that Nicolas had gone to bed at six o'clock and hadn't yet woken up.

"He's making his own beer? I can't wait to try that."

"You're braver than I am. How's everything with your family?"

He hesitated. I pondered the way the time of day and planetary alignments affected our conversations. We were in such different places, both physically and emotionally. I loved that modern technology allowed us to speak like this, but we also had such different energy.

"Max?" I prompted. "Are you still there?"

"You remember I told you about how when I was a kid my granddad used to take me treasure-hunting along the coast near my house?"

"I do. Because you loved a movie about kids looking for a pirate treasure that was filmed in your hometown."

Max had been born and raised in Astoria, Oregon, a town on the coast two hours away from Portland. His paternal grandparents had emigrated from China and lived in Oregon until Max's grandmother passed away and his grandfather moved back to China when he was a child. Max's own parents got divorced and Max grew up with his mom, Mary Jasper—a Texas native with a rancher father and Chinese immigrant mother—and sister Mina, both of whom I'd gotten to know. Max had initially been hesitant to introduce me to them, and to date me at all, because he thought he was too old for me. I couldn't tell him at the time how wrong he was.

"Granddad told me a story about a local legend called the Wizard of the West," Max continued. "A pirate who eluded capture at every turn, so they called him a wizard. Since it was a made-up story, he knew we'd never find a treasure. The process of searching was the whole point. But one summer, he buried a treasure chest himself for me to find."

"I remember you telling me that story. He filled it with blocks for you to build a castle." I imagined Max's still-boyish grin and how filled with boundless energy he must have been as a child.

"I never told you what else was inside it." He paused. It could have been for dramatic effect, but I had the strongest suspicion it was because he was weighing whether or not to tell me. "My grandmother's iron teapot."

That brought a smile to my lips. "The one you have in your kitchen now?"

"The very same. I didn't realize as a kid that it was the real treasure inside that wooden chest. Those blocks are long gone, donated to a thrift shop so another kid could build castles with them, but that teapot was the lesson of the treasure hunt. He tasked me with finding my grandmother's beloved teapot, which he said the Wizard of the West had stolen and hidden along with his other pirate plunder. My grandmother agreed to the game, knowing I'd find it for her. I followed Granddad's clues and found the treasure chest. I handed my grandmother her teapot without another thought before building my castle. I didn't see at the time that their legacy was the real treasure in there."

"You were a good grandson to both of them."

"I'm glad I made it to Granddad's 100th birthday celebration earlier this year."

"And that you can be there with your family now."

Another pause.

"Family drama?" I asked when he still hadn't replied.

"A different kind of drama. There was a small fire. I don't know if I can do this."

"Do what?"

Max didn't reply.

"Are you all right, Max? Oh no. Is anyone—"

"Nobody was hurt. But a fire of any kind spooks me. From all these years on the force, I've seen the damage fire can do, and so quickly. It can trap you before you realize it's out of control."

I knew the feeling. I'd lived through more of them than Max had, including a devastating fire at the apothecary shop I used to run in Paris.

But at the same time, fire is essential to alchemy. From the athanor furnace at the center of alchemical transformations to the symbols of fire depicted in alchemical texts, fire is both death *and* renewal.

"What tea are you drinking tonight?" I asked, trying to bring us back to safer territory. It was clear he didn't want to talk about the fire.

"I've got the dried mint from your garden keeping me company."

I smiled. "And I've got your jasmine green tea."

One of our favorite things to do when we were both in Portland was to sit on the back porch of one of our houses, looking at our backyard gardens while drinking tea. Both of our lives were dramatic enough that it was a simple pleasure. A respite from the world. Together.

Our young friend Brixton was looking after Max's garden while he was away. I'd taught Brixton some gardening skills shortly after I'd moved here. Weeding was the teenager's penance for breaking my window on a dare from his friends to check out the lights in a creepy old house that was abandoned until I bought it. In the end, the punishment turned into a joy, as I'd hoped it would.

I watched the plants waking up as I was. I'd recently pruned back the rambling mint to make space for a pigment garden for Perenelle. Woad, madder, and yarrow were now nestled into one corner of the yard. The plants would yield the organic matter for a vibrant blue close to indigo, an earthy dark red, and a deep yellow. The more expected trinity would have been woad, madder, and weld instead of yarrow for yellow—but weld and I had never gotten along. What can I say? I understand plants well enough to know when they dislike me.

I don't, however, understand people quite as well, even after all these years. Max hadn't replied. Normally this would be companionable silence if we'd been sitting together on the back porch. But now all I heard was crackling. *Crackling?*

"Is that the sound of flames?"

"Of course not." He chuckled, but it was nervous laughter. "But I should go."

"Max—"

"Take care, Zoe."

The line went dead.

CHAPTER 4

"Surely you know how to fix this piece of metal." My housemate held a bent shaft of steel between his fingers and looked at me across the broken Remington typewriter resting on an antique marble end table.

His accent was French, as were his facial expressions. Though I've lived in France and other countries for many years, and I speak several languages with various degrees of fluency, my accent has remained as American as it was when I was a kid. The edges had softened over the years, which was a good thing, since my original English was outdated and spoken in a style people would now find stilted. But the foundation remained the same.

I absentmindedly took the piece of smooth, twisted steel. I was distracted both by the unsettling way my conversation with Max ended that morning—and Nicolas's relapse. We'd pushed him too far yesterday. He'd slept in until 11 a.m. and barely touched his lunch.

"You must have an idea where it goes," Dorian insisted. "Every other piece appears to be accounted for. We cannot see the truth because it is twisted. Once we know its purpose, then we will be able to fix it properly."

"Just because I was alive when the first Remington was made in the 1870s doesn't mean I know how to fix the typewriter."

Dorian clicked his tongue. "You are not even trying, Zoe."

"I'm too stuffed from that exquisite lunch."

Dorian chuckled. "It is true. I outdid myself with the marinaded mushroom paella." His healthy ego was justified in this case. Dorian was a trained chef. He didn't always prepare such fancy lunches, but I suspected he was trying to impress Nicolas and Perenelle. He'd gotten off on the wrong foot with Perenelle last month.

I handed back the bent typewriter part and stood up. "I should check on Nicolas." He'd gone to sleep again after lunch, and I'd promised Perenelle I'd look after him while she worked on her art and alchemy at Elements Art House.

"Ah. This is the true source of your distraction, *n'est pas?*"

"We shouldn't have walked so much yesterday." I stood. "Or let him have a second beer."

"Let the man sleep. He is simply tired. And he is not a child. He is a grown man. If he wishes to stretch his legs and imbibe a beverage, you must let him do so."

I hesitated for a moment. "You're right. And Tobias will be checking in on him later this week. Oh!" I snatched back the piece of metal from Dorian's fingers. "It's not broken at all, Dorian."

"Have you lost your mind, *mon amie*? It is clearly bent." Flustered, Dorian flapped his wings. The left one clipped the edge of a wooden crate. He jumped up as it teetered, catching it before it fell.

Did I mention that Dorian is a gargoyle? A few other people know that Dorian exists, which they learned more by accident than design. Dorian had to remain hidden from the public. That's why we were fixing a typewriter in my windowless attic, the only natural light from a skylight above that served as an escape hatch and back door for Dorian.

He was originally carved as a stone chimera for Notre Dame Cathedral in Paris, but was accidentally brought to life through a strange form of alchemy that no longer existed. Backward alchemy. A dangerous way of creating transformations that Dorian had no hand in himself, yet it's why Perenelle remained wary of him. Every person who'd willingly participated in backward alchemy had not been a good person.

A little over a year ago, Dorian sought me out to help him figure out why his body was returning to stone. The opinionated gargoyle took a while to grow on me (did I mention his healthy ego and his penchant to borrow my credit card for "essentials" such as truffles?), but he was now my best friend.

"*Pardon*," Dorian said, folding his wings back in place. "I did not mean to damage your box. Yet what am I to do? You have filled my room with so many of these trinkets."

The attic wasn't entirely his room. It was the storage room and photographic staging ground for the small antiques I sold. Half of the large attic was also Dorian's space. I wouldn't exactly call it a bedroom because he didn't need sleep. But one corner held a desk with a working typewriter he used, an armchair for reading, a few of his favorite pieces of art, and now a set of broken typewriters and framed paintings he'd recently purchased online from a local thrift store. There wasn't enough room for everything we were accumulating.

"I'll get the boxes from the estate sale catalogued this week," I said. That would free up at least a little bit of room.

"I do not know why you purchased five chess sets from the estate. You do not even like chess."

"Because I *sell* them, as you know perfectly well." I run an online business called Elixir, and most of the antiques I sell used to be things I'd purchased new at the time. Lately, though, with a renewed public interest in high-end antiques, I'd sold off so much of my stock that I had to go hunting for treasures at estate sales and flea markets. "Don't you want to know about this rogue typewriter part?"

Dorian flicked his clawed hand through the air. "You mock me, stating the part is not broken."

"It's the carriage return lever. It's *supposed to be* bent."

He gasped. "How did I not see this?"

"Because you were too focused on the important interior pieces, I suspect. Why are you buying typewriters you need to fix anyway? I thought you were busy writing a novel on the one that works." At least he no longer used my credit card without permission. He had his own card now, since he was making money baking pastries for Blue Sky Teas.

He sighed. "I have writer's block. With the vast number of penny dreadfuls that were once produced, I thought, *how difficile could it be?* Yet… the great Dorian Robert-Houdin may have been mistaken."

"I seriously doubt that. I'm glad you took up writing instead of painting. It doesn't need as much space or as many materials."

"Ah." Dorian frowned. "You wish I were a master painter like Madame Flamel."

I frowned back. "I said the exact opposite."

"Yet you value her contributions more."

I sat back and observed my friend. I thought I knew him well by now, but he was behaving so strangely. "What are you talking about?"

"She painted a portrait of you and your beloved brother."

I smiled. That explained it. "I do love that portrait she made of me with Thomas. I wish it hadn't been stolen during her imprisonment."

"The reproduction hanging on the wall of your bedroom is not the same?"

I shook my head. "She put her love and intent into the paints and canvas as she created it. Only the original has that quality."

"Yes... you were quite sad that day you spoke with the small museum in France under your 'cover' of being an antiques dealer."

It wasn't a cover, but he was right about it being a cover story. I had no interest in selling the painting through Elixir. If I ever got it, it would be my most cherished possession. Perenelle had captured Thomas's angelic face with the hint of mischief that never left his eyes. But the museum had no interest in selling the painting for a price I could afford.

"I don't understand why they think it's so valuable," I said. "As their listing says, it's by an unknown painter." I wondered if they thought the artist was an apprentice of Philippe Hayden. Perenelle, Nicolas, and I were the only living people who knew the truth about Philippe. I hoped Perenelle and I could set the historical record straight one day, but that would be a much larger undertaking.

"If only you were better at making gold," Dorian mused.

"Or *any* of us." We really were terrible alchemists in some ways.

Whether or not you considered us awful alchemists would depend on what you wanted from alchemy. I know how to coax plants to grow and thrive, Dorian can transform ingredients found in the most barren cupboard into a scrumptious feast, Perenelle's artwork made with hand-mixed pigments is so imbued with life it feels magical, and Nicolas is a clever inventor. I don't think any of us would have traded our main talents for the ability to easily make gold. Nicolas and Perenelle both used to be able to make gold more readily, but it was a skill neither had regained.

"*Très bon.*" The gargoyle chuckled gleefully as he secured the carriage return lever.

I frowned as another sound reached my ears. Not from the typewriter, but an unmistakable noise from beyond the attic door. It was the sound of running footsteps slamming the stairs leading to the attic.

A fiery-haired woman crashed through the doorway and upset the antique table, sending the typewriter flying. Errant metal parts clattered across the hardwood floor. As a round letter key rolled to a stop and the room fell silent, I caught Perenelle's eye. She was terrified.

CHAPTER 5

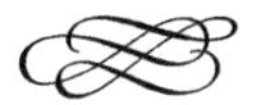

Perenelle's long hair hung loose, her messy auburn curls moving as her chest heaved, looking as if they would come to life like tendrils of fire. The hem of her midnight blue dress was covered in fresh mud. Most distressing were her hands, which clutched a package so tightly that her knuckles had turned white.

"I had nearly fixed that," Dorian huffed, wriggling his gray horns.

"What's happened?" I leapt to my feet and ran to Perenelle, ignoring Dorian and the broken typewriter.

"It was the wrong decision to ignore the blackmailer." Her grip relaxed, but only slightly. Wrapped loosely in Kraft paper, the package was large, but only a couple of inches thick.

"Are you hurt?"

"Hurt?"

I knelt and inspected the dark brown mud on her skirt. She must have fallen somewhere wet from the rain that had fallen during the night, but the muck didn't appear to be mixed with blood.

"No," she said finally, shaking her head and clutching the package tightly again. "When you weren't in the main part of the house, I was worried they'd gotten to you, too."

"I told Nicolas I'd be in the attic with Dorian." Had he forgotten? Or was he in worse shape than I'd imagined? I should have believed

Tobias when he told me Nicolas was still recovering from his injuries and needed to take it easy. Still, I didn't think his mind had been affected.

"He's asleep. I didn't want to wake him and worry him."

"What's happened? Have they gotten in touch again?"

"You were being blackmailed, Madame Flamel?" Dorian turned his gaze to me as well, his black eyes narrowing as he did so. "You knew about this blackmail, Zoe, and you did not tell me?"

"Let me check that the house is locked," I said. "I'll be back in a couple of minutes and then we can talk about what's going on."

Five minutes later, after making sure each door and window of the Craftsman house was secured, plus all of the curtains drawn, I climbed the narrow steps to the attic again.

Perenelle had set the package down next to her, but she and Dorian stood at opposite ends of the attic, not speaking. It was incredibly frustrating that they hadn't gotten along since I rescued Perenelle and Nicolas and invited them to stay with me while they got their bearings on 21st century life.

It's not like there wasn't enough room in the house. I'd bought it as an extreme fixer-upper and had partially fixed it up over the past year. Dorian had the attic to himself, I'd given Nicolas and Perenelle the master bedroom, and I was sleeping in one of the two additional bedrooms. My friend Tobias, who Dorian enjoyed playing chess with, stayed in the guest bedroom when he came to visit. Trips that were half social and half medical in nature. Tobias had both medical training and knew the truth about alchemy. He was an alchemist himself, and a trusted friend and confidant. Perenelle was understandably wary of backward alchemy. It still wasn't right to take it out on Dorian.

I had thought that Dorian and Perenelle had established a truce, of sorts. Perhaps even a grudging admiration. With the feasts he cooked in the kitchen, Dorian satisfied Perenelle's voracious appetite as she replenished her body after her long imprisonment. But this?

"Stop glowering at each other," I snapped. "Perenelle, tell me what's going on?"

"*Non*," said Dorian. "Since Madame Flamel is uninjured, you two must first tell me who was blackmailing you—and more importantly, *why* you did not tell me about this."

"You," I said, "would have investigated in an attempt to uncover who the blackmailer was."

Dorian gave a curt nod. "*C'est vrais.* Of course this is true. You did not investigate? What other option is there in such circumstances? You would simply let this immoral person get away with such treachery?"

Dorian, in addition to being an accomplished chef, thinks of himself as a modern-day Poirot. He was always eager to help solve any mystery in our lives, usually using methods he'd read about in classic detective fiction or Gothic novels. Since he's made of stone, he literally has "little gray cells," as Agatha Christie's Poirot liked to say.

We'd all discovered the Elixir of Life, which grants a degree of immortality. But we're not immune to disease or violence. We simply don't age normally. So it's not like we can investigate with abandon. We could meet with a violent end as easily as anyone else. The one thing we had going for us was a longer history of being around people and understanding human motivation. Though the details change over time, human desires remain the same.

"You have the blackmail note?" Dorian asked.

Perenelle took it from one of the pockets built into the voluminous skirt of her dress.

I know what you are. I will keep your secret in exchange for 10 pieces of gold.

Dorian took a monocle from a shelf and examined the crumpled note. He really did bear a striking resemblance to Poirot as he did so. I've always felt it's the expressiveness of a face which leaves more of an impression than the physical features themselves.

"You have no doubt ruined any fingerprints," he mumbled.

"We used the kit when it arrived," I said. "There were no prints."

Dorian grunted his approval. "*Très interresant.* Letters formed with a thin paintbrush. Perhaps to disguise any hint of their true handwriting. The paper appears to be common. But the paint... it is old."

"It was delivered to me at Elements Art House, where I'm renting studio space since Zoe's basement alchemy lab is being used by my husband."

I'd given Nicolas my basement alchemy lab, leaving me without my own space to practice. I didn't mind. Both because I had fallen off the alchemist wagon years ago, and because I had my backyard garden. That's where I felt the energy of plants most closely. If I'd had a space to work, I could have also harvested plants and turned them into herbal remedies. But I was no longer dispensing tinctures in Victorian England, or helping nurse back to health wary people tired from their arduous journey through the Underground Railroad in the mid-19th-century United States, or attending to the needs of those too ill to escape pre-war France in the lead-up to the occupation. My personal tinctures were less important now that so many more people had rediscovered knowledge that had been lost to modernity.

"What is this code at the end?" asked Dorian.

"A website," I said. "Showing a video of Perenelle making gold, ending with a phone number to call for instructions for where she should deliver the gold."

"You have paid them?" Dorian asked her.

She shook her head.

He sniffed the paper. Did he think he was Sherlock Holmes in addition to Poirot these days? He'd read a huge number of classic mysteries in the past year. Everything I could check out for him at the library—before he annotated too many cookbooks and got my library card revoked.

"You performed alchemy in a space with a window for people to see?" He looked up at Perenelle. He's three and a half feet tall. Tall enough that I don't kneel to speak with him, but short enough that he needs a stool to cook in the kitchen. Carved out of stone as a prototype for the Gallery of Gargoyles at Notre Dame Cathedral of Paris, he was too small to be seen from the street, so the final gargoyles were slightly larger.

"I did not know I could be observed." Perenelle sighed. "The windows there are too high for anyone to look into. Nobody should have been able to see inside—not unless they were purposefully spying."

"Now that Dorian is caught up," I said, "what's happened today?" I followed her gaze to the package. "Something to do with this package?"

"The package," she cried. "This is the one *good* thing in the midst of this mess."

"How so, Madame Flamel?" Dorian reached out his hand to touch the package.

Perenelle moved it out of his reach. She peeled open the Kraft paper, revealing a framed painting of a seascape on canvas.

"This painting," she said, "was created by the blackmailer."

"You figured out who it is?" I asked.

"The artist used lake pigment, handmade from organic matter," Perenelle said. "The essence of one of the blues used in the ocean is identical to the paint used in their notes."

Notes? Before I could ask if she meant there were multiple notes or if it was a slip of the tongue, Dorian spoke.

"You are certain?" he asked.

"I know I haven't been at my best as I've recovered." Her voice was prickly. "I'm unable to make much gold, it's true. But this? Of this, I am certain. Just as certain as you feel about the ingredients in your kitchen. As sure as Zoe feels about the plants in her garden. That's what I feel when surrounded by the elements that make up pigments and paint."

In the past, before stable binding agents were discovered, artists mixed their own paints. Or, more commonly, tradesmen called "colormen" created paints from raw minerals, after obtaining their ingredients from apothecaries. Alchemy and art had much in common.

Dorian gave a grunt to acknowledge these truths. "So, Madame Flamel, if you have identified the blackmailer, why are you so distressed?"

"I think I know," I said. "You don't know *who* painted it." I watched the anguish on her face turn her cheeks scarlet.

"The painting was in the general racks in the common space of Elements. I don't recognize the style, yet I know what it means: Someone close to me is the blackmailer. That's why I stole the painting." She groaned. "I don't know why I did it. It's a clue, yet it doesn't actually tell me who it is. I have no way to find them."

"This," Dorian said, "is where you are wrong. You have come to the great Dorian Robert-Houdin, whose little gray cells will solve the case!"

CHAPTER 6

"I cannot believe I have been relegated to the attic!" Dorian's claws tapped on the attic floor as he paced back and forth. *The effrontery*, the gargoyle thought to himself.

Madame Flamel had insisted she needed fresh air, yet he knew the truth. She did not wish to confide more in him. Only Zoe.

He stopped pacing and picked up the functioning antique telephone. His fingers did not work well on the screen of modern cell phones, so Zoe had let him choose a suitable telephone.

"I have been confined to the attic so the *adults* can talk," he said when his young friend picked up.

"Don't you like your attic?" Brixton asked.

"That is beside the point. I am more than 150 years old!"

"Um, Zoe and the Flamels are way older."

Dorian sighed. "Do you wish to hear about a mystery that is afoot or not?"

"Be there in ten."

Brixton was not a "good" boy. This is why Dorian appreciated his friend. Brixton was loyal and stalwart, not "nice" or the type of boy who would do something simply because an adult asked him to. He had done many illegal things—through no association with Dorian, long before they met—but not immoral things. The act that had gotten the boy arrested at age thirteen was because he *was* doing the moral thing, protecting his mother from a predator.

Now fifteen, Brixton appeared more mature than that mother of his. He was learning about plants and gardening from Zoe—originally as a punishment for breaking her window, when they first met—but now because the boy truly enjoyed seeing how plants would blossom if you knew how to take care of them.

Brixton arrived seven minutes later. Dorian watched from the rooftop as the boy unceremoniously dumped his bicycle in the sloping driveway; then he scampered downstairs to let him into the house. The boy's arms and legs were lankier than they had been when Dorian first met him a year before, causing Dorian to crane his neck further to converse with his young friend. Brixton's curly black hair was longer as well. Dorian would have suggested a haircut if it had been his place to do so.

"Perenelle Flamel is hysterical," Dorian explained once they'd reached the attic, "because someone at Elements Art House is blackmailing her." Zoe would no doubt have kept the boy in the dark about the blackmail as well, which was terribly shortsighted. Children could do things he and adults could not. He would never put Brixton and his friends in harm's way, of course. He simply gave them the credit they deserved.

"Why is someone blackmailing her?" Brixton plopped down in the 1970s bubble chair that Zoe obtained at a recent estate sale. Dorian didn't like it because his claws caught in the fabric.

"They saw her practicing alchemy. *Pfft*! Such a careless woman."

"Zoe says people see alchemy all the time, but they never believe it. So it's not like it matters if someone posts on social media that Perenelle is an alchemist."

"The blackmailer does not know this. Yet this is not what transpired today."

"'K."

"That is all you can say?"

"I figure if you're going to tell me what's going on, you'll tell me what's going on." Brixton pulled a phone from his pocket and scrolled on the screen.

Dorian did not give the boy enough credit either. He was quite clever. The gargoyle sighed. "You are missing the overall point."

"Which is?"

"Perenelle was not careful. It would be dangerous for all of us if our secrets were to be revealed. Zoe should not let them continue to live here. It endangers us all."

"You don't like Zoe's stepmom much, do you?"

Dorian glared at the boy. "She is *not* Zoe's stepmother."

"She pretty much is. Not legally, I guess, but she's totally like an almost-mom, right?"

Dorian narrowed his black eyes. "Zoe does not need a false mother."

"Whatever."

"Chess?" Dorian asked. "Or perhaps a game of Go?"

Brixton smiled. "I'd rather poke around that broken typewriter. You're trying to fix these things, right?"

The boy helped Dorian lift the heftiest of the typewriters onto the table.

"How can Zoe take her side? I am the great Dorian Robert-Houdin! I have solved numerous baffling mysteries single-handedly. How can they think of acting without my assistance. How can—"

"Ego much?"

"Yes, my ego is quite healthy. Thank you."

"Um, that's not what I meant."

Dorian studied the inscrutable expression of the young man. "I cannot discern whether you are mocking me. This would not be a respectful thing for a friend to do."

Brixton focused on the stuck keys. "What did you do to this thing? No way you can write those cranky letters to the editor to newspapers on this thing. You can't write a letter without an E. Maybe without the N."

"That no longer interests me. I am working on a novel." Dorian was glad for the boy's easily distracted nature. He did not wish to think more about Zoe's betrayal.

"Wicked. You're going to be like Stephen King?"

"More like Agatha Christie." He tapped his right horn. "With my little gray cells."

Dorian related to the French-speaking detective Poirot. He'd read Zoe's old paperback books, which before meeting Zoe he dismissed as pulp not worthy of his attention. He was very rarely mistaken, yet this was one rare instance in which he was wrong. He treated Zoe's books with care, as he knew she did not keep many possessions in her Airstream trailer.

Zoe did not own a full set of Agatha Christie's novels, so she borrowed the remaining books from the library for him. That was before she had her library privileges revoked. She blamed Dorian for having her library card canceled, yet he was not at fault! He was merely attempting to correct terrible advice in the library's cookbooks. How was he to know that his helpful corrections written in the margins would lead to Zoe being accused of defacing library books? Yes, his notes had been quite thorough, and frequently scratched out the bad advice on the page. But this was for the greater good. Perhaps this was why Zoe had not told him of the blackmail. To punish him. She had loved having a library card. She said she had forgiven him, but he knew people bore grudges.

Yet he was Dorian Robert-Houdin, with far more little gray cells than Poirot. Not only were his ideas greater than the great man, but he was real, unlike Poirot. Real life was messier than fiction, especially when the fiction was an Agatha Christie closed circle mystery.

They poked around the broken machine for a few minutes, with Brixton watching online tutorials and Dorian jabbing his claws into spaces that did not appear as they should be.

"Did you see that?" Brixton asked. "I got the Q key to work."

"One rarely needs a Q."

Brixton swore. "Do you want help or not?"

"It is quite frustrating to only be able to purchase items sight-unseen."

"Zoe didn't buy these herself to sell through Elixir?"

"*Non*. The other stacks of antiques are for her business, but these typewriters, and the pitiful paintings bundled with them, are my acquisition. As I told you, I am writing a novel."

"You need more than one typewriter to write a novel?"

Dorian flapped his wings in a shrug. "Creative inspiration benefits from variety."

"You should be focusing on staying in Zoe's good graces to keep this place. Not hiding up here writing on old-fashioned machines."

"You think she means to *evict* me? But it is Perenelle she should be evicting."

Brixton swept his arm across the attic. "She's already filling your room with other stuff."

"The room," said Dorian, "is only crowded because Zoe recently discovered many high quality antiques at an estate sale in Beaverton. Hidden gems that others missed."

"Uh huh."

Dorian shook his head and wriggled his horns. "I do not believe this will be a problem. If Perenelle believes she is about to be exposed as an alchemist, she will move on from here. This is what alchemists do."

"Yeah. I just hope Zoe doesn't go with her."

CHAPTER 7

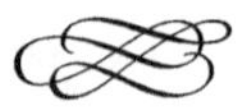

"I knew it was a mistake to confess so much in front of the gargoyle." Perenelle paced back and forth in the small space of my Airstream trailer. "At least I came to my senses before telling him about the terrible revelation in the second note."

In the tiny kitchenette of the Airstream trailer parked in my driveway, I was fixing us cups of tea. She'd feigned needing to get outside for fresh air—because she knew Dorian was incapable of joining us during daylight hours—though I suspected he saw through the charade.

I held a mug of steeped peppermint tea under Perenelle's nose. "You'll need to let go of that painting if you'd like tea." Though it lacked caffeine, peppermint always gave me a boost of energy and helped me focus. The latter was something I desperately needed to coax from Perenelle.

She eased the painting to the floor, leaning it against the shelf I once used as a mini pantry when I lived here in the trailer. "I'm being ridiculous, aren't I?"

"I don't know yet. You haven't shown me the second note. Only the seascape with paint that matched the note." The painting evoked no particular emotions in me. Could she really identify its style strongly enough to know how this artist would write block letters with a paint brush? Unlike Perenelle's paintings, all of which were rich with detail and a hint of secrets that pulled you in, this one told a straightforward story. A view of sand, a few jagged rocks sticking out of the ocean, and ocean waves that were neither large nor small. A reflection in the ocean water made it look like the artist had meant to add something else above, but had abandoned the idea. Everything about it struck me as an average amateur painting.

"I should have paid them." Perenelle shook her head. "They no longer simply want me to create gold riches for them."

Dread prickled my skin. "What else do they want?"

"The reason they know I'm an alchemist is because they saw me create a small amount of gold out of the elements I use to mix my own paints."

"You told me that much already."

"What I didn't tell you," she said, "is what the gold *looked like*."

"What did you do?" I whispered.

Perenelle reached into a hidden pocket of her voluminous skirt and removed a large gold nugget. A nugget I recognized. A nugget that everyone in Oregon would recognize.

I groaned. "You didn't create a transformation that resulted in unformed, unrecognizable gold. You based it on the most talked-about gold in Oregon."

"I wasn't able to create much. Only one piece of the much larger find."

"It's real." I touched the soft surface of the largest nugget of gold I'd ever seen, nearly the size of my palm.

"Of course. You know I'm still getting back in shape after all these years. I needed something to focus my intent on. An unformed mass of gold was not inspiring enough. So I mimicked the gold recently stolen at the Oregon Gold History Museum. I focused my intent on that shape as I did my transformation. I failed at transforming much, and I only ended up with a tiny fraction of what I was hoping to create. Yet..."

"This is clearly recognizable as one of the uniquely shaped oversize nuggets stolen from the museum." I lifted the nugget of gold.

Perenelle nodded sadly. "The blackmailer believes I can replicate the valuable gold nuggets recently stolen, since they saw me do it once. They don't realize how much that took out of me! Yet now, because I did not meet their first demand, they want me to create *the whole set* for them, otherwise—" she broke off and handed me the letter written in red paint with a delicate paintbrush.

Bring me 20 gold nuggets or my next note won't be red paint—it will be written in the blood of someone you care about. Instructions to follow.

I sucked in my breath. I'd like to say my life isn't usually this dramatic, but I'd be lying to myself.

I discovered the Elixir of Life when I was 28 years old, studying under Nicolas Flamel's tutelage, but didn't realize it at the time. I was working frantically to unlock the secret for my brother who was dying, not heeding Nicolas's advice that alchemy is a personal transformative process and I would not be able to give my knowledge to my brother. Nicolas was right. I was grieving after Thomas died and only realized I'd found the Elixir when I saw I hadn't aged in years. Only my hair had changed, turning completely white. People assume I dye my hair to be trendy, but in truth it's as natural as the rest of me. Not all alchemists experience their hair turning white like mine did. The Elixir of Life is such a personal transformation that it's difficult to make generalizations.

When the first letter came, I had been so sure that it wasn't necessary to engage with the blackmailer. The fact that alchemy is real isn't exactly a secret. The truth has been revealed countless times, yet the world has never been ready to believe it. People fall back onto their world view to explain what they see. But if the blackmailer was willing to resort to violence? That was something completely different.

I wasn't overly concerned for my own safety, but we had people in our lives like 15-year-old Brixton. And Nicolas, who could normally have defended himself, wasn't doing well.

"This is bad," I said.

"Exactly," Perenelle said. "If we don't give them the gold I'm not able to create, they'll not only expose me but harm people close to me, like you and Nicolas."

CHAPTER 8

"*Non*," Dorian insisted. "Zoe has a life here. She would not leave so soon. She has you and myself. And Max." He spoke the name disdainfully. It did not go unnoticed by the boy.

"What have you got against Max?" asked Brixton. "This typewriter doesn't even have a 'B' key that works. I can't type my name."

"Besides the fact that he is *un flic,* he does not accept Zoe for who she is. Yet he does make her happy. For this I am grateful. No, Zoe will not leave. It is Perenelle who will leave."

Brixton glared at the smiling Dorian. "You can't really be happy that Perenelle could be forced to run away."

"Her husband is a charming man. I will be sorry to see him go."

"You're really not going to help them?"

"I might point out that *they* are the ones who declined my assistance." Dorian sighed. "Perhaps you are right. Yes, you are becoming a wise young man. I do not wish Madame Flamel ill. Though a moment of *schadenfreude* is expected, is it not?"

"What? Never mind. I just realized something. You said it was someone at Elements Art House that's blackmailing her. That's the artist space my mom took her to. One of the people there is blackmailing Perenelle? That means we can help. We have, like, inside knowledge. I know it would mean asking my mom... but we can find a way to do that. We should—"

"No," Dorian growled. He needn't have spoken so sharply. "If Zoe and Madame Flamel wish to confide more in us and seek our assistance, they will."

"You shouldn't not help just because you're jealous of them."

"I am not *jealous* of the Flamels," said Dorian. "What an imbecilic idea." Although this is what he said outwardly, he was far more concerned than he dared express. Was the boy right? Was Zoe replacing him with the Flamels?

"You're totally jealous. I get it. They're taking your place in Zoe's life. Your food is really good, but not the same as how she looks at the portrait of her and her brother."

The boy was not wrong. And the portrait of Zoe and her beloved brother that Perenelle Flamel had painted was Zoe's favorite possession, even though it was a cheap copy.

"So what's your book about?" Brixton asked.

Dorian knew the boy was asking to distract him. Still, it was pleasant to be asked about one's work.

"It is a most thrilling Gothic novel," Dorian began, "featuring a mystery based on a Portland landmark and a great fire. You have heard of the Witch's Castle?"

"Sure. Some of the seniors at school go there."

"High school students are interested in the ruins?" This was surprising. The people of Portland thought of it as historical ruins, but from examining the remains of the structure, he could discern it was not much more than a century old. The wood from the roof, doors, and windows had long since been destroyed, leaving only moss-covered stone stairs and walls.

"Um, not exactly. Back in the 1980s, a group of high school students accidentally found the stone ruins on a hike in Forest Park. They thought it would be perfect as a late-night spot for parties, since their parents didn't know about it. I haven't been, but I hear it's the same deal today."

Dorian clicked his tongue. This explained the graffiti on some of the stone. No matter. There would be no desecration of the Witch's Castle in his Gothic novel, which was set in the past, when the house was a grand estate.

True, he did not know if this was *actually* the history of the structure, the layout of which was too small to have been a true castle. Dorian had purposefully not researched the history of these stone ruins further. No, sitting at his typewriter he used his imagination. In his mind, he conjured a once-stately house burning as its eccentric owners fled for their lives. Wood turned to kindling and eventually there was nothing left except smoldering ruins. Ruins ready for new life.

Fire was not only destructive. It was life-giving. It had given life to Dorian, and his own use of fire gave life to simple ingredients, transforming them into exquisite feasts. It would definitely be fire that destroyed the Witch's Castle in his novel.

Dorian was so absorbed in telling the boy his brilliant ideas that he did not think about the creaking on the stairs until it was too late.

He did not notice that the footsteps were not those of one of the inhabitants of the house, but two uninvited guests. Not until two shadows —one tall and thin, the other of average height—crossed the attic threshold.

By then, it was far too late to hide.

Dorian's secret, which he had worked so hard to protect, was exposed.

CHAPTER 9

Perenelle's secret, which she'd protected for centuries, was precariously close to being exposed.

I knew we could do damage control, because I still believed people only see what they're ready to understand. I was far more worried about the threat of violence.

Bring me 20 gold nuggets or my next note won't be red paint—it will be written in the blood of someone you care about.

"I would say we should pay them and figure everything else out later," I began.

Perenelle finished my thought. "But we both know it's not that easy. Not any longer. Not for any of us."

Aside from our alchemical specialties, only Nicolas had ever been a natural at creating gold. And there was no way he'd be up for this. The creation of gold was such a full transformation of the impure into the pure that it could drain even a healthy person. For someone recovering from a grave injury, it might even kill them.

I looked around my sanctuary. I'd lived out of this 150-square-foot trailer for decades. I customized it over the years, making sure the sunny back window had a built-in planter box for my kitchen garden. When I'd rolled into Portland a year ago, my clay pot winter garden herbs ranged from more common herbs like lemon balm, cottage rosemary, and sage, to plants less familiar to most people in the modern U.S., like shiso and chervil.

Every plant has a story. A personality. I had no specific agenda to grow herbs and vegetables that had been popular in my youth but fallen out of favor in recent years. I made my selections by intuition. By listening. Some of the most commonly grown herbs didn't speak to me, but if they did, I would grow them—even if they were weeds that could easily take over a yard, like mint, nettles, and blackberries.

When I lived out of the trailer, I would hang dried herbs in a spot I kept dark with a curtain. A custom-carved wooden shelf housed my herb-infused salts and oils. The kitchenette was small, but having indoor plumbing of any kind still felt like a luxury to me. As did the feel of soft foam. The couch converted into a bed, and storage below it held the smaller antique items I used to sell at flea markets, which I now sold through my online business Elixir. None of the items were vintage when I bought them, but now something as simple as a poster from the 1920s would sell for enough money to keep me going for a month. If I'd anticipated the internet, I would have hoarded even more posters and postcards.

I placed my hand on the shelf that had once held lavender and breathed deeply. Though I'd either used up or brought nearly everything into the house and the trailer was mostly empty, the faint scent of the calming flower remained.

"You really *lived* here for decades?" Perenelle asked as she shifted her skirt on the narrow couch-bed-storage unit.

"You've lived longer in stranger places."

She pulled me into an embrace and spoke into my white hair. "It's wonderful to know you as an adult, Zoe." She let go but held onto my shoulders for a moment, inspecting me as if I were a model for one of her paintings.

I never imagined I'd be in my 1950 Airstream with Perenelle Flamel in the 21st century. I'd lost touch with her and Nicolas so long before that my head was still spinning from them being back in my life this past month.

Perenelle sniffed the air. "I smell purple."

I laughed. "You mean lavender."

She wrinkled her nose. "I've always thought that flower was misnamed. The plant gives up pigments as bright as deep violet."

An idea was beginning to bubble up in my mind.

"This," Perenelle continued, "is a perfect example of why alchemists need their own laboratories. The remnants of the dried cuttings in this steel box are pleasant, but quite distracting."

"I have that new alchemical corner set up in my bedroom. I could try to create some gold—"

"I appreciate the thought, but you've never been adept at transforming any element into gold. Now isn't the time to expect miracles."

"You already made one nugget."

"I do have the *tria prima*." Perenelle shook her head. "But it's not enough."

The *tria prima* of alchemical elements are mercury, sulfur, and salt. They're the core elements for any physical transformation in an alchemy lab. Thinking of those elements alchemically as they related inwardly, our bodies are salt, our spirits mercury, and our soul is sulfur. That's why alchemy can refer to so many aspects of ourselves and the physical world, from the Elixir of Life to extend one's life, to the Philosopher's Stone to turn lead into gold.

"We might not be able to create gold," I said, "but I have an idea for how we can catch the blackmailer."

CHAPTER 10

Two people stood in the attic doorway. The raven-haired girl was far taller than the boy, and her eyes wider. The blond boy's mouth hung agape.

Dorian knew with certainty these were Brixton's teenage friends, Veronica and Ethan. Dorian had never met them in person, but he had seen them from afar, plus he had spoken to Veronica on the telephone.

"*Zut alors*," Dorian muttered.

Veronica opened her mouth. Dorian knew the magnitude of a scream that could emerge from the mouth of a teenage girl. He braced himself, but the sound did not come. Brixton jumped across the floor and clamped his hand over her mouth.

"Please, V. Don't scream." Brixton kept his hand over her mouth. "I can explain."

Dorian thought for a moment that she might faint, but no, she was not a weak girl. It was the other boy he needed to worry about.

"I don't feel so well." Ethan stared at Dorian as he backed away. Not toward the stairs, as Dorian had initially feared. He knocked into the wall near the door frame, but instead of turning around, he slid down the wall until he was sitting on the floor.

"I have no smelling salts," Dorian said. "Perhaps a cookie?" He tried to make himself look as friendly as possible. He did not need Ethan running screaming from the house as soon as he recovered.

Dorian was as friendly and polite a gargoyle as you could meet, but reactions like Ethan's were why he remained hidden. Always.

Brixton let go of Veronica's mouth as she tried to speak words that were clearly not a scream. "Dorian?" she whispered. "Is that you?"

Dorian smiled. Veronica remembered his voice. She had spoken to him on the phone and corresponded with him over email, when he had enlisted her help with previous investigations—with Zoe repeatedly reminding him she was a child not to be endangered. Veronica believed him to be a Frenchman (which he was) who was deformed and preferred not to be seen. In spite of everyone's protestations that this was Portland in the twenty-first century and people would not be judgmental, he knew his true visage would be too much.

"At your service." The gargoyle bowed as Veronica gaped at him.

"I can't even..." Ethan trailed off.

Veronica pushed her own fears aside for a friend in need. She knelt in front of Ethan. "Get some water for him, Brix."

"What do I tell Zoe?" Brixton asked.

"I believe," Dorian said, "she and Madame Flamel have departed. If she is in the kitchen, simply say hello and that you were playing chess with me and became thirsty."

"Chess?" Ethan repeated, then groaned. "The gargoyle plays chess?"

"Are you sure I should leave you?" Brixton looked at Ethan's pale face.

"Go." Dorian nodded. "It will be all right."

Brixton gave a worried glance at his friends before hurrying down the attic stairs.

The blond boy sprawled on the floor looked younger and far more fragile than Dorian had believed Ethan to be. The boy had the easy confidence that comes with having far more money than one needs, yet he was not as sure of himself and the world as his outward appearance suggested. From the boy's expression, Dorian expected him to pull his oversize coat around himself like a cocoon, yet the dark coat hung open as Ethan stared at the gargoyle, barely blinking.

"It's okay, Ethan." Veronica brushed a lock of his hair from his face. An intimate gesture. "I know him. *We* know him. It's Zoe and Brix's friend Dorian."

"Brixton wasn't joking," Ethan croaked. Speaking jarred his senses loose and he scrambled to push himself further against the wall. "That first night when we all met Zoe last year, he tried to tell us about… about a gargoyle."

"I thought he was being a toad." Veronica looked from Ethan to the gargoyle. Her long black hair fell forward as she tilted her head. "I thought he was making fun of a man with a deformity. But he wasn't…" Her shoulders began to heave. She had been calm for her friend's sake, but now that her attention was back on Dorian, her apprehension was returning. Perhaps it was a miscalculation for Dorian to have sent Brixton away.

Fast footsteps sounded on the steep stairs leading to the attic. Brixton appeared a moment later, water sloshing over the side of the glass of water in his hand.

"Drink this, E."

Ethan accepted the water and downed half of it quickly. So quickly he began to cough. "Is this drugged? You put something in here so I'd forget what I saw? Forget Dorian?" He shoved the glass away, and the remainder of the liquid spilled over Brixton.

Brixton glared at him. "I got the water from Zoe's pitcher with lemons and cucumbers floating in it. That's what you taste."

"You will find, Ethan," Dorian said, "that I am unforgettable." He chuckled, hoping he was taking the right tone with the boy. And the girl. She was still shaking.

"You tried to tell us," Veronica whispered, staring at Brixton, her eyes even wider than before. "But then you stopped. You let us think—"

Dorian stepped closer. "I would not allow him to tell you the truth. I have been alive long enough to know not to let people see my true self."

"I'm drugged," Ethan mumbled. "Is this what drugs feel like? I tried vodka from my parents' freezer before, but that was nothing like this. It didn't make me hallucinate."

"You're not drugged," Veronica said. "I'm seeing the same thing as you. A small man who looks… like a gargoyle." She tilted her head again and gasped. "I recognize you. You're from Notre Dame in Paris!"

Dorian beamed. "*Oui*."

"OMG, are all of those stone gargoyles people who are trapped in—"

"No. Rest assured, *mon amie*, that they are not trapped in stone. My body was originally carved in stone, meant to be one of the grand chimeras in the gallery of gargoyles atop Notre Dame Cathedral. I was *un petite peu* too small, so I was not used for the cathedral. Instead, Viollet-le-Duc gave his creation to his magician friend Jean Eugène Robert-Houdin, who brought me to life through alchemy."

"Wait." Ethan looked calmer now. "That magician Houdini was an alchemist?"

"Houdini named himself after the great Robert-Houdin," Dorian explained.

"So this other not-Houdini magician was an alchemist?"

"It is… complicated," Dorian said.

"You have to tell us everything," Veronica insisted.

"What you have seen," said Dorian, not raising his voice, but enunciating each word, "and what I am going to tell you, cannot leave this attic. If it does, there will be serious repercussions."

Ethan pushed himself further into the corner. "What does that mean?" His gaze turned to Brixton. "What does he mean? He doesn't attack people, does he? Oh God, those teeth."

"Of course not," Brixton snapped. "Don't be a toad."

A swell of pride arose in Dorian. Brixton was a good friend. And growing into a good man. "You must depart before Zoe and Perenelle return and realize you are here," Dorian said.

"She doesn't know your true form?" Veronica asked. "How does she not—"

"Of course she knows," Brixton said. "But I don't think Zoe would be happy if more people knew his secret. Nobody else can know, you guys. Um, how did you get inside? She didn't let you in, did she?"

"You weren't answering our texts," Veronica said. "You were supposed to meet up with us after school. We thought you might be working in Zoe's garden, so we came over. Nobody was in the garden, but the front door was open and we heard your voice coming from upstairs."

"Madame Flamel," Dorian muttered. "In her distress she neglected to close the front door. Zoe would never be so careless."

Veronica was still staring wide-eyed at him, but her expression had softened from fright to wonder.

"Zoe and Perenelle will be gone for a while if they've gone looking for Perenelle's blackmailer," Brixton said.

"A blackmailer?" Veronica repeated. "Why do I get the feeling things are even weirder."

CHAPTER 11

"There's no way to search the private rooms." Perenelle tapped her foot on the floor mat of my green 1942 Chevy. "That's the whole point of this studio set-up."

"Wait here for three minutes," I said, "then close your eyes."

"What?"

"Humor me. I'll be back in a few minutes."

She gave me a skeptical look, but didn't follow me out of the truck.

Perenelle and I had driven to Elements Art House, where Perenelle had found the painting that used the same paint as the blackmailer's note that had been sent to her.

Elements was a study in contrasts, both inside and out. Located in a nondescript strip mall of concrete-clad shops, the nicest thing that could be said about the outside was that it was walking distance to a nearby park. But Sameera Reddy's vision had transformed the harsh space into a magical oasis. By clever placement of the windows, she'd essentially created a mirage. The art studios felt as if they were in the center of a lush forest—when in reality a hillside park was two blocks away. There were no eye-level windows to look out over the harsh view of an asphalt parking lot filled with potholes and an alley of dumpsters. Instead, huge windows began eight feet off the ground, letting in plenty of natural light. Most importantly for this space, the high windows were strategically placed to show only the tree-filled landscape of the nearby park. Thus, despite its urban location, the only views from inside Elements Art House were of nature.

The two largest rooms hosted art classes, and five smaller rooms were available as rental spaces for artists. The private studios weren't cheap, but there was a room available that was perfect for Perenelle to practice both painting and alchemy. Luckily, she'd had a bit of gold with her in the hidden pockets of her dress when she was imprisoned, so we had enough funds to help get her and Nicolas set up beyond what I was able to provide. They hadn't yet figured out what the future held. We were taking things one step at a time as they recovered.

With Perenelle waiting for me in the truck, I hurried to the park and picked up a fallen walnut tree leaf and a river-washed granite pebble, then took a satchel of tea from the depths of my bag. One more thing… I ran to the drugstore on the corner and bought a cheap kids' set of paint.

When I returned to the truck, I didn't open any of the doors or even ask Perenelle to roll down her window.

"Keep your eyes closed," I said. "What's in my hand?"

Through the glass, I held up the cheap watercolor set.

"There are strange chemicals in this one," she said after a pause. "Not in the pigments, though. The plastic it's kept in."

"How about this?" I held up the pebble.

"Granite. With traces of clay."

"And this one?" I lifted the satchel of tea up to the window.

Tilting her head back into the seat, she breathed deeply. "That one is a trick."

"It's not." I sniffed the chamomile tea. Even breathing in the scent was calming.

"It is," she said. "It's chamomile. I knew that within a fraction of a second. I'm quite familiar with chamomile. I've used it to make a yellow dye. No, this one is a trick because there's so much more than chamomile." She smiled and opened her eyes.

"It's truly only chamomile," I said after walking around to the driver's side and stepping inside the truck.

"It's far more than that," she insisted. "*You* made it. I can tell. The dried leaves are filled with your energy and intent. You didn't simply harvest and dry the flowers. You worked with them to coax all of their strength."

"I'd say you passed the test."

"Remind me never to drink a brew made from these, or I'd become so relaxed I'd never deal with the problematic matter at hand. You've made your point, dearest Zoe. Let's go on a walk through a foul alley."

We walked along the alleyway behind Elements, stopping in front of each studio. We couldn't see inside, but we could smell the faint scents of the types of paints and solvents they each used. I wouldn't say it was easy—the trash bags in the dumpsters contained an assortment of unpalatable odors—but we were both used to tuning out the elements of the outside world to focus our intent on our quarry.

Without the benefit of sight or close proximity, Perenelle was still able to identify several elements inside each art studio.

"Egg tempura binder," she murmured. "Wheat paste. Quicksilver. Phosphoric acid."

I identified many myself—most strongly elderberry, beetroot, and currants in one paint mixture—but Perenelle was most attuned to the elements that didn't involve plants.

My heightened sensitivity to elements in the form of plant alchemy I excelled at had gotten me into trouble in the past. Shortly after I moved here, I sensed a poison that nobody else detected. It's what had drawn police attention my way. But it's also how I met Max. After everything that had happened today, even though there was something slightly stilted about our phone conversations across the world from each other, I looked forward to talking to him the next morning.

"It's not here," she hissed as we reached the section of the alley in front of the last studio. "The paint that was used for my blackmail note and that painting. Your idea was a good one, but it's not here. We have no way of proving who's threatening us."

"What are you two doing out here?" The sharp voice came from behind us.

CHAPTER 12

Veronica hesitated for only a moment before stepping forward to help Dorian with the snacks he'd procured from the kitchen.

He had thought the children needed a few minutes to talk amongst themselves, so he left them in the attic while he locked the front door and checked on the whereabouts of Zoe and Perenelle. The two women were not in the house, so Brixton was most likely correct that they had departed to investigate Madame Flamel's blackmail threats. Before returning to the attic, he picked up snacks from the kitchen. It would be more difficult for the children to fear him if they saw he was the same baker and chef they knew from Blue Sky Teas.

Dorian could see it took courage for Veronica to lift the tray from his hands, but she wished to show him she was unafraid. That he was still the same friend she had helped with research when he needed assistance with previous investigations.

"It's good to meet you in person." Veronica set down the tray of snacks and extended her hand.

Dorian smiled and clasped her hand in his. She tensed, but only for a moment. She squeezed his clawed hand and shook it, a smile appearing on her face.

"What are you doing, V?" Ethan croaked.

"Stop being such a toad."

"This is so messed up," Ethan whispered. "I don't even care that you two use the same insult you've used since you were 6 years old."

"Seriously, Ethan," Brixton said. "Dorian is a friend who just happens to be a gargoyle."

"Am I the only person who hasn't gone insane?" Ethan scrambled up as Brixton slammed the attic door. "I agreed to hear him out, but now you're trapping me in here? You can't—"

"Sit down and listen," Brixton said to his friend before turning back to Dorian. "Um, what can I tell them?"

"I believe," Dorian said, "the only thing we can tell them is the truth. We must impress upon them the seriousness of not letting anyone know." He looked to Ethan and Veronica. "You see, I am alive because of alchemy."

"Zoe doesn't think it's weird to have a secret gargoyle pet?" Ethan asked. "How does someone even find—"

"I am not a pet!"

"Whatever, Scooby."

"I am *not* a talking dog," Dorian huffed.

"It's a term of affection," Veronica said. "Scooby is very highly revered in this country."

"I will not dignify this with a response." Dorian straightened his wings. "I am a great alchemist, capable of transforming lead into gold." He held his tongue before he could add 'and turning little boys into toads.' He did not think that Ethan would appreciate that he was joking.

"You can turn lead into gold?" Ethan blinked at him, his fear replaced with interest.

"In theory," Dorian replied. "Alchemy is a finicky science." He did not wish to share how he was still only able to transform the smallest amounts of gold. He had previously mocked Zoe for this deficiency, so it would not do to share the same fault. He had believed that once he found true alchemy it would be easier, yet nothing about alchemy was *easy*.

"Can you teach us?" Veronica asked.

"You are too young."

Ethan groaned. "We're fifteen. In the old days, that was totally an adult, right?"

"You wish to remain in the body of a fifteen-year-old forever?" Dorian asked.

"Forever?" Veronica whispered.

Hmm. Perhaps it was not the best idea to discuss such matters with children. How did Zoe manage this with Brixton, he wondered.

"You can't hold back on us," Ethan said. "How does Zoe not freak out that there's a gargoyle in her attic? Come on, Scooby."

Dorian felt his cheeks flushing black. He breathed to calm himself, suppressing his urge to spread his wings wide. He should not frighten the boy. He needed to explain things, not simply plead for secrecy. He also knew he should not overstep. He considered how much he could reveal without endangering Zoe. She had fiercely protected his own secret. How could he reveal hers? Yet he needed to tell them at least part of the truth, so they would not be even more suspicious.

"Zoe is an alchemist herself," Dorian said in what he hoped was a calmer voice. "She understands such things." He frowned at his cryptic explanation. Such inelegant words were beneath him.

"Alchemy turns you into a gargoyle?" Veronica asked. "But Zoe isn't a gargoyle... is she?" Her voice trailed off and she bit her lip. "I'm not under a spell to see her differently than she really looks, am I?"

"You guys," Brixton said, "alchemy isn't magic. There are no spells. And Zoe looks just like we see her. Just like Dorian does."

Dorian sighed. "I am a gargoyle because this was always my original form. Zoe is a plant alchemist, meaning she extracts plant essences to transform plants into different energies."

"Alchemy just means transformation," Brixton said. "I learned about it after I met Dorian. No magic. Just intention and practice."

"But Dorian," Veronica said, "if you were built for Notre Dame, wasn't that ages ago?"

"Then how old is Zoe?" Ethan asked.

Dorian was not sure that the situation was improved now that Ethan was more engaged. Dorian knew full well that Zoe was over 300, and he could calculate the math in his head—he was a brilliant gargoyle, after all—so this was not the cause of his hesitation.

"It's not polite to ask how old a woman is," Brixton said, saving him. "Didn't you learn manners from your mom?"

"Of course not. My mom is the worst. You've met her. Now that she and my dad are getting divorced, she's even more annoying."

"I thought you said they were only separated." Veronica put her hand on Ethan's shoulder.

"They're separated for now, living in opposite ends of the house, and sure to get a divorce. They can't stand each other. They haven't for years. I don't know why it took them this long. Nope, I do. They were both so busy with their jobs they never had to hang out with each other. As soon as they had a little more time to spend together, they remembered they couldn't stand each other."

"My mom took her to one of her painting classes," Brixton said. "I really hope they don't become friends. No offense."

"My dad's family doesn't get along with my mom," Veronica said. "It makes family gatherings horrid. And it's my fault."

"How could it possibly be your fault?" Dorian asked.

"Because V uses both her parents' surnames," Brixton said. "Her dad's family doesn't think she should be Veronica Chen-Mendoza. Just Veronica Mendoza."

"This is very backward-looking. My own father joined his name with that of his wife, becoming Jean Eugène Robert-Houdin."

"Your father?" Ethan stared at him. "You have a father? He has a father."

Dorian was glad they had forgotten about the question of Zoe's age, yet concerned for what Brixton's friend was thinking.

"We're getting off track," Veronica said. "Alchemy and blackmail? Dorian, you have a lot to explain."

CHAPTER 13

Sameera Reddy stepped into the alley with a scowl on her face. "Hi, Perenelle. And it's Zoe, right? What are you two doing back here?"

Sameera ran Elements. Perfectly round glasses with copper frames slid down her small nose. Tattoos of art supplies crept up her forearms. A chunky, unlit cigar hung from her bottom lip, which was pierced, instead of the nose piercing her family would have preferred. Both styles, she had told me when we first met, were to expand the minds of her parents. Since she did marry a nice Telugu engineer as they'd hoped, she had to at least diverge from their expectations elsewhere. "Gotta keep them on their toes," she'd said.

She tossed a bag of trash into a dumpster, then turned back to us.

"We thought we heard an injured cat back here," I said, "so we took a detour before coming inside."

"Turned out it was nothing," Perenelle added. "It must have been the sound from someone's phone." She was practiced enough at deception to follow my lead without hesitation.

"That's a relief." Sameera smiled and we followed her to the front entrance.

Similar to the private studios, the effect of a light-filled entryway was created not with floor-to-ceiling windows, but thanks to high windows that looked up at the tops of trees and the sky rather than the parking lot.

Sameera sat down behind the main desk, located next to a mini snack bar with a coffee maker, water cooler, selection of teas, and a bowl of fruit. In the workshop to the left of the entryway, visible through a glass wall, ten women and two men sat and stood at easels arranged in a circle around an oversize flower bouquet in a two-foot ceramic vase.

"Zoe!" squealed a woman who turned around with a half-eaten Fuji apple in her hand. Brixton's mom Heather was always squealing. She'd had Brixton in her teens, so she was barely in her 30s, but acted even younger. Her fair hair was in two braids tied behind her back with an emerald green bow.

Heather threw her arms around me. "I'm still pinching myself that I'm painting here at Elements this year."

One of the five art rental spaces was endowed with a grant for an emerging artist who would not otherwise be able to afford the rental space. Heather had won this year's grant, which is how I'd learned about the space. Since there were so few units available, applicants weren't accepted simply based on their ability to pay; acceptance was a combination of payment and a curated review. After Heather had seen one of Perenelle's sketches, she told us as soon as a space opened up two weeks ago, and suggested Perenelle apply. Perenelle's application was approved within days, and she'd been practicing art and alchemy in the space for over a week now.

Heather gave me a final squeeze before letting go and giving Perenelle a quick hug. Though Heather was a free spirit who showed enthusiasm for many things, the only thing in her life I'd seen approach her fierce love for her son Brixton and her husband Abel was her artwork.

"Zoe, have you met Ashleigh?" Heather asked after releasing Perenelle.

"You're Ethan's mom, right?" I said. "Nice to see you again." I wasn't sure that it was, but what else could I say? Besides, maybe I'd been wrong in my first impression. Or perhaps she'd been having a bad day. I'd only met Ashleigh Eriksen once, but I'd heard more about her from Brixton.

Ashleigh's already perfunctory smile tightened. "Yes. I suppose that will be my identity until the day I die."

"Isn't it wonderful?" Heather beamed, oblivious to the sarcasm in Ashleigh's words. "Our boys are thick as thieves." She laughed. "I don't even know where that expression comes from. Zoe, do you know? You always seem to know that kind of thing."

"I should be going," Ashleigh said. She tightened her grip around her small designer handbag that looked out of place at the art studio. I was surprised to see her wearing tailored dress pants as well, until I noticed my mistake. They were yoga pants cut with fake pockets and pleats to get away with being office-work-friendly. I hadn't been completely won over to wearing stretchy clothing myself, but I did love the ethos of comfort that had been embraced in this century. I certainly didn't miss the scratchy clothes of my youth.

Heather's face fell. "I know your roses didn't turn out to look anything like roses today, or even flowers, really… but it takes time to get back into the craft of painting. Especially when you switched mediums from the photography you used to do in college." Her face perked up into a grin. "The journey of a thousand miles begins with a single step. Right?"

"I'm too old to start over and recapture something I loved 20 years ago." Ashleigh sighed. "What I want is to forget life. They say you lose yourself when doing art. So far, wine is much more effective." She gave us all a curt nod and sashayed toward the front doors. "Coming, Heather?"

"One second." Heather took a last bite of the apple and tossed it into a trash bin, then gave me and Perenelle quick hugs before following Ashleigh out the door.

I'd given Ashleigh the benefit of the doubt, but today's encounter was in line with my expectations. She and her husband Spencer didn't seem to pay much attention to their son, Ethan. They both had high-power jobs I didn't understand, even after Brixton attempted to explain it to me. But now they were getting divorced. Ashleigh was seeing a therapist (for anger management issues, according to Brixton), who recommended she take an art class. Heather had suggested Elements Art House. Ashleigh had loved art in high school, but abandoned it in college.

Perenelle watched them until they disappeared through the front door. She didn't know the teenagers nearly as well as I did, but was she worried about Ethan as well? Once the two women had vanished from sight, it was as if a spell had broken. Perenelle shook herself and turned abruptly.

"Watch out for—" I began as a woman emerged from the door of the private studio next to where we stood. Perenelle jostled the woman and sent her can of paint brushes clattering to the floor.

"My apologies," Perenelle said as she knelt to pick up the fallen brushes.

"Entirely my fault, Perenelle." The woman's voice was friendly, yet tentative. She was dressed in an oversize dress shirt covered in smudges of paint. "And thank you to your friend for trying to warn us. It's nice to meet you..."

"Zoe," Perenelle said as I scooped up the last errant brush that had rolled away. "Zoe, this is... "

The timid woman gave us both a smile. "Don't worry. Most people don't remember. It's Lucy. Good to see you again, Perenelle. Pleased to meet you, Zoe."

"Are you and your brushes all right?" I asked.

"Right as rain. I'll just get these cleaned up." She gave a small wave and stepped back into her studio.

"Right as rain," Perenelle repeated quietly as we walked down the hallway toward her studio. "I don't remember that phrase. Did she mean I ruined her day?"

"It means she's in good health."

"Such a strange and marvelous world," Perenelle murmured.

"One you'll be able to experience a lot more of."

"Only if we can figure out what's going on."

"We'll figure it out," I said.

I have a talent for learning languages. Not the formal structure, but the peculiarities that can help you fit in. Blending in is how my brother and I survived in those difficult years after fleeing Salem

Village, and led to the opportunity to apprentice to Nicolas Flamel in France. Just as Perenelle would say creating art is about looking so closely at your surroundings you can't *not* paint the world as you see it, learning languages is about listening carefully enough to what others are saying. Not just the words, and definitely not the grammar. It's in their intonations, their body language, and the spirit in their eyes as they speak to you. If you have enough time, and truly listen, that's how to truly learn a language.

We reached the door of Perenelle's studio. She unlocked the door, but immediately froze.

Another note from the blackmailer had been slipped under the door. This one had been hand delivered.

Deliver the 20 pieces of gold to the Witch's Castle, under the blue rock, at noon tomorrow. Any less, and I will reveal your secret.

CHAPTER 14

"The Witch's Castle?" Perenelle shivered.

"It's not as ominous as it sounds," I explained. "It's the name a bunch of teenagers gave to some abandoned ruins in a park across town."

"Why are you smiling?"

"Because we have an advantage the blackmailer doesn't know about."

"We do?"

"Dorian. That's one of his favorite spots to explore at night. He's decided to set a Gothic novel there, so he's told me all about it—including where there's a hidden spot not many people know about, where we can hide. We can watch to see who the blackmailer is."

"You don't understand, Zoe. I can't possibly make enough gold by tomorrow at noon. Neither can Nicolas. He's far too weak. It would kill him. We already discussed this. I can't—"

"I know. But you can make *fool's gold* with your pigments." I pointed to the elaborate laboratory set-up along one wall.

Her eyes widened with hope, but only for a second. "They'll know it's fake."

"It doesn't matter. Because we'll catch them. I just need to ask Dorian about the spot—"

"No." Her voice was firm. "Don't tell the gargoyle about this latest note. He'll insist on knowing why you're asking. He'll come up with a wacky plan, when what we need is calm and measured."

It was always Dorian who came up with a plan. It would undoubtedly be a ridiculous, untenable plan. But one that I could use as a starting point to rein in. Unlike Dorian, I do not think of myself of a modern-day detective. I'm a modern-day plant alchemist.

Yes, I happen to have solved a number of crimes. But my gargoyle best friend was always at my side. He must have rubbed off on me.

"I don't like your silence, Zoe. You're still thinking of telling the gargoyle, aren't you? I don't understand why. You said he can't be trusted."

"I said no such thing. I said he can't be trusted to not investigate if there's a mystery at hand. But we *are* already investigating."

"Why do we need him? You already came up with a great plan. We're two capable women. We can catch the blackmailer."

"I'll find a way to ask Dorian without telling him what we're doing. All right?"

"You have never been good at hiding your emotions, Zoe. You know what a disaster it will be for the blackmailer to reveal I'm an alchemist. It's nearly as bad as being in jail—because we'd be on the run. You'd be forced to leave your home."

"You misunderstand the worry on my face. I knew I could never stay here forever. I accepted that reality long ago. I'm more concerned about what the blackmailer might do to make good on their threat. They've threatened violence. I'm wondering how far they're willing to go."

"We shouldn't underestimate them," she agreed. "It worries me that you and your generous spirit believes it's a threat. I'm old enough to believe in human nature. Most people won't believe we're true alchemists even if presented with facts. But most people would never stoop to blackmail either. Those who are desperate enough or immoral enough to do so are also capable of far more dangerous things." She gripped the edge of the wooden table holding the elements to make both art and alchemy.

"Create the fool's gold," I said. "While you're doing that, I'll be creating something of my own. Our back-up plan in case it doesn't work to watch for the blackmailer to take the fool's gold."

"Which is?"

"I'll tell you once I've made sure I can do it. You need to focus on creating 20 pieces of fool's gold by noon tomorrow."

"That, I can do." She rummaged through the shelf of ingredients to transform raw materials into paint. The ingredients looked so much like alchemical materials—because they were. "Iron pyrite," she murmured. "Cadmium sulfide." She turned to me. "I need thirty minutes alone to set up the preparations that will rest overnight while I sleep. I'll need to return at dawn to complete the transformation."

"I'll try my part once we get home. You just need half an hour?" I glanced at the high window showing the line of trees and the darkening sky beyond. Technically, the sun had already set, but there was still plenty of light in the sky. It would be nearly dark by the time we got home. My energy wouldn't be at its peak in the darkness, but I didn't need to be at full strength for the transformation I had in mind.

"We need to get that window covered," I said. "Is there butcher paper in here?"

She gasped. "One of the artists is a butcher?"

I could never guess which word usage she wouldn't be familiar with. "A roll of thick paper that's used underneath something you're painting, so you don't get paint on the floor or a table."

"Ah." She sorted through a tall bin that looked like a covered trash can but contained rolls of paper and random miscellany. She tossed two rubber figurines over her shoulder to extract the roll of paper that looked to be the right size to cover the high window.

I crouched to pick up the red toys that landed at my feet. "Why are there Superman figurines in that bin?"

"The man who rented this space before me was nicknamed Superman."

"A strong guy?" I held the back of the chair for Perenelle while she taped paper across the high window.

"Quite the opposite, apparently. A very small man called Kent Clarkson. Heather felt bad that he thought he was being teased.

Apparently he shares a name with a character who's a strongman? That's why he left. Heather worried that they bullied him out of the space by giving him these figurines of this man with a broad chest wearing a red cape."

"Clark Kent," I explained, "was the name of a character named Superman. It's too bad Kent Clarkson's parents didn't think more about their choice of name for their son."

"I'm sorry if he felt persecuted, but surely a grown man should have been more accustomed to how the world saw him. Or he always could have changed his name." She jumped down from the chair. "I can see your energy lagging. Go on a walk in the park and meet me back here in thirty minutes."

I only hoped the haphazard plan would be enough. And that I had the alchemical ingredients I needed for my half of the plan.

CHAPTER 15

Before the children departed, Brixton and Veronica had convinced Ethan not to reveal anything he had seen or heard, at least until they could speak again. Dorian believed they would hold Ethan to his word, yet he grew nervous as the day stretched on. They could not meet again to discuss the situation further until nightfall, once the other alchemists of the house were asleep. Only then could the teenagers safely return.

In the meantime, Dorian busied himself cooking dinner for Zoe and the Flamels.

With Nicolas looking on, Dorian was preparing artichoke and potato canapés when Zoe and Perenelle returned.

As Perenelle pushed open the kitchen's swinging door, he caught a glimpse of Zoe behind her, looking distressed and alone. Before Dorian could say hello, like any civilized gargoyle would do, Zoe disappeared up the stairs. Was she retreating to be with the painting of her brother, he wondered?

Perenelle knelt in front of Nicolas, who sat at the small kitchen table, and took his hands in hers. With the abundant fabric of her full skirt, it was a good thing Dorian kept the kitchen floor spotless.

Nicolas blinked at her through his thick glasses, which Zoe had explained he had not needed in his life before his injury and imprisonment.

"How are you feeling, my love?" Perenelle asked him.

"I cannot complain." Nicolas smiled at her, yet the usual sparkle in his eyes was dull and there was a slight tremor in his voice and hands.

"He hasn't needed a nap since eating farmhouse soup for lunch," Dorian said.

"I would never have known his last soup did not contain pork." A bit of the sparkle was back in his eye.

Dorian chuckled. "I did not tell him it was seaweed until after he ate it."

"Most enlightening," Nicolas murmured. "Most enlightening." He scribbled a note into one of the journals he had returned home with after his overtaxing day out, then paused. "How do you spell the seaweed you used?"

"D U L S E," Dorian spelled.

"*Très interresant*," Nicolas murmured. "This is an interconnected new world indeed." His eyes were alive, yet the tremor in his hand grew more severe as he wrote.

Nicolas's body was more damaged than the alchemist wished to admit. Dorian observed that he slept the majority of the hours of each day. When Nicolas said he was practicing alchemy in the basement, Dorian knew he slept. Through the pipes, Dorian could hear when Nicolas ceased performing experiments and took a nap on the small cot in the basement.

The man was a good actor. Dorian gave the old alchemist credit for this. It is how he had survived for so long, even in the open before his imprisonment. Now, this skill was how he hid the extent of the damage from his wife and from Zoe. Even from his medical team, Tobias and Mina.

But not from Dorian.

Dorian did not wish the Flamels to replace him in Zoe's life, yet he did not wish for Nicolas to be in chronic pain—or worse. Dorian Robert-Houdin was no monster. He was a talented chef with access to high quality ingredients (and who would have had a Michelin star if he had been able to show his visage to the world). As he scrubbed red potatoes, he knew what he could do. Dorian would help Nicolas recover through his greatest talent: cooking.

Yes, the great Dorian Robert-Houdin would bring the great alchemist back to good health by nourishing his body and soul.

It was through Zoe that Dorian had learned about the healing powers of food. And that one needed to be flexible. Taught the craft by a visionary French chef who had lost his sight, Dorian was trained as a proper French chef, using traditional methods to produce feasts of the senses. He was a gourmand. One who was horrified when he found out he had stowed away in the crates of a plant alchemist who did not cook with animal products. The great Dorian Robert-Houdin rose to the occasion (yes, perhaps he attempted to circumvent it at first, but who in their right mind would not?). He accepted the challenge and had become one of the U.S. West Coast's most accomplished vegan chefs and bakers. He was certain his belief was correct, even though it was strictly true he was not able to sample the cuisine of chefs beyond their radius of meal delivery.

Yet he was still primarily concerned with taste. What good was living if one could not savor the perfectly balanced combination of flavors exploding on one's tongue?

Now was his chance to learn more from Zoe's philosophy of cooking. To properly care for Nicolas, a guest in his home, he needed to think of foods where the primary focus was healing—but which tasted every bit as good. No... better! Dorian savored a challenge, be it using his little gray cells to catch a criminal or unraveling a culinary mystery.

Zoe had cooked and eaten simply before he had entered her life. Her high-speed blender was her biggest extravagance. He approved of the device for making decadent creams out of beans or nuts, but it was only one of many tools.

Zoe's form of cooking involved her ongoing practice of growing vegetables and herbs, regardless of how small a space she was afforded, then cooking beans and vegetables on the single burner in her Airstream trailer, adding dried herbs and infused oils she'd made herself, and blitzing everything together into a soup. Or making fresh-picked seasonal fruit and raw greens into a smoothie. To accompany her simple meals, she bought fresh bread daily from a local baker. Buying bread! How foolish, when it was so much better to make it oneself. He understood this was impossible when she lived out of her trailer (well, not *technically* impossible, as she could have used a Dutch oven in a campfire), but now that she had a proper house and he was her roommate, he baked bread daily.

Portland boasted many plant-based cooking courses that focused on nutrition and healing. Dorian could not join in-person classes and his fingers did not work well with modern electronics, so he preferred to learn from books. Yes, the great Dorian Robert-Houdin was not above admitting he had more to learn. He had mastered French cuisine and vegan baking. It was only natural that he would turn to lessons to glean information that might aid the process of Nicolas's body healing through food. He would peruse online bookshelves to determine what to buy. Now that he had his own credit card, which he funded through baking for Blue Sky Teas, it was far easier to make purchases.

Dorian finished washing and chopping vegetables. His *mis en place* of ingredients was ready for tonight's feast. Now it was time to begin the most alchemical stage of cooking: fire.

Cooking came easily to Dorian. He had no doubt his skills could help Nicolas recover from his ordeal. The far more difficult task ahead of him would be convincing the children not to reveal his existence. And as soon as the reality of his existence sunk in, he knew they would have more questions. They would want to know more about Nicolas and Perenelle Flamel, born in the late 1300s, two of the most powerful alchemists of all time. And Dorian's own origin through dangerous backward alchemy. No, the feast he was cooking was most certainly the easiest part of his day.

CHAPTER 16

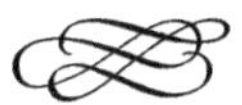

I closed the door of my bedroom. To get into the right mindset to practice alchemy, I took a few minutes to sit with my brother. The likeness Perenelle had painted into the portrait was truly remarkable. I didn't feel his energy in this copy, but I let my memories wash over me.

"Thank you, Thomas," I whispered before getting to work. "Thank you for saving me."

My part of the plan was inspired by a simple technology that had been used for the past 50 years by banks.

I found the ingredients I needed to create what was essentially a do-it-yourself version of the dye-packs banks used to foil bank robbers, by having an exploding pack of permanent ink dye inserted into a stack of bank notes given to a thief. Many banks were moving to a more modern system of small GPS tracking devices, replacing the dye packs that became ubiquitous after being invented in the 1960s. I didn't know how to go about using technology in a way our blackmailer wouldn't outsmart, but I had alchemical experience on my side.

If I was merely mixing ingredients to create a certain color, it wouldn't have been necessary to focus. That was the difference between art and alchemy in this context—if I were simply combining the elements that would create Prussian blue or Tyrian purple that someone could paint with, I could have all sorts of distractions around me. But if I wanted colors that behaved differently once touched by another person, I had to focus my intent on the result I wanted to achieve.

Using the flame of a candle I'd created myself, I heated elements in glass vessels until the colors bubbled and changed. Elemental sulfur, salts, and plants from my garden transformed into a rainbow of colors. I acted quickly, ensuring the pigments would be unstable.

As each color transformation was completed, I poured a swath of color onto the cloth we'd use to wrap our fool's good. This wasn't a mechanical trap that would release when tampered with. Instead, the elements of these unstable alchemical transformations would respond to the touch of another person, releasing color into the air as soon as the blackmailer opened the bundle.

When I came downstairs, Nicolas and Perenelle were seated at the dining table as Dorian carried out two serving platters of food. I needed to ask Dorian about his hiding spot at the Witch's Castle, but for now, breathing in the aroma of his cooking reminded me how hungry I was.

I smelled leeks, artichokes, potatoes, cassoulet beans, thyme, rosemary, and lots of garlic. Mingled with something else… Ah. The heavenly scent of a loaf of fresh sourdough bread reached my nose before I spotted it resting on the table.

"You've already filled nearly the whole notebook." I pointed at the notebook Nicolas was scribbling in.

"Do you remember our evenings around the hearth?" He closed the notebook and tucked it into his pocket. "Until my captivity, I wrote of the world around me, and my experiments, every day of my adult life. I regret that the journals I kept over the years were lost. At least many of Perenelle's paintings have survived."

"Even though they're not where they should be," said Perenelle.

"The museum gave me a reproduction that's quite beautiful," I said to reassure her.

"I can see in your eyes," she said, "that it's not the same to you."

Nicolas took Perenelle's hand before turning to me. "Like my wife, you can feel the energy of the ingredients used to make the paints. You know that if you were to have the original painting of you and your brother she painted, you'd also feel the love she put into the painting. I wish our ability to make gold hadn't been diminished from our captivity. If I could make gold again, I would buy it for you."

I shook my head. "You have nothing to feel guilty about. I'm only sorry it took me so long to find you."

Dorian cleared his throat. "Might you visit the painting one day?"

"I hope to," I answered. "The small museum in France is open to the public." I didn't add that I didn't yet feel comfortable leaving the Flamels on their own. I'd visit as soon as I could.

"A brilliant idea," said Nicolas.

Dorian dished up the potato canapés, a beetroot salad with farro, mint, and pepitas, and a main dish omelet made from mung beans and chickpea flour.

"Zoe," said Nicolas while he picked at his food, "do you care to explain why my wife was pestering Dorian about his hiding place near a local castle?"

To her credit, Perenelle didn't actually choke on her water. Yet I did see her throat constrict.

"Still curious about exploring Portland?" I caught her eye. "I know I promised I'd take you on a hike in Forest Park. I'll take you tomorrow."

Thankfully, Nicolas changed the subject and asked Dorian all about his cooking methods. He was still trying to determine how best to replicate the delicious beer he'd tasted earlier that week. Nicolas possessed a boundless enthusiasm for knowledge. He was never going to buy a beer fermentation kit—although many stores in Portland sold them—because even that felt like it was skipping a step in the process of transformation.

"Friends," Dorian said after we'd cleaned our plates, "would you prefer a baked apple tart or chocolate cookies for dessert? I baked both."

"It does not matter, my good man."

"No chocolate for me after dinner," I said.

"Ha!" Nicolas slapped his hand on the table. "I know why you said that. When we served you and Thomas drinking chocolate shortly after you arrived with us, you'd heard about it from the chocolate houses springing up in London, but you had never been afforded it yourself. Well, you didn't sleep a wink! The house was spotless when we woke up."

Dorian's eyes grew wide. "You forced her to work as a scullery maid to earn her keep?"

I laughed. "I always had to clean my alchemy lab where I was being tutored, not the rest of the house. But since I couldn't sleep or concentrate, I decided to be productive."

Nicolas laughed until it turned to a cough. "Perhaps I should get some rest before dessert is served." He tucked his handkerchief into his pocket. I don't think Perenelle or Dorian caught what he was trying to hide—but I did. A spot of blood on the pristine white handkerchief.

CHAPTER 17

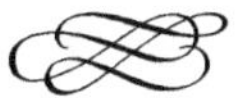

Dorian paced back and forth in his attic, hoping the children would be able to sneak out of their homes as planned.

The alchemists had gone to sleep hours ago. Nicolas was the earliest, but each of them grew tired when the sun went down. Zoe and Perenelle were asleep by 10 o'clock. Since discovering the Elixir of Life himself, Dorian understood the shift in alertness—yet for him, the pull was the opposite. He was most alive at night.

He continued pacing, hopping over an errant walking stick that had rolled away from one of the over-stuffed shelves.

Dorian's attic, normally a refuge, felt so confining! It was not because of the new items that Zoe was cataloging for Elixir. It was the oppression of this shared house. He and Zoe were a good team. She did not need the Flamels. They had meant a great deal to her at one time in her life. If he did not do something, they would replace Dorian altogether.

Not only that, but Zoe and Perenelle had left the stolen painting in the attic for "safe keeping," knowing Dorian would look after it even though they did not wish to involve him in its importance. He had not yet moved it from the spot on the floor where it was resting against the wall.

He'd placed it with the paintings that had come with the three antique typewriters he had purchased from an Oregonian shop owner who'd bundled the possessions of a deceased local writer. It was only the typewriters he had desired, but the acquisition came with the five framed paintings that had been hanging on the wall of the man's writing studio. Dorian thought Zoe might be able to sell the artwork through Elixir, but she had declined, stating they were not antiques and did not fit the store's ethos.

The sound of creaking on the stairs interrupted his silent rant. The attic door creaked open a moment later.

"I read up on the gargoyles of Notre Dame." It was the first thing young Veronica Chen-Mendoza said upon stepping through the attic's narrow doorway with her two friends. She dumped her backpack at her feet. "I also asked my parents about them over dinner. Your history is so fascinating, Dorian! Eugène Viollet-le-Duc was a polymath—"

"He had more than one wife?" Brixton asked.

Veronica rolled her eyes. "That means he was a person who's good at all sorts of things. Like a Renaissance man, you know? He was an architect and an artist, and it was his vision to renovate the cathedral way more than a simple renovation. He basically rebuilt the whole building."

This, Dorian knew, was not strictly true. Yet the idea she expressed was correct. Until Victor Hugo had rallied public sentiment around an idealized version of a medieval cathedral as imagined in his famous novel *Notre-Dame de Paris*, later renamed *The Hunchback of Notre-Dame*, people had not considered fantastical gargoyles, chimeras, and grotesques to be essential features of the Paris cathedral. Only his smaller, waterspout kin carried out a practical architectural necessity on the medieval cathedral. The new gargoyles from the mid-1800s did not replace lost carvings, nor did they serve a functional purpose. Yet they fulfilled another important goal: they inspired the good people of Paris.

"There was no gallery of gargoyles before the restoration," Dorian agreed. "People think of my brethren as being medieval, yet we are not. We gargoyles of Notre Dame are only 150 years old."

"*Only*." Ethan slouched in the doorway, not venturing further into the room. The boy still looked anxious and rather pale today, but he was no longer shaking, and he could look Dorian in the eye, at least for a couple of seconds at a time. When he caught sight of the table of food Dorian had set out for his guests, he forgot his wariness. "You cooked all this?"

"*Oui*." These were not sloppy discards from his baking for Blue Sky Teas. Dorian did his baking for the teashop at 3 a.m. His safety inspections, which he did not attend, were always rated 100%. He was meticulous. When he left the kitchen before dawn each morning, the teashop's kitchen was spotless and the shelves of Blue Sky Teas were brimming with an assortment of perfect pastries for the coming day's patrons. Any pastries that did not emerge from the oven ready for a photo shoot (he knew the younger patrons photographed their food before enjoying it) he took home in a picnic basket.

But this midnight snack he had cooked in his home kitchen, especially for the children. Freshly baked sourdough bread, which could be eaten with a creamy hazelnut chocolate spread or a savory white bean and paprika dip. Dates stuffed with cashew cheese. Spiralized vegetable salads in cupcake tins with a spicy vinaigrette. A pitcher of water flavored with fresh mint and a large thermos of cocoa. A perfect midnight snack, if he did say so himself. Ethan must have agreed. He helped himself to a tall glass of iced tea and spread a hearty dollop of chocolate spread onto a warm slice of bread.

"Neither of you told anyone?" Dorian asked cautiously, stealing a glance at his skylight, in case he might need it. The window served as Dorian's front door—and an escape hatch. When Zoe had purchased this crumbling house, part of the damage was a hole in the roof large enough for Dorian to squeeze through. A thick blue tarp had been affixed to the roof until proper roofers had fixed it and added a skylight. If any of them wondered why an attic needed a skylight, they did not raise their question with the woman paying in cash.

"No!" Veronica balled her hands into fists. "How could you think Ethan or I would tell anyone? You trusted Brixton this whole year—"

"Not," Dorian said, "by choice. Remember, he had broken into this house on a dare from the two of you."

Veronica reddened. "We didn't think he'd actually go inside, or literally *break* anything."

Brixton remained silent but popped one of the stuffed dates into his mouth.

"It is natural," Dorian said as he turned to Brixton, "to wish to be believed..."

"That was before I knew you." Brixton looked at his sneakers instead of at Dorian.

"Nobody would have believed us," said Ethan. "Brix learned that. I still can't believe he kept this from us for so long."

Brixton shrugged. "I didn't. Not really. Once I realized how much it would hurt Dorian and Zoe for word to get out about them being alchemists and him being, well, a gargoyle, I stopped trying to get him on video. But everything else I told you was true. He's a friend of Zoe's who's originally from France, and his appearance makes him scared of meeting up with people. V spoke with him on the phone a bunch of times. You both just assumed what everyone else did."

It was how Dorian, Zoe, and other alchemists had survived independently for so long. They stayed hidden in some ways, but in other ways they relied on human nature. People saw what they wished to see. If certain elements of what they saw did not comport with their world view, such as an unmoving gargoyle statue who looked as if he was watching them or standing in a pose that was slightly different, they would simply assume it was their imagination. They would not truly wonder if Zoe was 350 years old or if her gargoyle statue was in fact a living gargoyle.

"It's so romantic that you were carved for Notre Dame Cathedral," Veronica said. "Do you remember it?"

"The cathedral? Yes." Dorian smiled at his many memories of the cathedral over the years, including his recent trip with Zoe to stop an art thief. "But being created there? No. I was not yet alive."

"So you were created but not alive? How did you stay hidden? Oh! Brixton said you go around the city at night. Did someone see you? Is that why they're blackmailing Zoe? How long do you stay out each night? I don't see a bed in here. Don't you need to sleep? Is that why someone is blackmailing you? Well, not *you*, but Zoe's stepmom? She's an alchemist too?" The questions poured out of the girl almost as a single breath.

It would not be long until Veronica began asking pointed questions about alchemy. He would need to decide how to address this. For now, he fixed himself a hearty sandwich with two slices of sourdough with bean dip spread on both sides and the vegetable salad resting in between. He hopped onto the chair in front of the chess set and took a bite. Veronica could not expect him to speak with his mouth full. That would be rude. He pointed at his jaw to indicate the reason for his failure to answer.

Brixton pointed at the paper in the typewriter Dorian was using to write his novel. "New chapter?"

"Don't spy," Veronica said, sitting down across the table from Dorian and pulling up her legs to sit cross-legged, resting her hands on her knees, in rapt attention. Waiting for him to regale her with stories. Oh, the stories he could tell. What was appropriate for a 15-year-old? He would have asked Zoe, except she did not know Brixton's friends had learned of his existence. Hmm... He had thought it would be more difficult to keep the secret from her, but she had been so busy she barely noticed him anymore. Nobody was paying any attention to the gargoyle who cooked and cleaned, slaving away for their benefit. Well, to be fair, the cleaning only consisted of cleaning up in the kitchen. But it was still a great contribution to the household.

Brixton grabbed an ottoman and sat down in a spot where he could watch both of his friends. He knew Dorian's story already. Dorian suspected he wished to watch his friends' expressions as they listened.

"Can I touch your wings?" Veronica asked. "Oh! Sorry. Is that like asking to touch someone's hair?" She reddened.

"These?" Dorian finished his bite of food and unfurled his wings. The gray wings were unlike those of others who possessed them—neither feathers like a bird nor fur like a flying squirrel, not stone like a gargoyle or skin like a bat.

Ethan dropped his glass and stumbled backwards.

Unlike earlier that day, the boy was not backing into an empty section of wall. He was heading right for the set of six framed paintings resting at an angle against the wall.

Before Dorian could act, Ethan crashed into the pile of artwork. The first frame teetered, then propelled all of them to fall. The glass from five of the six shattered.

"Merde," Dorian muttered. He scampered from his chair and inspected the damage.

"Nice one," Brixton said to Ethan.

"What? You've had a year to get used to a monst—a gargoyle. It's not like I can't pay for new frames for all these paintings. I'll cover it."

Dorian ignored them. He knew that Ethan had money enough to buy a new frame, whatever the cost might have been. And also that the boy had been about to say "monster." It was nothing new.

Dorian inspected the damage. The boy had not only destroyed the frames. More than one of the paintings was torn. Dorian lifted a broken frame from the pile of rubble.

An item that was neither glass nor paper dislodged and fell. It rolled across the attic's floorboards.

"That's a really rusty quarter," Brixton said as he stepped on the coin to stop it.

Veronica picked up the coin. "It's not rusty. This is, like, old. Like the kind of thing that should be in a museum."

"Let me see." Ethan rested his head against Veronica's to get a closer look at the coin. "Whoa."

"See?" Veronica held it up for everyone to see. "It looks like one of those pirate doubloons from Max's favorite movie."

"That's not all." Brixton knelt at the pile of rubble, incautiously ignoring the glass. He lifted two worn pieces of paper with the indentation of a coin. He lifted them up and showed them to the group.

The first was simply notes written with a neat hand. But the second... The second was something else entirely. The faded paper. The rudimentary sketch of an old-fashioned ship just off the coast of a long coastline, its sails and hull engulfed in flames. A set of rocks emerged from the water next to the flame-filled ship. A dotted line began on land, circled the rocks, and ended in an X.

Brixton looked from the old, faded paper to Dorian. "It's a treasure map."

CHAPTER 18

At dawn, I dropped Perenelle off at Elements Art House. A light rain was falling. She needed her private space to create fool's gold for our noon assignation with the blackmailer. I would only hinder her progress, so I returned home.

It was nearly time for me to call Max. I had just enough time to steep a cup of tea to take with me to the covered back porch.

Dorian was preparing a loaf of fresh sourdough bread when I came into the kitchen. He wriggled his horns as he inspected my sleep-deprived self. "You did not sleep well?"

"That obvious?" I turned on a burner under the kettle, then ran my hands through my white hair.

"I am terribly sorry," he said, bowing his head in shame, "that I must report I broke one of your paintings kept in the attic. I feared it may have woken you." He looked at me expectantly.

"That's not what kept me awake. And as long as it wasn't Perenelle's portrait of Edward Kelley, you don't need to look so guilty." Nothing else in the attic was as dangerous as that portrait. I might lose a little revenue from a broken item I could no longer sell, but that didn't worry me.

"I tripped, and I broke my fall on the large pile of paintings we had resting in the corner—the ones I obtained with my typewriters that you rejected, from the collection of Oregon writer Hamlet Coltrane."

I abandoned the mug I was lifting from a cabinet and ran to my friend. "Are you all right? Did the glass cut you?" I wasn't sure how his body would react to cuts from shards of glass, but he didn't look injured.

Dorian chuckled. "Thank you for your concern, *mon amie.* My skin is quite thick, so I emerged from the wreckage unscathed. Alas, the paintings did not fare as well. Including the one Madame Flamel showed us yesterday."

"The seascape painting?" The frame didn't matter, but if the paint had been tainted… I shook off my worry. Perenelle had already gleaned what she needed to from the painting.

"Only the frame is damaged. Not the painting itself. I will replace the glass—"

"Don't worry, Dorian. But why do you look like there's something else you need to tell me?"

Dorian was rocking back and forth on his heels. His look was now giddy, not worried. "I am so pleased you are not concerned about the frame. Now I can share with you that the mishap has a silver lining. I have made a discovery in one of the paintings you unwisely deemed unworthy of Elixir." He grinned at me. "A discovery that could render your business unnecessary in the future." He paused again. "You are not going to guess?"

The kettle whistled and I removed it from the flame, giving it a minute to cool before pouring it over a bundle of mint leaves. "A hidden Picasso?"

Dorian clasped his clawed hands together. "Even better. *A treasure map.*" He wriggled his horns in glee.

"A treasure map," I repeated. "Like a scavenger hunt game?"

"*Non,*" he sputtered. "A *real* treasure map." He lifted it gently toward me, close enough for me to see a basic black ink drawing of a clipper ship in flames. "Never let it be said that Dorian Robert-Houdin did not share his spoils with his dearest friend."

"I need to call Max before he goes to sleep. I'm five minutes late already. Can we look at this when I'm back?"

Dorian grumbled but assented.

I took my tea and stepped onto the covered back porch. The light rain had turned into a stronger tumult, but the wind hadn't joined the rain, so the covered porch remained dry.

I called Max, but the call went to voicemail. I sipped my tea in serene silence while I waited for him to call back. Through the rain, I couldn't quite tell if a light dusting of powdery mildew threatened some of the leaves of my squash plants. I'd take a closer look later, once the rain had ceased.

My gardens flourished wherever I lived, but the weather of the Pacific Northwest was especially conducive to thriving plants. The colorful assortment of winter squash—long-necked butternut, knobby-skinned kabocha, and multi-colored carnival squash—peeked out from beneath their oversize leaves on the sprawling vines.

It was a few more minutes before Max called me back.

"Sorry I'm late."

"I don't mind. I'm enjoying the garden."

"I miss your garden. And mine. I'm tired. I wish it was time to come home."

"But you're enjoying your time there?"

There was a slight pause before he answered. "Enjoying isn't quite the right word. But it's fulfilling. I miss you. I heard you take a sip. What tea do you have this morning?"

"Ginger for a rainy day."

"Lapsang souchong for me."

"Made from fire," I murmured.

Max coughed. "What did you say?"

"Isn't that pine-smoked tea?"

"Yeah." A pause. "You're right."

"I know you're tired," I said, "but I can't help thinking there's something strange about your voice."

"I love that you can tell when something isn't quite right. It was like that from the start, when we met. I didn't believe what you said about your observations at the time. But I should have." His words were flowing more freely now. "You're an amazing woman, Zoe Faust. I love—"

The last word was cut off by the sound of my phone beeping at me.

The infernal device was informing me that Perenelle was calling me. I hated to leave at that moment, but we had a ticking clock to produce the gold and catch the blackmailer.

"I'll be just one second, Max," I said. "I have another call I need to take. Hang on."

I clicked over to Perenelle.

"It's not working, Zoe," she hissed.

"What's not—"

"The fool's gold. I know what I need to do. I need you. We don't have much time. Can you pick me up?"

"On my way." I clicked back to Max. "Max, I'm sorry. Something urgent has come up."

"Everything OK?"

"It will be. I know we don't have much of a window to talk right now. I'm sorry I can't—"

"It's OK. Go."

CHAPTER 19

Zoe stomped through the back door of the house and rushed through the kitchen, barely stopping to drop her mug in the sink. Before Dorian could inquire what was wrong, she was out the front door of the house.

Dorian gaped at the empty room. Zoe had forgotten about the treasure map he had so generously told her about!

If Zoe did not wish to involve him in her plans, why should Dorian try harder to bring her into the fold with his discovery?

The previous night, the discovery of the treasure map had thankfully distracted Brixton and his friends from questions of blackmail and alchemy. Dorian had kept the map and coin, but promised to update the teenagers after he spoke with Zoe. He had not anticipated it would be *quite* so early, but without Zoe's interest... Dorian called Brixton's cell phone from his attic telephone which the boy referred to as 'the dinosaur.'

Fifteen minutes later, two tired-looking boys and one chipper girl arrived. Droplets of rain clung to their hair and clothing, yet they did not seem fazed by this. In this, they were more like Dorian than the adults in his life.

"You locked the door behind you?" Dorian asked.

"Of course," Brixton said. "And I made sure Nicolas didn't see us before we came upstairs."

"*Très bon*."

"You're really French," Ethan muttered, looking far more awake than he had moments before. "And you're really *real*. Truly. I haven't had anything to eat or drink in this house in the last 12 hours. You can't have drugged me."

Veronica dropped her backpack on the attic floor and gently punched Ethan's arm. "Stop it already. Dorian, did Ms. Faust have any ideas?"

"Unfortunately," said Dorian, "she was not interested in our map."

"You mean she determined the gold coin isn't real?" Veronica asked.

"I did not have an opportunity to show her the rest of our discovery beyond the map," Dorian began.

"You didn't show the gold coin to her?" Brixton gaped at him. "We've really gotta tell Zoe. I could text her—"

"Stop." Dorian held up a clawed hand. "Remember, Zoe cannot know that your friends are aware of my existence. She will worry. This is why I told her I discovered the map myself."

"But you didn't show her the coin," said Brixton. "That's why she doesn't care about the map."

"This is not the reason for her disinterest," Dorian said.

"Does he always speak so formally?" Ethan whispered to Brixton.

"Zoe has other concerns at present," Dorian continued, ignoring the boy's comment. There was nothing wrong with speaking in a dignified manner. "We must figure out what we are dealing with on our own."

"We have to go to school in a few minutes," Veronica said. "My parents will kill me if I skip class again."

"I will begin research using Zoe's computer," Dorian said, "and you can help after school."

"Wait," Ethan said. "Zoe's pet gargoyle is giving us orders?"

"I am not a pet!"

"It's not orders," Veronica said. "Don't you want to know what's up with this treasure map that was hidden for some reason? I mean, if it wasn't real, why was it hidden behind a painting?"

"Yeah, but Fred should be the one making the plan. Not Scooby."

Veronica crossed her arms. "Blond hair doesn't make you Fred. Besides, Velma's way smarter. If anyone is in charge, I'm going to be the one to come up with the plan."

"Children," Dorian said, "you speak in riddles."

"Children?" Ethan glanced warily at Dorian. "If he can call us children, I can call him a pet."

"You guys," Brixton said, "this isn't helping. Dorian, did you find out more about the painting the map was behind?"

"I sent a missive to the online shop owner where I purchased the set of typewriters that came with these paintings. I have not yet heard back."

"A missive?" Ethan repeated. "You mean an email?"

"*Oui*. There was no phone number given, so I must await a reply on Zoe's laptop. All I know is what it says on the archived listing." He opened Zoe's laptop and found the digital receipt. It took a minute, because the keys were too small for his fingers. At least they responded to the touch of his fingers, unlike the screens of cell phones. Typewriters were much more civilized.

"The thrift store owner got them from the estate of writer Hamlet Coltrane," Brixton read.

"Never heard of him," Ethan commented.

"He doesn't have a digital footprint," said Veronica as she scrolled on the screen of her phone.

"Because he wrote during the time of typewriters." Ethan pointed at the broken Remington.

"We're going to be late for school." Veronica hefted her backpack onto her slim shoulders.

"While Dorian waits for the seller to get back to him, Veronica is the best one to come up with a plan on our end." Brixton turned to her. "V, you come up with our next steps and we can talk when we meet up at lunch—Ethan, you know I'm right it should be her—and then we can call Dorian. We'll all help after school."

"Yeah, whatever," Ethan said. "But what are we going to learn besides that these were props for some party game? That's why the map doesn't look like anywhere real."

"What about the notes on that other piece of paper?" Veronica hesitated in the doorway before her curiosity got the best of her. She hurried back to them and spread out the piece of paper that was not a map. "It looks like a real researcher's notes."

They gathered around the paper and read the curious words:

Dating confirms sixteenth-century coin.

Why didn't they say "based on a true story"? Would have made for better promotion.

Unless—what if they wanted to find the treasure in Oregon for themselves? Good reason to hide truth that the wizard is real.

Already found? But why no record? Fair to keep, so no need to hide.

"Right," Ethan said. Was that sarcasm in his voice? "A researcher who believes in wizards." Yes, definitely sarcasm. "And how would you know what a real researcher's notes look like?"

Brixton coughed. "You know her mom is a professor."

"Everyone has a cooler mom than me. Even Dorian's. Zoe is pretty cool."

"*Bon*," Dorian said stiffly, trying his best to ignore the barb. Zoe, his mother?! He was too dignified to respond. "I am not certain whether we should meet here at the house again. Even if Zoe and Madame Flamel are out on one of their secret errands, Nicolas will be awake but staying in the house later. He should not find out we are all friends now."

"Friends..." Ethan murmured, "with a gargoyle."

"Tonight," said Brixton, "after our folks are asleep, let's meet at midnight. I know just the spot where we can talk without prying eyes."

CHAPTER 20

I stepped into the shambles of Perenelle's private art studio. It was more difficult than it had been last night. This morning I had to be careful to avoid the metallic slime that covered much of the space.

I had been known to accidentally create copious amounts of a green sludge when my alchemical experiments went awry. Perenelle's pigment-centered alchemy had generated a far more beautiful metallic sheen, but the copper goo covered a swath of the concrete floor as well as two splatters on the wall and the butcher paper we'd used to cover the high windows. I was relieved to see the window coverings still in place. Though in some spots it could have been sludge covering the glass.

I stepped gingerly over the glob of bubbling copper on the floor to get a closer look at the table where she'd created three chunks of fool's gold. Though as large as golf balls, the lumpy, sticky shapes looked nothing like the true gold that had been rediscovered, which she'd been tasked with recreating.

"I've found," she said, "that I cannot replicate even fool's gold accurately enough without getting closer to the gold itself."

"The *missing* gold," I clarified. "Which we have no idea where to find."

A thin smile formed on her lips. "Have you forgotten everything Nicolas taught you?"

I closed my eyes and felt the elements in Perenelle's studio. It wasn't strong, but it was there. "The *energy* of the gold would remain. Not at levels most people can perceive. But for you—"

"I hope so," she said. "I certainly hope so. It's our chance at catching the blackmailer."

"Then let's get going."

The rain was pummeling down by the time we reached the Oregon Gold History Museum. My old windshield wipers gave a last squeak as I killed the engine of my truck in the museum's parking lot.

While the buried Gold Rush gold had originally been discovered in a location a few hours south of us, the museum where the gold had been housed and the theft had taken place was here in Portland.

Rain pelted my silver raincoat as we ran to the door of the small museum. The internet had conflicting information about the hours of this family-owned-and-run museum, so I didn't know if it would be open. The sign on the door said the museum would be open at 10 o'clock. It was only 9:30 now. We were scheduled to meet the blackmailer at noon.

"If we wait," I said, "you won't have much time to finish making the fool's gold."

Perenelle lifted her hood, allowing me to see the mischievous gleam in her eyes. "I've faced far more ominous deadlines. I've prepared all of the elements. I don't need more time than that. What I need is energy and intent. We wait."

While we waited in the bucket seats of my truck for the museum to open, Perenelle pulled up photographs of the gold on her phone. Though Nicolas was the one who'd expressed more curiosity about modern technology, Perenelle was the one who'd adapted to technology more quickly. Though I still couldn't convince her to wear trousers. I, for one, was pleased to be living in an era where I could dress however my mood struck me. Aside from my beloved silver raincoat, most of my small wardrobe had been destroyed earlier in the year, so Heather had taken me clothes shopping. Most of my purchases were green fabrics, as green had always been my favorite color.

Perenelle pinched and spread her fingers across the screen of her phone, enlarging a photograph of the largest of the gold nuggets. "Useless. This device is utterly useless. It only conveys one of our senses. What good is sight without scent and touch to sense energy?"

"Just because it's not perfect, doesn't mean it's not incredibly useful. We can read all about the origins of the gold—which I know will help you."

Gold was originally discovered in southern Oregon in 1852, shortly after it had been found in California. The Cabot family had been in Oregon since then, when one of their ancestors struck it rich in southern Oregon. The original prospector's great-grandchildren established the Oregon Gold Rush Historical Society in 1952, on the 100-year anniversary of gold being discovered in Oregon, with a room of research in the family home. Fifty years later, in the early 2000s, Ginessa "Gin" Cabot and her husband Harrison expanded the tradition by building a small museum on their expansive property. They were philanthropists known for sponsoring fundraisers for homeless shelters.

"The Oregon Gold History Museum was robbed four days ago," Perenelle read aloud, "two days after the private museum and historical society's owners, the Cabot family, found the gold nuggets lost in the 1860s." She paused and looked up from the screen. "Why do people enjoy reading on such small devices? My eyesight is perfect, yet would it not be so much more pleasurable to read on paper? I wish you'd saved those newspapers."

"You know as well as I do it's better to get enjoyment from things in the present moment than to think you'll need something like a newspaper later." I'd already used the past week's newspapers to wrap bouquets of flowers from my backyard for several friends. If I'd hoarded everything interesting I'd come across in my lifetime, I would need a storage container half the size of Oregon.

"You were always wise beyond your years." She smiled before

sighing and continuing to read on the small screen. "The gold was discovered after a rainstorm dislodged part of a hillside."

There were no local banks near the payload sites in the 1850s, so prospectors would leave gold coins and gold dust with a dependable paymaster of a local company. Because there was no bank vault, the gold was hidden by the trusted member of the community, who buried it in a safe hiding spot. The prospectors judged properly that he was a trustworthy man. Unfortunately, he wasn't a healthy one. The paymaster didn't steal their gold—he had a stroke. He was unable to reveal the location of the gold before he died, so the secret died with him.

Because the natural landscape changed over time, an intelligent young man had thought to try again. Harry Cabot had been dismissed by many as a rich kid who got lucky, but in reading the descriptions of how he set about finding his historical discovery, I didn't think that was the case.

Conventional wisdom says that young people used to grow up more quickly than they do today. In some ways that's true, but that idea also dismisses how capable young people are. Harry Cabot was perceptive enough to make an educated guess that a large rainstorm in the area meant the land might have shifted. He wasn't a young child. He had just turned 16, the same age I was when I fled my life in Salem Village.

Various treasure hunters had looked for the gold over time, but nobody found it until last month, when Gin Cabot and her son Harrison III did. They had the gold authenticated and then brought it to their family-run museum.

"Look." Perenelle dropped her phone into her lap and pointed.

A person in a hooded raincoat was running through the rain toward the museum. The hooded figure stopped in the doorway for a moment, then disappeared.

CHAPTER 21

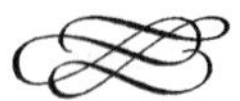

The dark-haired woman at the front desk blinked up at us with dark circles under tired eyes. She hadn't smiled when we followed her inside before she could lock the door behind her, but she didn't seem eager to keep us out either. Now that we were standing at the front desk, she was accommodating and let us buy tickets ten minutes before the official opening hours.

"It's too wet a day to leave anyone stranded outside," she said. "You can leave your wet coats on one of the coat racks."

I fought my impulse to think about what tinctures I might have to help her tiredness. A rumble of thunder sounded as we hung our coats. When I turned, Perenelle had already found an empty display case. A spot in the corner was blocked off by rope. I worried that Perenelle would ignore the barrier, but she stopped inches from the roped-off area. The space where the 20 pieces of gold had been on display sat empty, only a glass case remaining.

"It was here," she said softly as I reached her side. Though she'd spoken quietly and we were at the furthest end of the museum, I wondered if the woman at the front desk had heard her.

I thought for a moment that Perenelle would reach out to touch the glass case, which I doubted the museum employee would be happy about. Instead, she closed her eyes and breathed deeply.

One fragment of gold leaf remained underneath the glass. That was all I could see or sense. There might have been additional traces of gold, but I wasn't attuned enough to metals to notice. What I did notice was that the glass case was intact, though this was clearly the spot where the thief had taken the gold. Was it possible to lift the case without breaking it?

Ah. Several alarm triggers were visible if you looked carefully. The security appeared exquisite. Had that been installed after they put the new gold discovery on display?

I stepped away from Perenelle and let her absorb the gold's energy in peace. I doubted the museum was larger than a thousand square feet, but I was surprised by how spacious the building felt. Then again, for someone who'd lived out of an Airstream trailer for decades, that shouldn't have surprised me.

The layout was simple. This wasn't a museum of ornate columns and cornices, but of dark wood panels evocative of the Gold Rush era. It felt familiar because I recognized the museum layout from the news coverage.

The exhibits were divided into three sections: Oregon Gold Rush history, piracy in the Pacific Northwest, and a general section about the history of gold. The construction reproduced the feel of the 1850s, and made me feel as if I'd stepped back in time 150 years. This was in contrast to the signage on the exhibits, which looked like it was created for local school children.

I stopped in front of the section on the piracy of the Pacific Northwest. I was pleased to see that the explanatory placard next to the model of a ship explained the difference between primary sources and secondary sources. The placard noted further that although there was evidence privateers had plundered ships along this coastline, the infamous Pacific Northwest pirate "the Wizard of the West" was the figment of a writer's imagination.

I moved on to the section discussing Oregon Gold Rush history, filled with simple implements the prospectors had used to find gold, tools that would now be considered artifacts, from pickaxes to iron pans.

If you wanted to transform an item from pedestrian to priceless, all you needed was time.

Time was something we didn't have. I stole a glance at Perenelle. The clock was ticking.

Perenelle needed more time at the museum than I'd hoped. Once she was done, I drove as fast as I could as we rushed back to Elements.

We ran from the parking lot through the front door and kept our pace as we swung around into the hallway leading to the private studios. Unfortunately, the hallway wasn't empty. Once again, Perenelle crashed into the poor woman I'd met the previous day.

"I'm so sorry, Lucy." Perenelle knelt to pick up her brushes.

"I can help her," I said. "You go on to your studio."

Perenelle was gone in a heartbeat.

"Your friend is an interesting woman," Lucy said shyly, crouching on the concrete floor next to me. "Oh, this brush isn't mine. It must have fallen from one of Perenelle's pockets."

"I'll give it back to her." I accepted the brush.

"Do you know where she gets her wonderful skirts? They look like something out of an Elizabeth Peters novel that her character Amelia Peabody would wear when she's back in England, except with much more vibrant colors."

"Those are great books," I agreed. "You should ask her for the name of the tailor she found to make her skirts. They probably saved the pattern, since Perenelle added all those extra pockets. Sorry that we were in such a rush." I walked back with her to the main water cooler area.

"Aren't you going to give Perenelle back her brush?" she asked.

"I'm meeting up with her in a little while. I'll give it to her then."

I drove down the street to a coffee shop and ordered the only herbal tea they offered, a tart and fruity hibiscus. I had enough adrenaline pumping through me that there was no way I should introduce any caffeine into my body.

After finishing my mug of tea, I waited in my truck until it was time to pick up Perenelle. The storm couldn't decide whether it wanted to crash down or give up. The sound of the water hitting the truck alternated between deafening and a serene patter. Quite mercurial today. I hoped some of that energy was making its way to Perenelle.

She wasn't performing true alchemy, which is why I was cautiously optimistic that she'd be able to coax her malleable iron sulfide into the hardened shapes of fool's gold she intended. What she was doing was more closely related to mixing pigments than transforming elements.

Alchemists put the elements of earth, air, water, and fire through a series of steps to create transformations. It's necessary to calculate, dissolve, separate, conjoin, ferment, distill, and coagulate, all while being aware of planetary alignments and putting your own energy and intent into the process.

At eighteen minutes before noon, Perenelle slipped into the car with a wicker basket on her arm.

Her face was deathly pale, but her cracked lips formed a smile. "It's done."

CHAPTER 22

I parked near the Portland Audubon Society and we hiked on foot through sprawling Forest Park to the Witch's Castle.

The rain had mostly let up, yet a heavy mist hung in the air. My rubber-soled shoes squeaked as we hurried along the muddy path toward the ruins. Perenelle lifted her skirts to avoid being slowed down by wet fabric, but cursed every few minutes as a steep incline caused the fabric to slosh into the mud.

In the inclement weather, we only passed two hearty hikers, both dressed in hooded green parkas and sturdy hiking boots. I doubted either of them was our blackmailer, especially when they said a cheerful hello and I got a good look at their unfamiliar faces. Still, I wasn't letting my guard down.

Part of me had been worried that the blackmailer had been spying on my conversations with Dorian, since they'd suggested the Witch's Castle. But now, as we reached the ruins, I saw why the blackmailer had chosen this spot. We were simultaneously in the middle of Portland and also far from civilization. If the blackmailer needed to run away, they could go almost anywhere in the forest and disappear within seconds. There was also no way for there to be a mistake about what spot they meant—no confusion about calculating latitude and longitude or a particular tree in the woods. The Witch's Castle was unique, remote, and known to Portlanders.

We reached the base of the stone steps at five minutes past noon. The stones were slick with wet moss. As I lifted my foot toward the first step, Perenelle clasped her hand around my wrist.

"Look," she hissed.

Two people, their faces shrouded by hoods, stood at the top of the steps. Behind them was a window that no longer held glass and a domed doorway that had long ago lost its door.

As I tried to catch a glimpse of their faces, a clap of thunder sounded and the rain began to fall harder.

One of the two figures squealed. The other groaned. The pair ran down the stairs. A young woman paused briefly to say, "Careful on the slippery stairs!" then kept running.

I brushed wet hair out of my face and started up the stairs. My hoodless silver raincoat kept my body dry, but I shivered at the expectation of what we'd find.

Nothing.

There was nothing but moss-covered stones, slick with rainwater. No person. No message. Even the birds had fled from the rain for shelter.

"Here," Perenelle said. She ran to a stone that wasn't brownish-gray like the rest, nor was it green from moss. It was blue.

"Is that blue paint?" I asked. It didn't look like graffiti.

"Cobalt. Freshly painted. This is it."

I'd carried a Leatherman multi-purpose tool in my bag ever since Detective Vega used it to save our lives. I pulled out the knife blade and pressed it into the blue rock. The small rock popped out, revealing a laminated note and a brown linen tote bag.

Find a hollowed-out tree twenty paces north. Leave this bag there, filled with gold.

I groaned. "This is how they plan to get away with it." Even if we'd staked out a hiding spot near the Witch's Castle—which we had—it would no longer be relevant, because this wasn't the final destination.

Rainwater ran down the back of my neck as I made sure nothing else was hidden behind the cobalt rock.

We were soaking wet by the time we found the tree. It was in a secluded spot off the accessible path hikers used. Unlike the Witch's Castle, something left at this location wouldn't likely be found by anyone who wasn't the blackmailer. And it wasn't at all likely we could hide without being seen.

Luckily my back-up plan color bomb trap meant we didn't have to see them—but unless it was someone we knew from Elements, who we'd be able to see covered in color, we still wouldn't know who the blackmailer was.

We left the fool's gold and made our way back to the hiding spot near the Witch's Castle. It was now no longer a given that we'd see the blackmailer from here, but we had to try.

As we stepped around a thicket of trees, I jumped as my phone rang. I scrambled to silence the ringer, but as soon as I saw who it was I knew I had to answer the phone.

"Tobias?" I said.

"It's Nick. Are you with Perenelle? You two need to get back to the house right away. He's in bad shape."

We couldn't stay to see who the blackmailer was.

CHAPTER 23

Two hours later, I sat in the window of Blue Sky Teas, watching the rain cascade down the large front windows.

Located in my Hawthorne neighborhood, Blue Sky Teas was a cozy neighborhood gathering spot that was one of the reasons I'd known Portland would be perfect for me. It was a special place even on the outside. Above its welcoming bright orange door, a plaque read, "*'There is no trouble so great or grave that cannot be diminished by a nice cup of tea.'—Bernard-Paul Heroux.*"

But today, I wasn't sure even the greatest cup of tea could ease my worries.

After speeding home to get Perenelle to Nicolas and making sure he wasn't in immediate danger, I'd returned to the blackmail drop-off point.

It was too late.

The fool's gold was gone, and a vibrant rainbow of color coated the bark of the tree. The blackmailer had activated the explosion of color, but I wasn't there to see who'd emerged from the park in a swirl of colors.

Even if they'd scrubbed it off their skin, I should be able to detect the alchemical brew I'd concocted. And if someone at Elements didn't return for several days, that would be suspicious.

At least Nicolas was stable. Perenelle's presence had calmed him, so it was the right decision to abandon our quarry. I'd left him at home with Perenelle, and I'd come to the teashop with Tobias so we could speak freely.

Tobias was making his way back to the teashop table now. I breathed in the scents filling the air—dried rose petals, green tea with toasted rice, and cinnamon bark were most prominent—as he maneuvered around the line of customers and the old weeping fig tree that grew out of the ground at the center of the teashop. The tree's gnarled roots had pushed their way out of the earth next to the mosaic tiles that covered the rest of the floor, with gangly branches above stretching to the high ceiling painted like a sky with fluffy clouds. Eight tree-ring tables lined the walls. I was seated at the two-person corner table.

Tobias handed me a mug of turmeric tea.

"Doctor's orders?" I asked.

"Blue was out of my first choice, nettle tea. She told me someone asked if they could buy in bulk this morning and she sold them more than she should have. Blue could easily scale up. There's certainly demand for it."

"Which isn't what she wants out of life." I breathed in the warm, spicy scent, but gave it a moment to cool. Blue had fled her old life and had no desire to return to a more hectic pace. I couldn't imagine her expanding her already-bustling business. "Nicolas is really OK?"

Nicolas had called Tobias because he and Max's sister Mina were the two doctors who understood the ordeal he'd been through during his alchemical imprisonment.

"From what I can tell, what he needs most is rest."

"Which he's terrible at. You'd think he'd slow down after all this time."

Tobias chuckled.

Tobias Freeman was one of the few people on earth who knew my true age. A formerly enslaved man I first met in 1855, he'd discovered the Elixir of Life after we parted ways. I didn't know at the time how closely he'd observed my alchemy-infused transformations I used to help tired and weak people regain their strength, or that he'd go on to discover alchemy himself. He was around six feet tall, but he couldn't have weighed more than 100 pounds when I first met him. He was skin and bones then, but he'd transformed both his life and his body. When he gave me a hug today, he easily lifted me off the ground.

Until the Flamels returned to my life, Tobias had been my only human alchemist friend. And we'd only found each other again the previous year. He was still grieving the loss of his wife of several decades, Rosa, who had passed away recently. They'd been living in Detroit, and toward the end of her life they had to tell people that Tobias was her son or caregiver. They never would have believed a fit 50-year-old man was married to an 80-something woman. If their genders had been flipped, people might have raised an eyebrow, but they'd have believed it. It was only one of the many challenges of living longer than those around us.

Tobias had medical training, but had never wanted to be a formal doctor in the modern world because of the scrutiny. Like all alchemists, he wanted as low a profile as possible. He used his skills working as an EMT in places where hospitals were understaffed. After Rosa died, he was ready to leave his past life in Detroit. I suggested Portland, knowing we could both use a friend who understood. He'd stayed with me for a short time, but was now living in a small town not too far away, where the community was underserved with medical professionals.

Tobias's large hands covered the mug as he intertwined his fingers around the steaming vessel. "His injuries are *mostly* behaving as they would in any person, but because he was imprisoned with that horrible stab wound for so long, my best assessment continues to be that he just needs time for his body to readjust to normal life."

"I can't tell if you're optimistic or pessimistic."

"Neither can I. When I take a sip of this heavenly tea and sit here in this cozy window, I'm optimistic. When I step out into that heavy rain that returned unexpectedly, I'm pessimistic." He nodded toward the street.

He was right about our cozy spot giving us a false sense of security. The rain was perfect from our small table next to the window, underneath one of the sprawling branches of the weeping fig tree.

What made this spot less desirable to most businesses made it attractive to Blue, who was a wildcrafter and loved plants as much as I did. She'd both saved the tree and gotten a reduced lease.

He was wrong about the rain being unexpected. I'd gotten to know Portland well enough to never let the rain surprise me.

"His appetite is still pretty bad," I said. "Dorian has taken this as a challenge to cook hearty and healing meals that Nicolas will finish. We've got a lot of frozen soups and stews if you'd like me to send you home with some."

"I won't turn down Dorian's cooking. Make sure you've got enough for Nick, though. Eating well and resting is the best you can do for him right now. On his end, working in his alchemy lab will help him as well. That was generous of you to give him your basement space, including your athanor furnace. I know it means you haven't got space or an alchemical fire of your own."

I shook my head. "You forget I have my garden. Plus Nicolas insisted on giving me a wax candle lit from my athanor—he did something to it to ensure the flame doesn't go out. It's more than I need. My garden is enough for me. Especially since it's so overgrown at the moment, thanks to this rain." I'd never been someone who liked neat and tidy gardens. Chaos in nature wasn't disorder, but vibrancy. Life. "Can I send you home with some plants to help you get settled at your new place?"

"Mina said she'd bring some plants over, so I'm good. But thanks for the offer."

"I can give you some today. Who knows when she and Max will be back from their grandfather's funeral."

"Nah. They're back."

I blinked at my friend.

"At least Mina is," Tobias added, noticing my surprise.

"When did they get back?"

"A week ago."

A week? "You're sure Max flew back with her?" I thought back on our calls this week. He hadn't corrected me when I said "goodnight," but had he said where he was during our calls? Why wouldn't he have told me he was back? We'd been talking this whole time... Except for one day when he'd said he was busy. Was that when he was taking the long flight home?

"I assumed Max was with her, since that was the original plan. Maybe I'm wrong. I haven't seen him."

The tea tasted bitter in my mouth. Max and I always drank tea together. He had an impressive collection of teas he'd fix in his grandmother's teapot, and we'd savor it on his back porch while watching the night blooming jasmine unfurl as the moon crossed the night sky.

Max hadn't taken it well when I'd tried to explain to him that I was an alchemist. His sister Mina was far more open to the idea. Max and Mina's grandmother had been an apothecary. She'd taught Max and Mina some of what she knew. In Mina, it led to her becoming a medical doctor who specialized in integrative medicine. In Max, it was different. As he grew up he rejected things he couldn't quantify and sought concrete answers. They both wanted to help people, and Max's way was to become a detective to restore justice to the world.

Tobias finally met my gaze and saw the anger in my eyes. "I could have been mistaken," he added hastily. "Don't worry, Zoe. I'm sure there's a perfectly rational explanation."

CHAPTER 24

"Give me back the key." I lunged at the short figure in the red cape standing on the sidewalk.

Dorian jumped out of my way and held the key I was after behind his back. "He gave you the key to his home for a reason, Zoe."

"This is ridiculous. Give me the key. We shouldn't be outside either."

"You may go back inside. I will happily use this on my own. It is after nightfall. It is perfectly safe for me to be out in my cape. I know how to avoid people."

We were standing at the base of my driveway. The trees gave us a degree of cover, but not enough for comfort.

Dorian had hated the hooded cape at first, but he'd come around when he realized its practicality. He still needed to be careful, but it allowed a degree of anonymity. If caught on video or seen by anyone too closely, he looked like a child dressed in a Halloween costume.

Dorian used to use the hole in the roof to sneak out of the attic. The hole was now fixed and replaced by a proper skylight that hinged open. Unless hiding safely in my truck, he only went out at night, and always wore the hooded cape when he did so.

"I already went by Max's house earlier," I said.

"Yet you did not go inside. You merely knocked. This is true, yes?

You gave up when nobody answered the door. Max might be lying on his floor, slowly dying."

I rolled my eyes. "You don't believe that." I couldn't see Dorian's face beneath the hood of his cape, but I saw something more important. He shifted his arms. His hand holding Max's house key was now in front of his body.

I reached out and grabbed Dorian's wrist.

"*Mon dieu!*" He twisted away from me. The key slipped from his hand—and into the sewage grate next to the sidewalk.

I groaned as Dorian knelt at the grate and shook the iron bars with his clawed hands. The bars didn't budge.

"I guess I'm telling Max I lost his house key. At least that settles the matter of searching his house for clues."

Dorian chuckled beneath his cape. "When has something as trifling as a key stopped me?"

"I can't believe I'm letting you do this." It was fifteen minutes after we'd lost Max's key. I listened on my phone as Dorian's claws tapped on the lock.

Cell phone screens didn't respond well to the skin of his fingertips, so he didn't use a cell phone. But I'd bought phones for Nicolas and Perenelle (with a family plan discount), and, borrowing Nicolas's phone, rigged a headset that fit well over one of Dorian's ears with the microphone in front of his mouth.

"These claws were made for this, Zoe. You know this to be true."

"It doesn't mean you have to use them at Max's house."

"You are the one who said you were concerned. Something is amiss."

"I know. But it's not like I *really* think he's lying injured on the floor of his house and unable to call for help."

"You could have forbidden me to do this."

"Once I told you about his deception, I knew you'd do this even without me. Only in that case, I wouldn't be able to be on the phone with you to be your lookout."

He chuckled. "It is true. I do not need a lookout, though. His backyard is more overgrown with plants than yours."

I was now sitting in my truck halfway down the block. Far enough that it didn't look like I was parked at Max's house, but close enough that I could start the engine and swoop in to pick up Dorian if anyone called the authorities on a short intruder who looked like Little Red Riding Hood.

I'm no good at being awake when the sun is not. I've spent so much time nurturing plants, and they're how I found the Elixir of Life, that I respond to daily and seasonal cycles much like they do. I also respond to stimulants, so I'd fixed myself cocoa to take with me on my stakeout, to make sure I wouldn't fall asleep while Dorian burgled Max's house. *Ugh.* I hated to think of it like that. But I had to admit that's what we were doing.

Max used his garage as a small home gym, so he parked his jeep in the driveway. The jeep wasn't there. That was another sign he wasn't at home, so what was going on? Was he all right? Mina had confirmed that he flew back with her, but she hadn't seen him since. I was the only one he'd been in touch with—until a day ago. And until Perenelle's call had interrupted us, it sounded as if he was going to tell me he loved me. Then why was he lying to me?

The creak of a door sounded in my headphones.

"I am inside," Dorian reported. "This is how it should be. The two of us investigating together. I am a much better partner in crime than Madame Flamel, no?"

"Focus, Dorian."

"What do you think of me? Of course I have focus."

"No lights."

"*Pfft.* Do you think I am an amateur?"

"I dearly hope you're an amateur at breaking and entering."

"I broke nothing." A thud. "*Merde.*"

I gripped the steering wheel. "What is it?"

"I tripped on something."

Oh no. No, no, no. Please don't let it be—

"I was not," Dorian huffed, "expecting such a dark hallway. I pride myself on my nocturnal vision, you know. But there are no windows in this hallway. No moonlight filtering through—"

"Dorian."

"*Allo*? Can you hear me?"

"Can you see well enough to know what you tripped on?" Please let it be a *what* and not a *who*.

"I am uninjured. Thank you for asking."

"Dorian. Please. What did you trip over?"

"A suitcase."

"A suitcase?"

The sound of wheels rolling on a hardwood floor was followed by Dorian clicking his tongue. "My, my. I have confirmed the truth. Your boyfriend is no longer in China. The airline tag on this hideously ugly piece of modern luggage shows that Max Liu arrived at PDX eight days ago."

"Like Mina said."

"This house," Dorian said, "is much cleaner than ours. Almost too clean."

"I'm sure he cleaned up before leaving town. Nobody wants to come home to a house filled with ants." In a rainy climate like this one, I'd learned that even the smallest hint of sugar could create an invasion. "You don't need to report on the status of the house. Only to see what clues there are."

"Every single thing is placed in a cabinet."

"Except for his teapot, you mean."

"What teapot?"

"His grandmother's teapot. He leaves it on the counter. It's like a piece of art for the kitchen."

"There is no teapot, Zoe."

"I know it's dark—"

"*Non*. My night vision is exquisite. All I need is a sliver of light, which I have from the moonlight here in the kitchen. There is no teapot."

"Huh. He must have put it away. It doesn't matter. Forget about the teapot. Look for evidence of where he went."

"Like crumpled, half-burnt pieces of paper in the trash can."

"Perhaps," I suggested, "not quite so obvious." I heard the sound of numerous drawers swishing open and cabinets bumping shut.

"Nothing," Dorian said after a few minutes. "Unless he has hidden it away in the depths of his wardrobe, a teapot is not in this house."

"I thought we were going to forget about the teapot."

"You said this, yes," Dorian said. "Yet your voice made it sound as if this was important."

I scrunched my eyes shut. It was true. "Why would he take the teapot with him on a brief trip?"

"Thieves?" Dorian surmised.

"No. It's not worth more than $20. $50 at most."

"Then where," Dorian mused, "did the teapot go?"

Where indeed. It was the type of sentimental object someone would take if they were moving on with their lives. Moving on from me.

I gave a start as Dorian opened the passenger door of the truck.

He chuckled. "You did not see me approach, eh? I told you I am a stealthy gargoyle. I know how to maneuver through the shadows." He ducked down in the space in front of the bucket seat.

When we pulled into my driveway five minutes later, a man with wild hair, polka dot pajamas, and bare feet ran to meet us so quickly that he crashed into the hood of the truck as I screeched to a halt.

"Come quickly," Nicolas cried. "Someone has attempted to burglarize the house!"

CHAPTER 25

The irony was not lost on me that my house had been burglarized while Dorian and I were breaking into another house.

"They broke this window with a brick." Nicolas showed us the shards of glass on the floor of the kitchen. It wasn't the window box above the sink, but the one other window in the kitchen that faced the backyard.

"They got inside?" I looked out the window into the dark garden and drew the curtain across the empty hole where the window had been.

"No." Perenelle looped her hand through Nicolas's elbow and eased him into one of the kitchen chairs.

"I'm fine, dear," he said, but accepted the seat. "As Perenelle was saying, they did not get inside. It was a crude attempt, using the brick for speed instead of something less noisy. We heard the crash and glass shattering. I yelled that I was calling the police and Perenelle said she had a rifle. When I opened the blinds in the main room, I saw a figure dressed in black running away."

"What did they look like?" I asked, my gaze returning to the billowing curtain. Though the burglary concerned me, the secret of Dorian's existence was something we couldn't grow complacent about. Whenever there was a light on inside the house and Dorian was at home, I made sure the heavy curtains were drawn.

"Alas," said Perenelle, "they were neither large nor small in girth. Neither exceptionally tall nor short. A black cap—a ski cap, I believe you call it?—covered their hair and obscured their face."

"Did they think the house was empty because my truck wasn't here?" I mused. But if the burglar was who I believed them to be, why would they think the whole house was empty?

"They must have been watching the house," Dorian said. "They believe you live alone."

"They know, Zoe," Perenelle whispered. "They know."

"We knew they'd suspect it was fool's—"

"Yes," Perenelle cut in sharply. "We were fools." She clapped her hands together. "I should get Nicolas to bed."

Dorian clicked his tongue. "Not so fast, Madame Flamel. It is time for you to tell me what is going on."

"The full story, dear." Nicolas buffed his glasses on his shirt, then smiled innocently as he put his glasses back on and fixed his gaze upon Perenelle. "I know you have not told me what you and Zoe have been up to this week. You are still trying to protect me, but I assure you it is unnecessary. Have you not learned this by now?"

"They're right," I said. "This is serious. We can't keep this to ourselves. They're affected too."

"Very well." Perenelle sighed.

"I need to board up the window first. We don't know who could still be outside."

"They were alone," Nicolas said, "and fled."

"Zoe is right," Dorian said. "We cannot be too careful."

"I'll clean up the glass," I said. "Dorian, do you know where the extra boards and toolbox are?"

"*Oui.* I will return momentarily."

As I swept the last of the glass into the dustpan, a terrible thought struck me. Could the attempted thief have *planted* something? I sifted through the glass and inspected the surrounding areas. Nothing was amiss. The glass itself was simply glass from the windowpane, and nothing had been thrown through the window along with the brick. I lifted the heavy rust-colored brick and felt along its bumpy surface. It appeared to be a regular brick. Still, for good measure, I put the brick and the shards of glass in a trash bag and carried it to the far corner of the backyard before joining the others back inside.

By the time I was done, Dorian had returned with two boards and the toolbox with hammer and nails. We worked in silence until the window was secure, then moved to the living room, dark from the drawn blinds and pulled curtains. I turned on all the lights so our shadows wouldn't look quite so ominous.

"Begin," said Dorian, "at the beginning. That way, we will miss nothing." He steepled his fingers together.

"The beginning," Perenelle murmured. "That is perhaps too much for this conversation, Monsieur Robert-Houdin."

Dorian narrowed his eyes.

"Come now," Nicolas said. "You understand what Dorian is asking."

"Very well." She smoothed the folds of her skirt. "I have always been drawn to gold. In my workshop at Elements Art House, you all know I was observed and recorded creating gold."

Dorian clicked his tongue. "*Oui.* And you already know I believe this to be a careless—"

"It's not a public space," I cut in. "It's a private rented space. One that has high windows people can't casually look through, a door that locks, and assurance from the owner Sameera that the only cameras are in the entranceway facing the front doors. Someone used a camera without her knowledge, and without the knowledge of the people who use the space."

"Even so," said Dorian, "alchemical supplies—"

"Are the exact same supplies as I use for painting," Perenelle said. "Surely you know this, Monsieur Robert-Houdin. Apothecaries ran the first art shops."

I smiled at that, in spite of the situation. I remembered the artists' assistants who came to me for pigments, their skin covered in colorful mineral hues.

"That chunk of gold," said Perenelle, "was modeled after the Oregon Gold History Museum."

Dorian gasped.

"I needed something specific to focus my intent on," Perenelle continued. "But now the blackmailer thinks I can replicate famous gold—which is surely more valuable for whatever they wish to do with it. They left another note, which demanded I replicate the whole set of gold and deliver it to them earlier today. All I was able to create was fool's gold."

Nicolas took her hands in his. "Which you assumed they would not notice?"

"We thought we could catch them," I said. "I created a bundle of exploding color last night, which I hoped would stain their skin. But we had to leave before we could observe them…"

"Ah," Nicolas said softly, looking into Perenelle's eyes. "This was when I had my set-back and Tobias came to check on me?"

"They must know it's fake," Perenelle said. "We lost our opportunity to fool them briefly before we could identify them, and now they're taking matters into their own hands by trying to break in and steal whatever additional gold they believe me to have."

My earlier worry crept back. "Are you certain the attempted thief didn't get inside?"

Dorian gave a single flap of his wings. "I know that look, Zoe. You are thinking of something more troubling. What is it?"

"Could they have *added* something?"

"A listening device?" Nicolas asked. "It all happened so quickly; they didn't have time to do whatever they set out to do. Besides, unless such a thing is so small as to be invisible, the attempted thief left nothing behind."

"And why would they wish to do such a thing?" Perenelle asked. "Surely they wish to obtain gold, not to expose me and see me hang. I haven't been here long enough to make any enemies."

"Madame Flamel," Dorian said, "they no longer hang people. It would be a more modern form—"

"Dorian," I broke in. "You're not helping."

He wriggled his horns at me. "I am assuring your new houseguest that she is not in danger of a crude form of execution—"

"Thank you, my good man," Nicolas said. "Your words are most comforting. Might I trouble you for a spot of tea?"

Dorian scampered to the kitchen, grumbling under his breath. I heard the sound of a kettle being filled and a burner of the gas range being lit.

Nicolas sighed. "He is quite something, is he not? Quite something."

"For a creature brought to life through unnatural alchemy," Perenelle murmured.

"That was only his origin," I said for probably the fiftieth time. "His birth, which he had no control over. He made himself a true alchemist through his own efforts. You can trust him." But I knew she wouldn't listen. She and Nicolas had risked so much to stop the dangerous form of alchemy that had given Dorian life.

"Is it time for you to call your friend with the police?" Perenelle asked. "I know you weren't certain if we could trust him, but you were right: the blackmailer has acted more quickly than anticipated."

"He took leave for a family funeral."

Perenelle gave a resigned nod, then her face lit up. "You could try calling his untethered phone."

"You mean his cellular phone," Dorian corrected as he pushed open the kitchen door carrying a tray of tea. "I do not think that would do any good."

"We can't go to him," I agreed.

Dorian scratched his gray chin. "Madame Flamel. I believe you are not yet finished with your story."

"Am I not?"

Dorian glowered at her. "It is *you,* Madame Flamel, who this miscreant is targeting. What do *you* wish to do?"

"Creating fool's gold has depleted my energy," she said. "I would appreciate a midnight feast, to feed both our minds and souls. I, for one, am famished. Shall we raid the freezer?" Her eyes sparkled. "I have the correct saying, do I not?"

She led the way to the kitchen as the kettle whistled. Nicolas followed, while Dorian and I lingered behind in the living room.

Dorian sniffed. "With her voracious appetite and appreciation for my cooking, perhaps I have underestimated her intelligence. We might just get along yet."

CHAPTER 26

Dorian silently climbed the stone ruins of the Witch's Castle and looked out over Forest Park. It was one of his favorite places to visit when he explored Portland at night.

The Castle was not near the craftsman house he shared with Zoe—and more recently the Flamels—in the Hawthorne neighborhood of Southeast Portland, but it was worth the trek on his usual solitary nights. He had not expected the children to wish to travel outside of their neighborhood so late at night. But to them, this was a grand adventure. He appreciated their *joie de vivre*.

The perch was a well-placed lookout spot for Dorian as he waited for Brixton and his friends to arrive. He had been worried that the "midnight snack" he fixed for the Flamels would last past midnight, with Madame Flamel's voracious appetite, yet they had finished eating and returned to bed by eleven o'clock. Even after cleaning up, Dorian had plenty of time to arrive early for his assignation with the children.

The night air was crisp and damp, but the rain from earlier that day had ceased. A crescent of moonlight illuminated the sky, as did the faint glow of man-made light.

It was twenty minutes after midnight when the children finally arrived. Technically, this park was off limits at this time of night, yet Dorian had coached them on how to evade prying eyes.

The teenagers had slipped out of their bedrooms, leaving extra pillows stuffed into their beds in case their parents checked on them. At least, this is what Dorian had suggested. Veronica said it was a good idea. The boys claimed their own parents would not check on them. Dorian hoped they were right. They did not need the complication of the children being grounded. Not while they had a treasure to find.

Dorian peered over the edge of the moss-covered stone wall with no roof as Brixton jogged up the stone stairs, his friends behind him.

Dorian scampered silently down the sloping stones that had once supported a roof and landed with a muffled thud on the soft ground. "What have you learned?"

Ethan stumbled back. "Don't *do* that. Didn't anyone ever tell you it's not nice to scare people?"

"Sorry we're late," said Brixton. "Veronica's dad goes to bed so late that she couldn't leave on time."

"He'd kill me if he knew I was here," Veronica added, yet she did so through a wide grin.

They were each filled with energy, in spite of the late hour. Oh, how Dorian appreciated finding other beings who did not need sleep! He knew they would eventually need to sleep, but unlike Zoe, whose sleep patterns were tied to the sun, these young people were just as awake after midnight as they were in the daylight.

This spot that provided privacy through its stone walls was perfect for planning what they were here to do. Veronica spread a thick blanket on the damp stone floor, and the four of them sat in a circle around the coin, map, and note. They had divided up tasks. Veronica had researched the coin, Brixton the map, Ethan obtained supplies to keep their discoveries safe from the elements, and Dorian conducted extensive online research anywhere his "little gray cells" led him.

"I don't know if it's a pirate treasure," Veronica said, "but I've identified the coin as a doubloon. At least that's what it looks like."

"It would be so much easier to go to an expert to get it authenticated," Ethan said. "My parents know rare coin dealers and art museum curators. I could have asked for their help if you hadn't said we couldn't show this stuff to anyone. At least we'd know for sure the gold was real."

Dorian clicked his tongue. "This much we know."

"We do?" Veronica blinked at him. Her brown eyes were wide in the camp light.

"I am an alchemist," said Dorian. "I know real gold when it is in my presence. This coin, it is real gold. Yet I know nothing of its origins or age. Only that it is real gold. This is why young Veronica was tasked with researching its history. What exactly have you learned?"

"This coin resembles a doubloon," she said. "Spanish gold. From the 1500s or 1600s. Doubloon means 'double,' and historians disagree if it's called that because it was worth two 'ducats'—that's the word for a gold or silver coin used for trading in Europe in old times—or because it had a double portrait of Ferdinand and Isabella. The Spanish brought these coins to the New World on ships, plus a bunch of new ones were made from gold they got from slave labor in Mexico. A lot of them were lost when ships sunk."

"Or when pirates raided them." Brixton held up the treasure map. "We once had a teacher who was really into local history, so we learned about all sorts of cool stuff, like the Shanghai tunnels underneath the city. One of the things he taught us was to be wary of stories about local pirates. Most pirates didn't make it all the way here to the Pacific Northwest, but some privateers did. I couldn't find anything about specific hoards of doubloons around here, but a lot of what was pillaged isn't known, you know?"

"You were tasked with researching the map," Dorian reminded him.

Brixton shook his head. "I know. I did a bunch of image searches online, but nothing came up that matches this hand-drawn map. It's too general. Not drawn to scale, you know?"

"I feared as much," Dorian said. The outline of the map was the whole coast of Oregon, with details drawn out of proportion. He tapped his clawed finger on a faded sketch of a ship being swallowed by three curls of waves.

"It's clearly a sinking ship," Brixton agreed, "and then an 'X' along these rocks on the coastline. It's got to mean a hidden treasure, right? But even I know that looking for a ship somewhere along the northern Oregon coast is hopeless without more information."

"And without scuba diving licenses," Veronica said.

"Let's get back to the coin." Ethan flipped it into the air. "Is there any identifying information on this thing?"

"Not that we'll find out if you break it." Brixton caught it mid-air and handed it to Veronica.

"It's a coin." Ethan scowled at him. "Not a Fabergé egg."

"You're asking about unique markings?" Veronica held the coin into the glow of the camp light. "Nothing that stands out. No way to tell exactly where it's from. Not without consulting an expert, which we agreed not to do yet."

"We have three pieces of information," said Dorian. "This must be enough for now. Young Veronica... your eyes have grown wide."

She stood and looked out over the forest for a moment before turning back to them. "I know what the treasure is."

CHAPTER 27

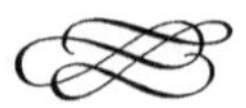

The antique clock in the attic struck midnight. So many of these antiques had been family heirlooms to their owners across continents and centuries. Now they were anonymous treasures for strangers to discover while scrolling the internet with insomnia.

Perhaps I was in a maudlin mood.

I shouldn't have been awake. The caffeine from the cocoa I drank earlier had worn off, but I didn't realize there was chocolate in the almond flour cake we defrosted as part of our midnight snack until I'd taken a second bite. By then it was already too late.

I normally pay more attention to what I eat and drink, but I'd been discombobulated by the burglary. Even the slightest bit of caffeine or alcohol affects me strongly. Perenelle was asleep in her and Nicolas's room. Since I was wide awake now, I thought I'd keep Dorian company. I hadn't been spending much time with him lately. I didn't like the current state of the relationships in this household. I needed to deal with that, but after the blackmail situation had been resolved.

But Dorian wasn't in his attic. He'd already gone out for the night.

I thought about cataloging the new items I'd purchased, but I was too distracted. Where had Dorian gone? A walk to stretch his legs, no doubt. It was perfectly normal for him to explore the city under the cover of darkness, even before he arrived at the Blue Sky Teas kitchen at 3 a.m. to bake pastries for the day. He wasn't confined to the attic, and he was a curious, adventurous gargoyle.

Still, why did I get the feeling he was keeping something from me? Probably just my imagination from the stress of the burglary, plus our plan to trap the blackmailer falling apart. I suspected it was also the items that needed to be catalogued and priced. Finds at estate sales were always bittersweet. Cherished items no longer valued, but that were once much beloved by their owner before they died. I always gave heirs a fair price, even when they did not realize what they had. In this case, the woman had no family and no will, so the state was selling her lifetime of possessions.

Max had told me his grandfather planned on dividing up his possessions among his family members who would appreciate different things, but we hadn't spoken about the details. Max had a complicated relationship with his family, as most of us did. He'd rejected his apothecary grandmother's teachings as he grew up, but last year when he and more than a hundred friends and family members had celebrated his grandfather's 100th birthday, he began to wonder more about his own life choices.

Where had Max gone after returning to Portland? And why didn't he think he could tell me? When he'd told me about his grandmother's teapot, it had seemed like he was about to open up to me, but then he'd shut down.

The clouds shifted and moonlight filtered through the skylight above, casting shadows over the shelves of small antiques. The shadow of the Underwood typewriter looked like a herd of animals climbing a hillside with castle ruins at the top, and the shadow of a clay vase resembled an anguished face crying out for help.

This was definitely not the right time for me to be in the attic. I clicked off the small light in the corner and closed the door behind me.

Back in my bedroom, I looked up at the copy of Perenelle's portrait of me and my brother. The green in my dress was my favorite color. A rich green that both flattered my complexion and reminded me of nature. Behind us, a fire was smoldering in a cozy hearth. As I looked more closely at the painting, I thought I saw something in the low flames. No, surely it was only my imagination.

I stepped closer to the reproduction of the painting. Even though it was a good copy, there was no way to see and feel the energy and details of the original.

In the small French museum where the painting was displayed, the placard's title read, *Brother and Sister, artist unknown, France, circa 1700.*

A scant, one-paragraph description by the curator speculated that the subjects were from a bourgeois family that had fallen on difficult times. Which wasn't true, yet was not a bad guess for someone who had no additional information. We didn't fit into the normal societal structure of the time, having money for the things most important to us, but not surrounding ourselves in opulence, and with no familial connections. Only our found family of Nicolas and Perenelle.

The curator noted the artist's choice of showing sunlight on the faces of the siblings, whereas the rest of the painting was dark, even the embers in the hearth. A study in contrasts. I loved the way Thomas's expression revealed the slightest hint of mischievousness in an otherwise angelic face.

I turned off the overhead light, leaving only the faint glow of the candle Nicolas had given me. A candle that didn't extinguish. I'd placed it in a hand-blown glass vessel and left it on my bedside. It was no brighter than moonlight from a crescent moon. The light was peaceful, yet I still had no confidence I'd get to sleep, even though it was now twenty minutes after midnight.

I let myself out of the back door and looked out over the peaceful backyard garden. Most of the plants had turned inward for the night, getting some rest before stretching once the sun would touch their leaves again in several hours.

I looked from the sleeping plants up to the window of the small bedroom I'd moved into after giving Nicolas and Perenelle the master bedroom. The eternal flame of the candle cast a barely detectable glow through the window. Flickering, it looked almost like a hidden face.

In the damp night air, I shivered as I looked up at the ghostly light.

Who was the blackmailer? Was it someone we knew? The explosion of paint had caught them, so we might know who it was as soon as the next morning.

The tail of a nocturnal visitor swished through the squash leaves. A racoon. It turned its head and I caught a glimpse of bright eyes peeking out from the fur striped like a mask across its furry face. Bored with me and the vegetable garden, my masked intruder hopped the fence, leaving me in silence, wondering if I'd be unmasking a blackmailer shortly after daybreak.

CHAPTER 28

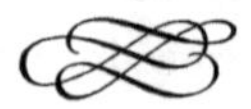

"There's a local legend about a pirate known as the Wizard of the West," Veronica continued. "It's like something out of that adventure movie *The Goonies* that Max loves."

"Boonies?" Dorian wriggled his horns. Why must the children speak in riddles?

"*The Goonies*," Brixton said as they all shed their backpacks and Dorian scampered down the smooth, weather-worn stone wall. "It's a famous movie from the 1980s. It was Max's favorite movie when he was a kid. It's set in Astoria, where he grew up. It's about a group of teenagers who find a pirate's treasure map behind a painting in their parents' attic. Haven't you seen it? It's wicked good."

"I read books," Dorian said. "Not watch television."

"The gargoyle *reads*," Ethan muttered as he set up a battery-operated lamp and pointed it at the items they'd discovered.

"V," Brixton said, "the Wizard of the West and *The Goonies* aren't *real*. This isn't a game."

Veronica scowled at Brixton and pointed at the faded piece of paper held in place by a rock. The nearly forgotten paper that was not the treasure map.

"You refer, young Veronica," said Dorian, "to the researcher's notes?"

He lifted the faded piece of paper in his clawed hands and handed it to her to do the honors.

She accepted it and read aloud:

Dating confirms sixteenth-century coin.

Why didn't they say "based on a true story"? Would have made for better promotion.

Unless—what if they wanted to find the treasure in Oregon for themselves? Good reason to hide truth that the wizard is real.

Already found? But why no record? Fair to keep, so no need to hide.

"No way," Brixton said.

"You see what I'm thinking?" asked Veronica.

"The note is talking about the movie being based on a true story, not a made-up legend." Brixton grinned.

Veronica nodded slowly, her eyes locked on the boy's. "They found out the Wizard of the West was real."

"The scriptwriter based their plot on a real treasure. *This one*." Brixton ran his hands through his black curls and looked up at the dark clouds above, a look of wonder on his face.

"It all fits," Veronica said. "Our map shows an X next to a pirate ship right along the coast, with a bunch of rocks. None of them look like Haystack Rock, but the scriptwriter wouldn't use landmarks about a real treasure if they wanted to find it for themselves—like the researcher's notes suggest. A pirate treasure of doubloons and other gold riches."

"I don't think it was him," Ethan cut in, holding up his phone. "He was a famous filmmaker who didn't need the doubloons for money. If he knew it was real, he would have totally used that info to promote the movie. He must've heard about it somewhere else and it made its way onto the page. Isn't that how writers' brains work?"

"This is a fair point," said Dorian, thinking of his own manuscript. He was still angry at Madame Flamel for breaking one of his new typewriters. But no matter. "We must focus on what we have. The map." Dorian tapped his claw on the X. "This will tell us *where* to search."

Brixton shook his head. "What we know suggests it's somewhere off the Oregon coast, but that's way too big an area to narrow down. Even if we waited until the end of fall semester, we couldn't search everywhere over our holiday break."

"These facts fit what we know," Dorian said. "The original owner of the painting with the hidden map is a deceased Oregonian. I have not yet heard back from the online seller. I will try to contact him once more, to see what he knows of this Oregon writer Hamlet Coltrane. If the seller does not have sufficient information, we can still compare this sketch to a map."

"You mean like digital mapping?" Ethan asked. "Brix already tried that. We'd need help to turn this messy sketch into something searchable to do more."

"Or we could use our eyes," said Dorian, "looking at real maps."

The children stared blankly at him. Had they ever seen a paper map before? One that showed topography and was filled with mapmakers' symbols?

"Whenever we figure it out," Ethan said, "my parents' extra car is in the garage. We could follow it—"

"With who driving?" Veronica scowled at him.

"Just because I don't have an official license doesn't mean I can't drive. My parents never notice when the car is missing."

"Why do you not simply get a license?" Dorian asked.

"That's a good one, Scooby," Ethan said.

"We're not old enough," Brixton said. "But Ethan is right. You only need a license if you get stopped. And we won't get stopped."

An owl hooted.

Veronica crossed her arms and glared at them. "This is ridiculous. We can't just steal a car and go in search of a treasure."

"I'm not saying we leave *now*," Ethan said. "We need to figure out where this map leads to. It's gotta be somewhere here in the Pacific Northwest. We'll have done more research to figure out where to go. That's how treasure hunting works, right? We call our contacts, do some online research, and then, um… then we know what's up. Right?"

"I still think this is a terrible idea." Veronica's icy gaze remained. "I mean, even if we figure out where the map leads, we'll need to tell Zoe to ask if she can drive us."

"I doubt," Dorian said, "she will take time away from her important life to help us." He may have spoken more bitterly than he intended.

Ethan and Veronica exchanged a look. Ethan was the one who spoke. "What are you talking about?"

"Dorian is jealous," Brixton answered.

Dorian clicked his tongue. "It is not jealousy." He would not admit this to the boy, even if he half feared it was an accurate description of his emotions. "It is concern. I do not trust the Flamels." This was also true. The longer an alchemist lived, the greater the danger became of losing their humanity. With Madame Flamel's lack of empathy for his own existence, perhaps this was to blame.

"Why don't you trust them?" Veronica asked. "If Zoe does, that should be enough for you. They seem really nice. Kinda strange, but that's pretty normal for Portland."

"Dorian," Brixton said, "you can't drive, can you?"

Ethan laughed. "A gargoyle at the wheel? That's a recipe to get stopped by the police."

"He'd be in a hooded cape," Brixton said, "like how he walks around to get here. That way he just looks like what we used to think—a man with a face he doesn't want people to see."

"Alas," Dorian said, "I never learned how to operate an automobile. I would say it is because my wings do not comfortably fit into the driver's seat of a car, but in truth it is for the reason Ethan stated. I should not be seen."

"Oh." Veronica frowned. "But you have to come with us."

"This," Dorian said, "is not a problem." He stood in a comfortable position, tucked his wings behind his back, and turned to unmoving stone.

Ethan stifled a scream. Veronica gasped, but did not appear frightened. She touched Dorian's shoulder.

"Stone. You're stone. You guys, he's real stone."

Dorian wriggled his horns and began to move. "A perfect way to hide, *n'est pas*?"

"I don't feel so well," Ethan murmured. "Are you sure I'm not drugged again and you guys aren't messing with me?"

"Get over yourself," Brixton said. "We're about to go on a treasure hunt."

"Patience, my young friend." Dorian steepled his clawed fingers together and stretched his wings. It was not as easy to transform between stone and flesh now that he was truly alive. "We narrow down the area in which we must search. There are clues hiding in this map we have not yet discovered."

Dorian felt he was on the verge of an important discovery. Not that he cared about the fame, for he could never take credit. Yet if he and the children found the missing doubloons, he could find the gold to buy Zoe the painting of her and her brother.

He would deliver her beloved portrait to her and prove his worth.

CHAPTER 29

A text from Max was waiting on my phone when I awoke.

Sorry I missed your calls. Can't talk today but will call soon.

I called him back. The phone went straight to voicemail. "I know you're back from China, Max," I said before hanging up.

I squeezed the phone. It was much more satisfying to let out frustration with a land line phone that allowed you to slam the receiver down. Cell phones didn't allow people to adequately express frustration.

I was grumpy at breakfast, even though the sun had come out full force this morning and I knew I might be close to learning who our blackmailer was. They'd have realized by now that we'd tried to trick them with fool's gold. It was even more urgent that we figure out who they were.

Dorian had returned from his pre-dawn baking in the Blue Sky Teas kitchen and insisted on fixing a feast for breakfast.

"I would be able to create an even more exquisite meal if a certain forgetful alchemist had not forgotten fenugreek seeds at the market." Dorian glanced briefly in my direction before ladling thick batter onto a hot cast iron skillet.

"There's been so much going on I know I haven't kept up with groceries. I'm sorry."

"*Merci.* I accept your apology."

As the batter heated and cooked, the scent of spices filled the kitchen, slightly improving my mood. I was almost optimistic as Dorian hummed an old French folk song as he sprinkled finely diced bell peppers and herbs on top.

The kitchen door swung open and Perenelle swept inside the cozy room. Her hair was unusually frizzy, making me suspect she felt as frazzled as I had when I woke up. "I'm ravenous." She headed straight for the fridge.

"No need to scavenge for leftovers," I said. "Dorian is making enough breakfast for everyone."

She peeked up at Dorian from behind the open door of the fridge. "Really?"

"A mung bean omelet," he said from his stepping stool in front of the stove, "with onions, bell peppers, parsley and cilantro from the garden, and a spice mix of turmeric, cumin, coriander, fennel, and pepper. Served alongside brioche bread and warm golden oat milk."

With the pan in his hand, he hopped off the stool and divided the omelet into four equal pieces. He handed the first plate to Perenelle, where she was seated at the small kitchen table across from me. "*Qu'est-ce que vous pensez?*"

"The omelet and golden milk are both a beautiful tint of yellow," Perenelle replied. "I would have thought those green-colored legumes you soaked overnight would have muddied the vivid yellow of the turmeric, but it has only made it more vibrant. Well done."

"You speak solely of color?" Dorian huffed.

"The flavor is excellent, too," I said, savoring a bite of the flavorful, fluffy omelet.

"Will Monsieur Flamel be joining us as well?" Dorian asked. "The omelet is high in protein and the spices will help awaken him."

"Nicolas will be down shortly."

Sure enough, as I took my first sip of the sweet and spicy frothed golden milk, Nicolas pushed through the kitchen's swinging door.

"You look stunning, dearest." Perenelle rose and kissed her husband on the cheek, letting her lips linger.

Nicolas looked dapper in a dark gray wool suit, white dress shirt with wide collar, and cuff links in the shape of skeleton keys. His glasses, which had been dulled by fingerprints by the second day he acquired them, sparkled with clarity.

"The foolish man fell asleep in his basement alchemy lab last week while wearing the suit," Perenelle said, "so I steamed the suit in the bathroom this morning. It's even better than it was when we found it at the thrifting store on Hawthorne."

That explained the frizzy hair. I was glad I'd been wrong in my assumption.

The kitchen wasn't large enough for the four of us, so we moved to the dining room. Dorian insisted on serving everything, and chuckled happily as Nicolas and Perenelle both requested seconds, whipping up a second omelet.

As Dorian cleared our empty plates, I felt fortunate we'd made it through the meal without any household infighting.

Perenelle lowered her voice to a whisper. "You're certain he's not using backward alchemy for his culinary creations? Elements that will backfire in our digestive systems?"

The sound of clattering dishware sounded from the kitchen.

I pinched the bridge of my nose. "His hearing is excellent, Perenelle."

"It was an honest question."

Dorian's situation was completely different than that of other backward alchemists, yet I didn't know what else I could do to convince Perenelle of that.

Dorian's snout poked out of the cracked kitchen door. "I would be happy to share the recipe with you, Madame Flamel. My culinary alchemy might be too complex for you to follow, but I will happily submit the evidence."

"Perhaps it's for the best if you two go out for a time," Nicolas suggested. "I'll help Dorian clean up."

We needed to go out anyway, so I accepted his suggestion.

Perenelle and I needed to arrive at Elements Art House as soon as the main area opened up at 9 o'clock. I was eager to see if anyone had paint on their skin or if anyone who should have been there wasn't because of their temporary accidental tattoo. Artists in residence had a key to work there at other times, but they would only spend time outside of their studios when others were around. It was Saturday, the busiest day of the week according to Perenelle.

A woman I didn't recognize, no older than her late teens or early twenties, sat at the front desk. She stopped spinning the swivel chair around when we stepped through the front door.

"I didn't believe Mom when she told me how early people would show up," the young woman said as her white sneakers came to a squeaking halt on the concrete floor. "Guess she was right that I needed to cover for her."

"We're the first to arrive today?" Perenelle asked.

"You're the alchemist who took over Kent's studio, right?"

I froze, and I sensed Perenelle stiffen beside me.

"Alchemist?" Perenelle repeated.

The young woman laughed. "Mom says you make your own pigments and paints. Which is pretty rad. I've watched some videos by this guy who says grinding your own pigments and transforming them into paints should be thought of as Alchemical Arts. So you're like a modern-day alchemist."

Perenelle's body relaxed. "I'm Perenelle."

The young women grinned. "I know. I'm Neisha."

I introduced myself and asked if her mom was all right.

Neisha shrugged. "Fine, I guess. Mom sets her own schedule. I go to Reed, so I'm nearby? I help out when I can? Especially on days when there are workshops that sound amazing?" She yawned. "Wish I didn't have to get up so early, though, you know?"

"You're here for today's bookbinding workshop?" Perenelle asked. I could tell she was confused by Neisha's style of ending sentences as if they were questions. I'd gotten used to the speech pattern that was increasingly common in this century.

Neisha's face lit up. "I've taken the instructor's workshops before and they're amazing. I have to sit where I can see the front door in case any patrons come in, but my generation knows how to multitask." She winked, and I could see so much of her mom Sameera in her.

Perenelle and I had been planning to linger near the central coffee station to see if anyone showed up with traces of my paint bomb. Since nobody else was there, we let ourselves into her studio.

Perenelle leaned against the studio door. "Why is Sameera hiding? I really hadn't expected her to be the blackmailer. Foolish, I know. But I quite like her."

"Maybe she's not here because she has paint on her skin, but maybe not. Her daughter didn't think it was suspicious for her mom not to be here this morning and I doubt Sameera would enlist her child in her own crimes. It sounds like it's normal for Neisha to cover the front desk."

"Perhaps," Perenelle agreed.

Her studio was still a mess from yesterday's transformations. It was terrible for the soul of an alchemist not to have an orderly alchemy lab, but our timetable to meet the blackmailer's demands couldn't be helped. Perenelle's glass vessels were filled with chalky pigments on the simple table. I hadn't previously noticed the wooden box beneath the table, but I knew that's where her alchemy supplies would be kept.

"You've only been here a couple of weeks," I said, "so you don't know what's normal for Sameera yet. We don't have enough information to know for sure."

"I know she needs money."

"She does?" I forgot about the wooden box and turned my attention back to Perenelle.

"She's thinking of getting rid of the scholarship studio space once Heather's year is up. Apparently the workshops they give don't generate as much money as they used to, because so many people take classes online."

"Just because someone needs money," I pointed out, "doesn't mean they're a blackmailer."

When Perenelle spoke again, her voice was the whisper of a defeated woman. "Our plan failed. We must accept that." She ran a fingertip across a glass vessel of bone black.

I shivered as the energy of the dark pigment reached me. She'd created the bone black herself. I could feel it. I could feel the power everywhere in this simple art studio that she'd only been in for such a short time. This was not a woman easily defeated.

"You don't mean that."

"I do," she insisted. "I should see if I'm ready to make gold after all. I can't live under the threat of the blackmailer harming you, Nicolas, Tobias, or anyone else we know. That's the challenge of finding community, isn't it? The more one finds, the more there is to lose."

"I don't want to lose you either."

"I can take care of myself perfectly well." This was the woman I knew.

"Who rescued you last month?" I raised an eyebrow, but ever since my hair had turned white the effect was far less dramatic.

She laughed at that. Laughed so hard a tear rolled down her cheek. "Thank you, Zoe. I needed you to remind me who I am. And who you are." She picked up one of the Superman figurines. "Why is this fellow dressed in red tights? I understood this fashion for men to have ended centuries ago."

I shrugged. "It's his superhero disguise."

"It must get terribly hot." She tossed it aside and peeled out of a hand-knitted sweater she had been drawn to at a thrift shop because she could tell that the knitter had dyed the yarn themselves. It was only shortly after 9 o'clock and already quite warm. "Let's go back to the museum. If I'm to make gold—"

"Only as one of our contingency plans," I broke in, "if everything else fails."

"Yes. I need time. And I need to be near the remnants once more."

She was the most powerful alchemist I'd ever met, even more powerful than her husband. But they were both still recovering. Was she capable of making gold once more?

"Can we stop at the French bakery down the street?" Perenelle asked as we stepped into the hallway and she locked the door of her studio. "I need a snack before you drive us to the gold museum." Perenelle's appetite was still making up for lost time after being imprisoned. I was still stuffed from Dorian's feast of a breakfast.

"You're going to the Oregon Gold History Museum?" a voice from behind us asked. Heather stepped out of her studio.

She wore a white sundress, colorful sandals, and flowers in her hair—her favorite type of outfit, regardless of the weather. There was no possibility she'd gotten my paint bomb on any of her skin. A streak of her own dark green paint did circle her right arm up to her elbow. Not that I believed Heather was a viable suspect. Well, maybe just a little. I'd been living with Dorian long enough to wonder if the least likely suspect was often the culprit.

"I didn't see you come in," I said. We hadn't been in Perenelle's studio for long.

"I was painting all night." She giggled. "Don't look so scandalized, Zoe. Abel was home with Brix. He's wonderful about supporting me when the muse strikes." She yawned, triggering another yawn from Neisha across the room.

"I remember those days of my youth when I could stay up for 48 hours or more finishing a painting that called to me," Perenelle said.

"I knew you were a kindred spirit." Heather hooked her green arm through Perenelle's. Perenelle didn't mind. "What a great idea about getting out of my head and going to a museum."

"Aren't you ready for your bed?" asked Perenelle.

"Too much adrenaline. I already texted Lucy and Ashleigh to meet me for brunch before I crash. But I'd love to see the museum. Brix has been talking about that theft there. I'll text the girls to meet us there before brunch."

CHAPTER 30

"Our next step in figuring out the location of our treasure," declared Dorian, "is to visit the Oregon Gold History Museum."

It was Saturday morning, and they had gathered in the attic the morning after their nocturnal discussion. Before inviting the teenagers back to the house, Dorian made sure that Nicolas was working in his basement alchemy lab and Zoe and Perenelle were out again.

Very suspicious, those two. He wished he could have learned more about what they were up to on their quest to thwart the blackmailer, yet he could tell Madame Flamel did not want him there, and furthermore, now he had his own mystery to solve. One that would put him back in Zoe's good graces more than inserting himself where he was not wanted. Especially when he knew a blackmailer exposing an alchemist would most likely not be believed. Why were they wasting so much energy?

"I've been there for a school project," Brixton said. "They've got a section on pirates. Because of all the gold they stole. That's a great idea."

"Sounds like a plan," Ethan said. "Don't worry, Scooby. I know you can't go with us, but we can livestream video for you, so you can see, too."

Veronica pointed to the website. "Looks like they're open, even after that burglary—or is it a robbery if there are people there? Either way, it's so awful that the theft put the owner in the hospital. The show must go on, I guess. The museum has information and displays about Pacific Northwest gold history in general, not only the Gold Rush but also the lure of gold that's brought all sorts of gold museum pieces to Oregon. Oh. But they've got a policy that says no video or photography."

"We'll have to stick the phone out of my coat pocket so they don't know we're streaming to Scooby." Ethan slid his phone into the pocket of his tweed coat, where it fell into a deep abyss. "Oh. Guess that won't work."

Dorian did not think wool was a wise choice for a climate that included many downpours, but of the three friends Ethan was the one who changed his style of clothing most regularly.

"Can you sew something so the top of the phone will stick out of his pocket?" Brixton asked Veronica.

The young woman's face turned bright red. She had just eaten an almond cluster. Dorian hoped she was not allergic. Blue always asked for his ingredient list to create signs to tell Blue Sky Teas customers which baked goods contained allergens. *Mon dieu*! No. As he observed further, an allergic reaction was not what was happening here. For a moment later, as Veronica threw one of the almond clusters at Brixton, Dorian understood the course of her discomfort. It was not an allergy. She was infuriated with her friend.

"What?" Brixton brushed off a sticky section of his shirt where the treat had landed. "Why'd you waste one of the almond clusters? They're too good to waste."

"Just because of my gender you think I can sew? How long have we known each other? Have you *ever* known me to sew?"

Brixton pointed at her backpack. "I saw a hand-knit scarf sticking out of your bag. It's uneven, not something you'd buy."

Dorian was impressed by the boy's deductive skills.

"Oh." But she was still frowning.

Ethan laughed. "That's one of my mom's creations. She's trying all sorts of art therapy. So far, she's terrible at all of them. But I knew Veronica liked the colors in this lopsided scarf, so I thought she'd like it. I gave it to her."

"I see how it is." Brixton scrambled up and walked to the door. "We're wasting time. I'm heading to the museum." He walked out the door.

"What was that about?" Ethan asked.

"He's a weirdo." Veronica grabbed her backpack and skateboard. The boys still used bikes, but she'd abandoned hers this year in favor of the skateboard. "But he's our weirdo. Come on. Let's follow him."

CHAPTER 31

Perenelle and I were the first of the Elements Art House group to arrive at the museum. We'd skipped Perenelle's requested snack in an attempt to beat the group to the museum so we could have some time on our own and give Perenelle time to feel the energy of the gold without questions. Today, a teenage boy was selling tickets at the front desk. I was glad it wasn't the same woman as the previous day, or Perenelle's interest would have looked quite suspicious.

While Perenelle spent more time with the gold remnants, I examined more of the exhibits. The Cabots had packed a lot of information and historical items into the small space. The last time we'd been here, I hadn't noticed the rotted timber from two ships that had sunk off the Oregon coast, or the miniature replica of a Gold Rush town, which the placard attributed to a local artist who was a miniaturist.

"Zoe!" An enthusiastic voice shook me from my thoughts. Heather gave me a hug, even though she'd seen me half an hour earlier.

Ethan's mom Ashleigh was with her. I couldn't tell if she was attempting to smile but failing, or if she wasn't even trying.

I also couldn't tell if she was our blackmailer. Dressed head-to-toe in black fabric, Ashleigh's clothing covered most of her skin. Above full-length yoga pants, a lightweight workout sweatshirt covered her neck as well as most of her hands with cuffs that looped through her thumbs. With her skin covered, plus the elements from the earth that surrounded us, I couldn't tell if any traces of my paint bomb remained underneath her yoga garb.

"I never knew this place existed." Ashleigh looked not at me but at the displays surrounding us as she spoke. "Spencer gave me a gold necklace and other jewelry. I wonder how much value I'd lose if I melted it down instead of selling it off as it is. I can't bear for it to still exist in the world, even if I lose money on it. It feels like it's tainted."

"It is," Perenelle said matter-of-factly as she joined us. "If a man for whom you feel such animosity is the one who gave it to you, it can't be salvaged. Not if it stays anywhere near you. You must melt it down. Or sell it to someone very, very far away."

Ashleigh gave her a malicious smile. "I knew I liked you from the first day you arrived at Elements." The mask on her face wavered. The malicious smile turned to a hesitant one, and for the first time I saw the woman Ashleigh could have been if she hadn't been so angry. "I like the symbolism of destroying it, but I should probably just sell it. I need money to start again. I don't want to put Ethan through a long, drawn-out divorce, so I know Spencer is going to win whatever he wants." She balled her hands into fists and the mask was back on.

Perenelle's stomach growled. "I apologize. I'm always hungry these days!"

Ashleigh laughed. "Let's get brunch."

"How about a picnic?" I suggested. "It's so warm outside that we can relax in the sun after the rains earlier this week. I have a thick picnic blanket in my truck, and there's a spot down the street where we can get takeout."

"I love that idea." Heather looked up at the ceiling as if she was already feeling the sun on her face. "But we've barely looked at the items in the museum."

"What is there to see?" Perenelle asked. "Most of this gold is fake."

"Really?" Heather asked, incredulous.

I gave Perenelle a sharp look. She wasn't wrong, but there was no way for us to know that.

"Or so I assume," Perenelle added hastily. "Museums don't keep their most valuable items on display. I assume these are replicas. Shall we eat?"

I watched Ashleigh's reaction. It was shaping up to be a hot day. There was no way she'd be able to sit outside with us and not take off her sweatshirt without being incredibly uncomfortable. Then I'd know if she was hiding something on the skin of her arms.

"Works for me," Ashleigh said.

I glanced over at the bored teenage boy sitting at the front desk. He was playing with his phone. Aside from a family with two young kids in front of the exhibit on the tools used for prospecting, nobody else was inside. "I thought you said Lucy was coming."

Heather shrugged. "She might have stopped at the hospital on the way here."

"Hospital?" Perenelle asked.

"Her fiancé is in the hospital, recovering from a stroke. She visits him a lot. His prospects aren't good, and insurance doesn't cover as much as it should. A picnic on a sunny day will do her a world of good. I'll text her to meet up with us in the park for a brunch picnic once she's done."

Every one of our main blackmail suspects needed money. Sameera to keep Elements alive. Ashleigh for her contentious divorce. Lucy for medical bills.

If the blackmailer had only asked for the gold they'd seen Perenelle create and hadn't elevated their attacks, I would have understood their desperation and wanted to help. But now that they'd threatened people I cared about and attempted to break into my house, they weren't getting off the hook. With me and Perenelle working together, they didn't know what they were up against.

CHAPTER 32

Dorian watched the children's excursion from a video feed in the attic. They were on bikes (the boys) and a skateboard (Veronica), so their trip to the museum had taken longer than it would have if he could have asked Zoe to assist their quest and drive them. The museum was not downtown, but in a mostly residential neighborhood. They rode a bus as far as they could go, and went on their own from there.

By the time they had called Dorian through an app that allowed him to talk with them on Zoe's laptop, the gargoyle had conceived of more terrible fates that could have befallen them than he could count on his claws. The prospect of being hit by a car was too pedestrian for his little gray cells, so he had instead worried that a cunning jewel thief had befriended them on the bus, or that a murderous pastry chef had lured them to his treacherous kitchen. How, he wondered, were parents not sick with worry every moment after their children were scheduled to return home?

Now that he saw none of his fears had come to pass, Dorian squinted at the laptop screen. There was nothing wrong with his eyesight. It was the video itself. The children had failed at adapting one of the cavernous pockets of Ethan's coat, so the camera was in a front pocket of Brixton's jeans. An imperfect solution, as fabric frequently obscured the camera feed. The youngsters could most likely build one of these computers, yet they could not sew a stitch that stayed in place! Dorian would speak to Zoe about this. He sighed and scratched behind his horns.

Glancing away from the screen, he scowled at the portrait of alchemist Edward Kelley hanging in the attic. He stubbed his toe on one of Zoe's many new acquisitions on his way to flip over the distracting portrait, which did nothing to improve his mood.

Dorian reached the canvas and glared at the portrait of the rogue. Dorian had tried to be a polite gargoyle and had engaged Perenelle in conversation about the infamous alchemist she had known many centuries ago. She had been reluctant to relive those trying times, so she had declined discussion, and Dorian had to read about the man to learn more. Edward Kelley was a charlatan and thief. Had he lived in the Pacific Northwest centuries ago, he no doubt would have teamed up with the pirates the children were researching now.

Hearing his name mentioned, Dorian scampered back to the laptop.

"Too bad Dorian couldn't come," Brixton was saying to his friends. "He'd surely be interested in this doubloon here."

"That one is actually just one *escudo*," a voice Dorian did not recognize said, "so not really a doubloon."

The camera turned toward the speaker. The thin boy who appeared on screen looked to be roughly the same age as Brixton and his friends. Dark brown curly hair obscured his forehead and eyes, yet Dorian could not help but think the boy looked familiar.

"I thought the gold ones were doubloons," said Ethan.

The camera was still tilted toward the new boy, who was shaking his head. "*Reals* are silver and *escudo* are gold. *Doubloon* was just a twice-as-valuable gold coin. I'm Harry. I could show you around, if you wanted."

"Veronica. This is Brixton. And Ethan. You give tours in addition to working at the front desk?"

Dorian could not see the boy's face, but he heard the change from confidence to a mumbled reply.

"Your *parents* are the owners?" Ethan's voice was much louder than the voices of the other boys. "You're Harrison III?"

"Harry," the boy corrected. "It's Harry. My dad is Harrison. Not me."

Ah. Dorian sat back on his haunches. This is why the boy had looked familiar. He had seen images of him because of his discovery of the gold.

Veronica wrung her hands together. "I'm so sorry about your dad. I heard he was still in the hospital."

The boy who did not wish to be called Harrison did not smile, yet he did not look overly bereaved. "Thanks."

"So you grew up at a museum?" asked Ethan.

"Yeah, kinda."

"What's your favorite part?" Veronica asked.

The boy's face lit up. He looked much younger when he smiled. "Over here."

The camera went dark. It must've fallen further into the pocket. They did not notice Dorian could no longer see. Yet he could still hear, and his hearing was superb.

"Here," the boy called Harry said. "When I was twelve, I found these tools used by prospectors 150 years ago. As soon as my mom realized what I'd found with our metal detector, she made me stop digging. She called the archaeology department of a local university, and I got to work with two grad students who showed me how to remove things from the earth while documenting and cataloging the discovery."

"Your own dig," Ethan commented.

"Ouch," Brixton said. "Why'd you do that, V. Oh. Right."

"You okay?" Harry asked.

"Um, yeah. Fine." Brixton's fingers covered the lens of the phone's camera, and a moment later Dorian could see again. Dorian chuckled. Veronica had noticed that he was no longer able to see them.

"After I found these," Harry said, "I was even more hooked on looking for history. But it took another three-and-a-half years for me to find something else as interesting." He looked away. Dorian deduced he was looking toward the now-empty case where the gold nuggets he had discovered used to be housed.

"You saw the thief running away, right?" Brixton asked.

The new boy shrugged. "From the house. I couldn't see anything except a figure dressed in black running away with the gold I found. And my dad attacking him."

"That was brave of him," Veronica said. "He wanted to save your discovery."

Harry snorted. "You don't know my dad. It wasn't brave. It was self-interested. No way was he doing it for me."

CHAPTER 33

Lucy smiled shyly at me through oversize copper-framed sunglasses. She arrived at the park just as we stepped onto the grass with an assortment of food and drinks for brunch. In a tank top appropriate for the sunny day, there was no paint on her skin.

"How's your fiancé doing?" Heather asked, giving her arm a squeeze.

"Same as before. This picnic is exactly what I need. Thanks for inviting me."

"Of course!" Heather kicked off her sandals and plopped down cross-legged at the head of the picnic blanket and lifted boxes of food from a paper bag.

Next to her, Ashleigh popped the cork of a bottle of champagne. "As soon as everyone takes a few sips of orange juice, I'll top it up with bubbly."

"Mimosas," said Heather. "Perfect."

"We're making flowers?" Perenelle asked.

Ashleigh clinked the champagne bottle against the small bottle of orange juice in Perenelle's hand. "You have the most interesting sense of humor. It's a breath of fresh air. Like this park." She slid off her hoodie. Her fitted workout shirt left most of her arms bare, as well as revealing a few inches of taut midsection. There was none of the paint from my paint bomb on any of her skin, or remnants of its essence.

Nobody at the picnic was our blackmailer. I was simultaneously relieved and disappointed. I was glad Brixton's and Ethan's moms weren't the blackmailer, but I was no closer to identifying them. Could our assumption that the blackmailer was associated with Elements Art House be wrong?

"Drink up," Ashleigh was saying. "I bought a second bottle of this expensive champagne. I've got Spencer's credit card." Her tongue loosened by drinking most of the first bottle herself, she told us about her wretched husband—"Spencer had not one affair, but *two*, and I don't know how I was so naive to believe he was working late…"—but didn't mention her son until Heather brought him up.

"How's Ethan doing?" she asked.

"Angry, but what fifteen-year-old boy isn't? I suspect it has more to do with liking some girl he won't tell me about."

I was still stuffed from Dorian's breakfast, so I sipped my orange juice and observed the group.

"I wish I had your metabolism," Ashleigh commented in Perenelle's direction.

Perenelle paused before taking a third helping of bread. "I'm making up for lost time after a fast." She went back to slathering the bread with black currant jam.

I wasn't too worried about Perenelle slipping up and saying anything about how she'd been imprisoned for longer than their life-times. She was even better at hiding her identity than I was. She'd lived through periods of time in which it would have been far more dangerous for her to reveal her gifts.

"What do you think, Zoe?" Heather asked.

"Sorry," I said. "I was lost in my thoughts. It's a gorgeous view. What were you saying?"

"It's true about the view," Heather said. "I want to set up my easel and paint that copse of trees. What I was telling Ashleigh was that she doesn't need a man. I was perfectly happy on my own until I met Brix's stepdad, Abel. But you're happy being single, right? Anyway,

Ashleigh, you'll be just fine. Oh... Oh, Lucy, I'm so sorry! How stupid of me. I wasn't thinking."

Lucy shook her head. "You don't have to treat me any differently. We've all got problems in our lives. That's why I spend so much time at Elements these days. Visiting Bill in the hospital takes a lot out of me, but painting helps me forget."

In the sunlight, Lucy looked different than she had inside. Yesterday I would have guessed she was in her 40s, but now I could see she was past middle age. Not that it made it any easier to have a loved one suffer a stroke.

Heather passed around a container of rolls. "Let me know if you ever want company to visit him. Or a bouquet of flowers. I love picking flowers from Blue's overgrown yard. She calls it weeding when I thin out the overgrown blossoms." She laughed as she tossed her hair back and lifted her face towards the sun.

Lucy gave her a sad smile and passed on the bread. "You're very kind."

"I think you'll find you're stronger than you realize," Perenelle said. "Both of you."

Nicolas was Perenelle's second husband. History had recorded that much properly, at least. She would have been perfectly contented to be on her own if she hadn't met him. Perenelle and Nicolas were lucky to have each other. I'd had that once. I thought I'd been lucky to find it a second time with Max. It was a second love for both of us. His wife had died young, and I'd lost my love Ambrose after he couldn't handle his beloved son growing old while he did not. Whatever was going on with Max, I'd figure it out once I made sure my loved ones were safe.

My phone rang. My first thought was Max. But an unknown number showed on the screen.

"Excuse me for one minute," I said as I rose and stepped away from the picnic blanket.

The caller wasn't Max. Nor was it the blackmailer. It was the window repairman.

The kitchen window that had been broken was a standard size, so the repairman didn't need to place a custom order. I could get it fixed later that day if I didn't mind paying his weekend service fee. I didn't want to go another night with a less secure house, so I readily agreed.

"I need to get back to the house for a repair," I told the group.

"We can give Perenelle a lift home after we're done with lunch," Heather said. "I insist! She hasn't finished eating, and she's clearly starving."

Since none of the group had the color bomb on them, I felt safe leaving Perenelle with them. But that left the question: if they weren't involved, who was?

CHAPTER 34

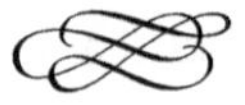

The children had returned from the museum excited—and hungry. It was lunchtime, and Dorian was happy to feed them.

The kitchen phone rang. This was the phone number Dorian used, since the screens of cell phones did not work for him.

"*Allo*," he said, tucking the receiver under his chin as he continued stirring.

"He uses the phone?" Ethan whispered to Brixton.

"I'm looking for Dorian Roberts," the voice on the other end of the line said.

"Speaking," Dorian replied, not correcting the man.

"I don't usually call people back, but the message you left about your purchase made it sound urgent."

"Ah! Thank you. Yes, as I explained in my message about the set of typewriters and artwork from Hamlet Coltrane's writing studio, it is of the utmost importance," Dorian said in his most litigious voice.

The man on the phone did not speak for a few moments. Dorian was aware of the children whispering nearby. Realizing he might need to take notes, he thrust his whisk into Brixton's hands and hopped off his stool. He was beginning to wonder if the connection had been lost, when the man finally replied.

"Look," the man said. "I made it up."

"*Pardon*?" Dorian paused with a ballpoint pen poised in the air.

"The writer Hamlet Coltrane doesn't exist. I own a thrift store. I was listening to jazz while sorting a bunch of junk—er, I mean, while curating treasures—to list online. The typewriters weren't what customers like these days—not quite old enough to have that hipster vintage vibe and not new enough to be in working condition—so they hadn't sold. And nobody had bought these amateur landscapes."

"Where did the paintings come from?"

A pause. "A garage sale. I think. I go to a lot of them."

"You do not know? Yet your posting declared—"

"These typewriters and paintings had a 1980s vibe, so I bundled them together. They looked like they could all have been in a writer's workshop, so I named the writer Hamlet Coltrane. Since he wasn't real, nobody could claim fraud. I figured it would make someone happy to feel like they had an obscure writer's set-up. Maybe inspire them to write their own literary masterpiece, ya know? No harm in it."

"No harm?" Dorian sputtered. "This is an illegal business practice. Fraud."

"Look, I'm a nice guy. I get it if it's not what you were after. If you want to return the set, just pay the shipping and I'll return your money. You're not too far from me, so I could even come pick them up."

"I will consider it. Good day." Dorian hung up the phone and turned around to find the three teenagers staring at him.

"Don't tell me Scooby is a lawyer, too," Ethan said.

"I am not an *avocate*." Dorian narrowed his eyes. "One does not need to practice law to understand fraud is a crime. Yet pursuing the matter with the proprietor will get us nowhere."

"Fraud?" Brixton asked. "It was a game after all?"

"It's over?" Veronica looked more disappointed than Dorian thought the minor setback warranted.

"*Non*." Dorian held up a clawed hand as a faint squeak sounded in the distance. He paused for a moment. The sound did not repeat, so he continued. "The man I purchased the items from *himself* is a fraud. He does not know where any of the paintings came from. This means that wherever the map came from, we will never know. We must therefore act based on what the map *itself* tells us. We will have no additional information. We must start with what we know—that this is a map of the Oregon coast—and glean what we can from other sources. We must—"

The creak of a floorboard interrupted his thoughts.

Zut! The original squeak had been the basement door!

Dorian scampered to the swinging kitchen door, yet it was too late. Nicolas Flamel pushed the door open.

Dorian had believed Nicolas to be sleeping upstairs, a location that would have allowed Dorian to hear him on the stairs with time to disperse the children. Not working in his basement alchemy lab. Dorian's food must have helped Nicolas more than he realized. The pride in his culinary accomplishment was lessened by the realization that Nicolas now knew Dorian was being as incautious as Madame Flamel. He had revealed his identity to more people than was wise.

"Hello," Nicolas said with a broad smile. "I don't believe I've met everyone here. I'm Nicolas Flamel. Enchanted to meet you." He extended his hand to Veronica, then Ethan.

"It's an honor to meet you, Mr. Flamel," Veronica said. "I'm Veronica Chen-Mendoza."

"Yeah, nice to meet you," Ethan mumbled. "What? Oh. I'm Ethan Eriksen. Hey... you have the same name as a character in a series of middle grade books I read when I was a kid."

"How delightful!" said Nicolas. "What a serendipitous occurrence."

Dorian held his tongue. He did not wish to point out that Nicolas Flamel was indeed the real man about whom many stories had been based. Those questions would surely come soon enough from the children.

"I'm terribly sorry for disturbing your lunch party," Nicolas continued. "I wonder if I might trouble you for a spot of lunch for myself, Dorian. When you have a free moment."

"But of course," Dorian said. "If you will be in the basement, I will bring a tray down shortly."

"Most kind of you. Would any of you wish to sample the beer I am brewing downstairs? I have not quite perfected it, yet it is coming along well and quite invigorating."

"Um..." Brixton said as Ethan choked on his glass of water.

"No, thank you," Veronica said. "But we appreciate the offer."

"Very good, then." Nicolas smiled and gave a nod of his head to the children, then departed.

"That was weird," Veronica said.

"Understatement," Ethan added. "Everything is weird right now."

"In addition to offering us beer," Veronica said, "he didn't seem bothered by the fact that we're all hanging out with Dorian."

Dorian chuckled. "He is a brilliant mind, yet only in some ways. I should not have worried. While he is hard at work on his experiments, I doubt he would care if the president of France appeared in the house."

Ethan blinked at him. "Why would any of us care about the president of France?"

Dorian sighed. "Are you ready to eat? Let me fix Nicolas a tray of food, then I will return to serve our own lunch."

He curled leaves of basil into a roll, and sliced the leaves into ribbons, which he sprinkled onto the steaming bowl of farro and chickpeas tossed with kale and basil pesto.

"I can set the table," Veronica offered.

Dorian looked up from his chopping. "Since we do not need to worry about Monsieur Flamel, we may have our feast at the dining room table, not at this cramped breakfast table. Brixton, you know where the cutlery and serviettes are."

"I do?"

"Napkins," Veronica translated.

Dorian knew the English word for napkin, of course. There were simply some words he did not care for in the English language. He preferred to speak elegantly, though not as much as he enjoyed eating elegantly.

When Dorian returned from leaving a tray of food for Nicolas in the basement, the children were tossing balled-up linen napkins into the empty bowl in the center of the dining table. The dining room was an extension of the open living room area.

"There's no control to make the shot," Brixton moaned as his serviette missed the bowl and fluttered onto a dining chair.

Dorian scooped up the fabric and placed it on the table. "If you are done with your game of basketball, I will fetch lunch. Then you can tell me the rest of what you learned at the museum."

The children fell silent. This, he had learned, was not a good sign. "What is it? What terrible news are you shielding from me?" He prepared for the worst. That the treasure had already been discovered.

"I'll help you bring out food," Veronica said. She widened her eyes in silent communication with the boys, as if Dorian was not an observant gargoyle and would not see her.

No matter. Dorian knew his food would prove better than a truth serum. He chuckled to himself as he and Veronica brought platters of food from the kitchen to the dining room.

"How are you not over here for dinner every night?" Ethan asked Brixton as he took a bite. "This is so much better than takeout. So much better than *anything*."

"*Merci beaucoup*, young Ethan," Dorian beamed. "Perhaps you are ready to inform me of what I missed from the museum, since I could not see everything?"

Ethan set down his fork. "You saw that we met Harry Cabot today. He's really cool, and he knows a lot about treasure hunting—he's the one who found the 20 pieces of famous gold that had been lost for 150 years."

"Yes," Dorian said. "You have learned additional useful information from him?"

Again, the silent look passed between the children.

"Not yet," Brixton said. "But that's what we wanted to ask you about. We think he could help. If we could tell him—"

"We didn't tell him what we were doing yet," Ethan added. "We respected your wishes. But if we told him—"

"Absolutely not." Dorian held up his hand.

"I told you he'd say that," Brixton said.

"Why does he get to decide?" Ethan asked. "Just because he's the oldest? He's not even hum—"

"Don't go there," Brixton cut him off. "Just don't."

Veronica stood so quickly the legs of her chair squealed against the floor. Her jaw was firm, and she placed her hands on the table. Leaning over, she spoke in a voice Dorian knew well. Not from Veronica herself, but from knowing people for over 150 years. It was a voice that declared there would be no arguments.

"No single person is in charge. Don't you see that? We *all* need to be in agreement. Every single one of us. If we're not *all* comfortable telling Harry what we're up to, we don't do it. That's the only way any of this will work. Do I make myself clear?"

"Um, yeah," Brixton mumbled.

"Aye," said Ethan in an indeterminate accent.

Dorian bowed. "I am your humble servant, Veronica. You are very wise."

She failed at suppressing a smile. "After lunch, we go back to the museum to finish looking at everything they've got that might help us get closer to where exactly the treasure map points to. We can ask for Harry's help only if we don't reveal that we've got the map. Agreed?"

"As long as by 'after lunch' you mean after dessert," said Ethan, "I'm in."

CHAPTER 35

As I stepped out of my truck, a flurry of door-slamming sounded from inside the house. The repairman shouldn't have been there already. I hoped something else hadn't happened.

When I stepped through the front door, Dorian was clearing a set of dishes from the dining table.

"Wow," I said, eyeing the nearly empty family-size platter. "Nicolas has that more of an appetite now?"

"He requested a feast," Dorian said. "I believe I have perfected a dairy-free pesto."

"A window repairman is coming over shortly, so you can leave the dishes in the sink—"

"I shall hide in the attic." He sighed, then chuckled. "I will bring a chocolate mousse dessert with me. Chocolate decadence is the perfect accompaniment for the scene of my novel I am working on."

The repairman arrived half an hour later. Perenelle wasn't yet back from the picnic lunch.

"I'll be reading a book in the living room," I said, "so I'll be close by if you need me. I'll leave the front door open for you."

"The new window is in my truck. Back in a minute."

As soon as I sat down with a paperback mystery, *A Keeper of the Castle,* a knock on the front door sounded. I opened it and found the repairman holding the window. No, a second glance at the legs and shoes visible beneath the wrapped glass showed me this wasn't the same man.

"My boss asked me to bring this in," a female voice said.

"Through here," I said, showing her the kitchen.

"Thanks."

I was only two pages into the book when her boss appeared with a chagrinned look on his face. "I'm so sorry. I could have sworn I had the window with me, but I can't find it on my truck. Must've left it behind. I've gotta go back to get it, so I'll be about half an hour."

"Your assistant brought it in a few minutes ago."

He gave me a strange look. "My assistant?"

"Your colleague, I mean," I corrected myself. I shouldn't have assumed the woman was his assistant. But she had referred to him as her boss.

His confusion intensified. "It's just me today for this small job."

Oh no…

I ran into the kitchen. The window was resting against the fridge, but nobody was in the room. The stairs were near the kitchen. The swinging door barely made a sound, so she could have opened it without me seeing or hearing her.

I ran up the stairs. The bedrooms and second bathroom were empty, but the drawers of my bedroom and the Flamels were wide open with clothing spilling out onto the floor.

Someone had ransacked our rooms.

When I got downstairs, Perenelle was chatting with the confused repairman.

"Ah," said Perenelle with a smile. "Here she is."

"The window is in the kitchen already," I said. "One of my roommates must have thought they were helping by bringing it inside. We'll be upstairs, but call my cell phone if you need me."

I pulled Perenelle aside as soon as the repairman walked toward the kitchen, shaking his head.

"Where's the real gold nugget?" I whispered to Perenelle.

"It's safe."

"Show me."

"Zoe, this isn't like you. What's going on?"

"Please. Just show me."

We climbed the stairs together. She gasped when we entered her room.

"No!" She flew to the bed, where a wooden box lay upside down.

She held up the empty case. Not quite empty. In the spot where the gold had been was a note. A string of old French curses escaped Perenelle's lips as she handed me the paper.

This time, there was no paint. These were block letters with the ink from a blue ballpoint pen. I saw why the blackmailer had switched mediums as soon as I began to read. This was a longer message.

This is the last time I will ask nicely. Call this number when you are ready to hand over the rest of the gold you stole. You have until Sunday at midnight before I call the police and turn you in. Harrison Cabot isn't doing well. You're not only a thief but a possible murderer. Do not try to run. I will be watching.

"The repairman didn't have an assistant," I whispered. The events of the last few days played through my mind. The events we'd misinterpreted so badly. We were wrong about so many things. "*She* was our blackmailer. Here. In my house. She doesn't think you're an alchemist. She thinks you're the thief who pulled off a museum heist and nearly killed Harrison Cabot in the process."

CHAPTER 36

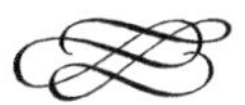

"The blackmailer believes that I'm the one who stole the gold nuggets from the Oregon Gold History Museum." Perenelle's skirt shuffled as she paced methodically back and forth. "They believe I'm the thief who nearly bludgeoned that poor man to death."

What a fool I'd been! I'd fallen into the same trap of assumptions, even though I believed myself above them. *People see what they already believe.*

The blackmailer *hadn't* thought Perenelle was an alchemist, even though they'd seen her perform alchemy. The first note had read: *I know what you are. I will keep your secret in exchange for 10 pieces of gold.*

I had taken it as fact that "I know what you are" meant they knew Perenelle was an alchemist. But it didn't. That was a false assumption. *They believed she was a thief.*

"When the blackmailer wrote that she would expose your secret," I murmured, "we jumped to the conclusion that made sense to *us*, not thinking of what a normal person would think. Of course they think you're a thief rather than an alchemist. It's what they know. We assumed anyone who saw her video wouldn't believe you were practicing alchemy, since it's not something they believe exists. We should have considered the blackmailer would think the same thing."

"Because the video wasn't high resolution, they believed it was a glitch?"

Perenelle adapted to the times quickly. Much more quickly than I had ever done. No, that wasn't quite true. To avoid drawing unnecessary attention to myself, I picked up modern vernacular for how languages evolved and were spoken in the present. But I hadn't kept up with modern technology. I loved my 1942 Chevy and fixed it myself. I couldn't imagine having a vehicle with a computer running it.

"She must have rationalized what was on the video," I said. "Maybe thinking that you're eccentric and like to play with your spoils."

"You didn't recognize her when she carried the window inside?" Perenelle asked. "You couldn't tell if it was someone from Elements Art House?"

I shook my head. "She stayed out of my sight. Expertly. I didn't notice what she was doing because her movements were natural. She hid behind the wrapped frame of glass, so I never got a look at her face. All we know now for certain is that it's a woman. I think." *Was I* certain? Could it have been a small man disguising his voice?

"Her voice? Speech pattern?"

"Nothing distinctive. It was muffled, which I assumed was from a protective mask that contractors wear when they're working with dust." Again, I'd jumped to the wrong conclusion. I'd assumed the wrong thing because of my own bias. "It's time to ask Dorian for help. He and Nicolas need to know the truth." I didn't add "in spite of Nicolas' health and Dorian's predilection to embark upon outlandish investigations."

Perenelle hesitated, but only for a moment. "You truly trust him, in spite of his origins?"

"With my life. You *know* this." I felt my voice rising in frustration. "You know he had no control over the backward alchemy that brought him to life, and that he's since overcome it. Why do you insist—"

"Because it's not only the *rational* part of my brain I must argue with, Zoe." She stopped pacing and smoothed out her full skirt, made from a purple dress she had found at a thrift store on Hawthorne and transformed. There were no wrinkles, yet she smoothed it out again.

"I know he can be a bit much."

"It has nothing to do with Dorian himself. It doesn't even have to do with the fact that we fought this dangerous sect of alchemy for so long. I can tell myself, rationally, that Dorian has nothing to do with that. Yet I lost someone I cared about very much. Someone who reminded me very much of you, in fact." Tears welled in her eyes. "She was intrigued by alchemy, but she wanted shortcuts."

There are no shortcuts. Not shortcuts that work. To create a transformation, we give our energy and intent. It takes time. Backward alchemy created the appearance of a shortcut, for it let the impatient instigator avoid work by channeling the energy of another person. It was cruel and immoral, and it corrupted the souls of those who went down that path. Dorian had been unknowingly brought to life because of it, but he'd found true alchemy on his own once he and I discovered his true origins.

"It broke my heart," Perenelle said, "what happened to her. She lived only slightly longer than what is considered a natural lifespan, but at so great a cost. She destroyed her soul and the lives of several others, for the prize of a few years longer on earth. Years in which she was miserable. My expectations that Dorian would behave similarly have not been borne out." A tear escaped and rolled down her cheek. "You are right. It's time to tell him what's happened. Everything."

We gathered in the attic and explained the latest development to Dorian and Nicolas.

Dorian gasped. "Madame Flamel! You are so drawn to gold that you must steal it when you are unable to transform it yourself?"

I failed at suppressing an eye roll. "She didn't steal the gold. The blackmailer *thinks* she did. That's why they had such an exact demand."

"You have done nothing wrong, my love," Nicolas said. "The thief will not find true gold here. Nor will there be evidence of a crime you didn't commit."

Dorian steepled his clawed fingers together. "This blackmailer is a formidable foe. Now she has not only a video of you with gold that can be plausibly identified as the true stolen gold, but she found a piece of the gold hidden in your home. She will not stop now. We must discover the identity not only of the blackmailer, but also the person who perpetrated the heist. It is the only way we will all be truly safe."

CHAPTER 37

"Dorian is right," I said. "Our best option is to discover the identity of the gold thief."

Huddled together in the cluttered attic, Dorian and Perenelle cautiously observed each other. Nicolas bore no grudge against Dorian, so he looked on hopefully.

"Let's go over what we know," I said. I began with what we knew of the gold that had been discovered and then stolen within a week, pulling up an article for reference. "Ginessa and Harrison Cabot's son, Harrison III, is an amateur treasure hunter. He had the money to do so. But like so many of the prospectors nearly two centuries before him, he lost the gold nearly as quickly as he'd found it. Just for a different reason. He gave it to his parents, who immediately put it in their museum—which, to be fair, had a security system."

"And they insured it," Dorian added. "The gold is lost, but they did not lose money. Insurance fraud is a powerful motive."

Perenelle took my phone from my hand. "I don't like the look of this fellow Harrison, the elder."

"The man who chased the thief and ended up in a coma for his efforts?" I asked.

She tapped on the screen of my phone for a closer look at the husband's face, launching another web page. She swore in old French. "I didn't mean to send the page away!"

"We can get it back."

"He looks like the type of man," Perenelle said, "who would make gold disappear just to spite his son."

"That's a terrible thing to think about a father," I said.

"Much of the world, my dear Zoe, is terrible." A smiled ticked up the edges of Perenelle's lips. "But so much of it is marvelous. Especially now. Water that doesn't need to be boiled to be safe to drink. Women with more freedom than I thought possible. Readily available art supplies." Perenelle's smile faded. "I do not wish to be imprisoned again."

Nicolas clasped his hands around hers. "We shall figure it out."

I took the phone back from her and looked at two photos published online. Harrison Cabot II looked the role of the wealthy middle-aged man that he was. Would he wake up from his coma and return to that life?

Perenelle pointed at the phone. "Look. He's wearing a corset, and this is false hair. This man is overly concerned with his looks."

"Though I agree with Madame Flamel that it does us no good to avoid speaking ill of the man simply because he is in a coma," said Dorian, "please do not judge a man by his appearance."

"You are right," Perenelle said softly. "I have judged you harshly for reasons that have to do with my own past. Not yours. Please, don't feel you need to call me Madame Flamel. Call me Perenelle. I would very much like to call you Dorian. And to apologize for my past behavior."

Dorian blinked at her for a few moments, then gave a small bow. "*Oui*. This is most agreeable, Perenelle."

I smiled as I clicked to another article from a reputable news source. "The museum next to the house was burglarized at 2:17 in the morning, with the sounds of breaking glass and a shrill alarm waking up Gin. Her husband slept through the initial blaring of the alarm next door, but awoke when she shook him. They found their son in the hallway, already on his way outside. Gin paused in the window and saw a silhouette at the side of the museum. She screamed as she saw the figure run away."

I then clicked on the accompanying video, evidently taken from the museum's outside security camera. We watched intently up to the point where the Cabots followed their son outside.

"This is when her husband gave chase," Dorian said.

"*After* the thief had already stolen the gold." I shook my head, thinking again of how something was wrong about what we were watching. "Something is off about the timing. The alarm. They woke up when the alarm went off. How did the thief get the gold so quickly?"

"Two shadowy figures captured on camera," Perenelle murmured. "The cameras show the thief carrying the bag of gold as he flees. He must be young and quick."

"Maybe..." Something strange was going on. All but one of us wore solemn expressions as we watched the video again.

"A challenging puzzle indeed." Nicolas chuckled.

"How can you be so cheerful?" Dorian asked.

Nicolas drummed his fingers together, considering the question. He looked around for a moment, then lifted an antique clock from one of my shelves. "I have lived for several centuries. Far longer than this 18th-century timepiece has marked the hands of time. It is long enough for perspective." His smile faded. "Perenelle and I lost many years at the hands of a nefarious alchemist. I am not worried about the machinations of an opportunistic criminal who thinks they can best my wife. With the four of us working together, I have no doubt *they* will be the one who is sorry in the end. Now, shall we solve this?"

We gathered around the screen of my laptop, again watching the video of the shadowy figure running away with a bag of gold. Widely shared security footage showed a thief, dressed from head to toe in black, approaching the rear window of the museum. There was no sound, and the window itself was not in view of the camera, but it was close enough to catch fragments of glass falling onto the grass, no doubt flung aside by the thief as they worked quickly to get safely inside.

And work quickly they did. I didn't know if the alarm that sounded was silent or blaring, but the thief must have known it had sounded. Twelve seconds later, they emerged on the screen again—this time carrying a small black satchel in their gloved hand. Light from the Cabots' nearby house clicked on. As the thief fled, the teenage son appeared in the distance of the frame, from the doorway of the house. He stepped forward, but a barefoot, pajama-wearing Harrison Cabot held him back. Harrison senior gave chase, coming closer in the video—and closer to the thief. As he lunged, the thief turned and attacked. I winced as I watched Harrison flung to the ground. He remained unmoving as the thief ran away and Harrison's wife appeared on the screen. Both an ambulance and a security guard arrived two minutes later.

I timed the robbery itself again. Twelve seconds, or perhaps thirteen, elapsed between when the thief went off camera and when they returned on the screen running away with the gold. Was that long enough for them to have grabbed the gold?

I knew that many museum thefts could be achieved in under a minute. Sometimes in as little as thirty seconds. But twelve seconds? It was reported in the news that the thief had disarmed the security cameras inside the museum itself before breaking in, so there were no videos to show how they'd stolen the gold so quickly and no videos that showed the thief up close. The small museum had stepped up their security before displaying the Gold Rush gold, but they hadn't planned on the types of security back-ups that larger museums employed. When one system failed, the external alarm wasn't enough to stop the thief.

The thief hadn't disarmed the external alarm, though, so they needed to move quickly. The window breaking tripped the alarm that alerted both the Cabot family and the police.

"It's too fast," I said. I couldn't let go of that fact. Had the recording been tampered with? No, the alarm had sounded and the family woke up. "Twelve seconds. How is that possible?"

The twinkle in Nicolas's eye was back. "Simply because something is difficult, that does not make it impossible."

"*C'est vrais*," Dorian cried. "I believe I have solved this mystery."

We all looked expectantly at him.

"Go on, my good man," Nicolas prompted as Dorian gloated and rocked back and forward on his heels.

"The thief," said Dorian, "is in the circus."

I groaned.

Dorian clicked his tongue and frowned at me. "You doubt my theory? Circus folk travel around the country, do they not? They are dexterous." He narrowed his black eyes. "They are not to be trusted."

I groaned again. "Traveling circuses aren't as popular as they were when we were younger, and what have you got against people who work in the circus?"

Dorian raised his chin and tucked his wings. "I am a dignified creature, am I not?"

"Of course," Nicolas replied.

"I have not," Dorian said, "even told Zoe this story before, because it is beneath me." He gave a long sigh. "Once, in Paris, I attended a traveling circus. From the rafters, of course. A man with the circus saw me. He attempted to capture me. To make me an exhibit to be gawked at. I was forced to flee before I could partake in the spectacle below." He straightened his back and flapped his wings once, before folding them again at his sides.

"Terrible," Nicolas said. "Absolutely terrible."

"You escaped," I pointed out. "And it doesn't mean everyone in the circus can't be trusted."

"Dorian has a point," Perenelle said. "A gymnast or someone with similar skills could have gotten in and out of the museum with the gold that quickly."

"Maybe," I said, though I wasn't convinced. "We need to go back to the museum."

"The museum?" Dorian's horns wriggled.

"The Oregon Gold History Museum. It's open again after the break-in."

"I did not realize..." he murmured.

"I'm sorry you can't come with us, Dorian."

"It is of no matter."

I eyed him suspiciously. "Why not?"

"I have my own life, Zoe. I will always help you when I am able to participate, but I can occupy myself when I am not needed. I am working on a novel. Were you not listening to me when I told you why I wished to use the typewriter? Do not worry about me. But remember, you are collecting reconnaissance and then we will regroup. I wish you a productive excursion at the museum."

CHAPTER 38

Dorian called Brixton from his land line phone as soon as Zoe and the Flamels had departed. "You said you were returning to the museum after our luncheon?"

"Um, yeah."

"Are you still there?"

"Nearby. We wanted to hang out with a new friend first."

"If you wish to do more research there today, you must finish your research *immediately*."

"Why?"

"Zoe and Perenelle are headed there now."

"Um, okay. So what?"

Dorian sighed. "They cannot know you are investigating the treasure."

"We've gotta get back to the museum now," Dorian heard Brixton say to his friends.

"The museum doesn't close for a while," a less familiar voice said. "We can finish the game before we go over."

"Um," Brixton mumbled, "I wanted to see something. You and Ethan can finish the game. Veronica and I will go back to the museum."

The sound of shuffling and footsteps.

"What was that about?" Veronica asked, her voice quiet. "Was it Dorian who called?"

"He's still on the line."

"Oh! Hi, Dorian."

"Once you reach the museum, telephone me with a video call I can open on Zoe's computer," Dorian said. He assumed it was now safe to speak freely, since Veronica had addressed him.

"We'll be there in two seconds," Brixton said.

"You are in the nearby park?" Dorian asked.

"Playing video games at Harry's house."

"The Cabot boy? You did not reveal your true motive for spending time with him?"

"He doesn't know anything," said Brixton. "At least nothing we could learn without telling him about the map. Okay, we're here. Hanging up now. I'll call you back on video."

Dorian paced across the attic. He wished to help Zoe discover the identity of the thief and blackmailer, but he was so close to finding a grand treasure that would solve so many problems!

Zoe's laptop rang, and Brixton and Veronica's faces filled the screen a moment later. The pair were outside, the setting sun behind them.

"Veronica has an idea about what to look for this time," Brixton said, "but she won't take the phone."

"Don't be a toad." She scrunched up her face at Brixton before turning back to the camera. "I'd take it if I could—even though it's against the rules, which is how much I care about this—but there's no way either of our phones would fit in my front pocket without falling out. I don't understand why Brixton's clothes have pockets that are so much better than mine."

Dorian cleared his throat. "You have a solution?"

"Yeah," said Brixton. "I'll have the phone in my pocket, but Veronica will tell me where to stand."

"*Très bon*."

It was a good thing Dorian was not susceptible to motion sickness, for watching a bumpy, angled video of a camera in the pocket of a teenage boy was enough to induce a seizure if one did not possess a strong constitution.

Veronica indeed knew where she was going. She led them through the central exhibits to a section of the museum where old maps of the Oregon coast hung on the wall.

"This map." Veronica pointed, and Brixton attempted to step closer, but a museum patron extended their arm to block him.

"Careful, young man." The woman was off camera, yet her clipped voice made her intent clear. "You aren't supposed to *touch* the exhibits. If you can't see the display properly, I suggest you ask your parents to take you to an optometrist."

"Um, sure. I was just looking."

"It's okay, Brix," Veronica said. "I have what we need."

"You do?"

She pulled him backward, and a few moments later they were outside. The jerky video showed feet scurrying away from the museum, first on paved stones, then asphalt. The motion came to a stop once they reached grass.

When Brixton took the camera from his pocket, Dorian observed a park behind them.

"Sorry I couldn't get a closer look."

"It doesn't matter," Veronica said. Though Dorian could not see her face, he heard the excitement in her voice.

"Give Veronica the phone," he demanded.

Black hair splashed across the screen, then Veronica's smiling face appeared. "I know where the treasure is."

CHAPTER 39

Nicolas had had too much excitement for the day and wasn't feeling well, so Perenelle stayed with him while I went to the museum on my own. It was mid-afternoon, and the museum would be closing in a couple of hours.

I struck up a conversation with the friendly woman working at the small information desk. It was the same woman who let us in early on our first visit.

"Nice to see you again," I said.

"You as well. I remember you looking carefully at the miniature Gold Rush town reproduction before. I can tell you appreciate the history. Not like some people who just come to crane their necks at a crime scene."

"It's a great museum. I only spotted one anachronism."

She smiled. "The one in the miniature town?"

"The telephone looks old-fashioned to people today, but that one wasn't in use until the 1870s."

"You're good. There's one more that I know of."

"Another mistake?"

"I prefer to think of them as keeping people on their toes. But yes, you missed one." She got up and took me to a case showing prospector clothing from the 1860s Oregon Gold Rush. "Levi's."

"Slightly too early. I'm ashamed I missed it."

"Historian?" she asked.

"History buff."

"I love showing people around. I wish I had more help, but our usual docent and ticket-taker quit after the robbery."

A sullen teenage boy walked through the main door. Instead of stopping at the now-abandoned ticket desk, he came right up to her.

"Is it cool if I have dinner with some new friends?" he asked.

"My son, Harry," she said to me before turning her attention to him. "You know we're heading to the hospital to visit your father once we close up here."

"Right." He gave us both a nod and departed.

"You're Ginessa Cabot," I said. She looked quite different from the photos of her that had been published by the press. I hadn't recognized her without makeup, in a plain T-shirt and jeans, and with her hair pulled into a ponytail.

"Gin," she said. "Just Gin. As long as you're not the press. Which I doubt since you spotted the phone in the miniature. Nice to have people here who aren't just here because of the theft. It was a madhouse when we reopened the week following the theft."

"I'm Zoe. And I'm so sorry about what happened."

"I'm so angry that someone stole Harry's discovery and hurt his father. I don't care about the monetary value of the gold. We have money through no doing of our own. Harry knows that. But this was his own accomplishment, not thanks to our name or money. He was the one who wanted to go to the site with his metal detector after the storm. He was the one who put the clues together. When he was little, we used to go camping and search for treasure. That's how he learned about history, as a proud seventh-generation Oregonian."

"Do the police know exactly what happened yet?"

She shook her head. "The more they find out, the less any of it makes any sense."

"What do you mean?"

"Because the thief was able to get the gold so quickly, one of the theories is that the gold wasn't real in the first place. That it was a fraud and we knew we were about to be found out so we removed it. Like they think Harrison would risk his life! It's absurd."

It was definitely absurd for a man to risk his life as he did. But… I looked more carefully at Gin. What if *she* instigated the fraud? If her husband didn't know his wife had staged the robbery, he would have wanted to catch the thief.

She gave me a strange look, and I wondered what my own expression revealed.

"I was just thinking how sorry I am about what happened to your husband," I said quickly. "Someone I care about is recovering from a bad injury as well."

"I wish I understood what happened. The money doesn't matter, but everything is such a mess now. Harry is at a complicated age where he's finding himself. He was so elated when his love of history and hard work led to a historical discovery. When it was stolen… I don't think I've ever seen him so dejected."

"How's your husband?"

"They don't know if he'll ever wake up."

CHAPTER 40

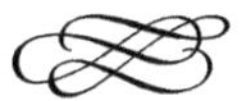

Dorian gasped. Not only at Veronica's statement that she knew where the treasure was, but at the time. This had taken longer than he'd realized.

"You must depart from the vicinity of the museum immediately," Dorian said. "Zoe may be there any moment. Is the museum visible from where you are?"

"Yeah," Brixton said. "We're not in the museum anymore. We're already outside. That witch kept glaring at us. We weren't even doing anything."

"You must move further away from the museum."

"Don't worry. We'll find another spot so we won't run into Zoe. Call you back in a sec."

When they did so, they appeared to be in the shelter of the porch of a house. Dorian would have asked where they were, but Veronica spoke so quickly that he did not wish to interrupt.

"We already realized that a treasure everyone thought was fictional was actually real." She fumbled for something in her bag. The letter that had been with the map.

Dating confirms sixteenth-century coin.

Why didn't they say "based on a true story"? Would have made for better promotion.

Unless—what if they wanted to find the treasure in Oregon for themselves? Good reason to hide truth that the wizard is real.

Already found? But why no record? Fair to keep, so no need to hide.

"Now is not the time to go over what we already know," Dorian said.

"I'm not finished," she said curtly. "What none of us thought about is the fact that although the researcher's notes mention Oregon, *Oregon wasn't yet a state* when a pirate treasure would have been hidden. What we *thought* was a map showing the coastline of Oregon is no such thing. It shows the general shape of a coastline, plus there's this ship and some rocks in the water, so it's immediately what we thought of. We were wrong. It's a much more zoomed-in view. It's a small area of coastline with distinctive rocks. Not in the ocean. In a much smaller body of water. That's where this ship caught on fire and sank."

"Whoa," Brixton said.

Whoa, indeed. Dorian sat back on his haunches. He knew Veronica was intelligent, yet he had not imagined she would crack the case so efficiently.

"One of the maps on the wall showed this inlet off the coast," Veronica said. "Brix, take your phone back. I need to look up something on mine." She was silent for a moment, then gasped.

"What did you find?" Brixton asked.

"I knew it. This rocky coastline looks different than all the current maps we looked at, but this old one here is the same. We should have guessed. We *knew* there was a connection to Astoria. Astoria isn't on the coast of the ocean itself—*it's a bay.* Where the Columbia River meets up with the Pacific Ocean. The treasure map isn't drawn north to south or top to bottom. East is on top. It's a different coastline. And now we know exactly where to go."

CHAPTER 41

I knew where I needed to go.

On my way from the museum back to my truck, I took a detour to the park across the street. I slipped off my boots and socks. Stepping onto the grass, I savored the feeling of the cool, prickly greenery. The skin on my feet was less calloused than it had been when I didn't live in an urban environment, but I didn't mind the pinpricks of nature.

Keeping my left foot firmly on the earth, I lifted my right foot and felt the soft leaves of dandelions with my toes. I closed my eyes, inhaled deeply and caught the fragrances of flowers, tree bark, and lemons. Lemons? I opened my eyes and spotted the branch of a lemon tree poking over the top of a fence of a nearby house.

I closed my eyes again. This time I listened as crows spoke to each other in the trees, traffic hummed along one of Portland's twelve bridges nearby but out of sight, and a baby gave a delighted squeal from a stroller.

A minute later, I opened my eyes. A brief respite in nature hadn't jarred loose any grand ideas. But it had reenergized me. I put my shoes back on. The brown boots were more than ten years old, and I always took them to a cobbler to repair them instead of seeking out a new pair. I was still getting used to living in a two-story house that also had an attic and basement, instead of living out of my Airstream trailer. In some ways, I'd adjusted quickly, filling the walls with art and the backyard with an edible garden. Heather had taken me clothes shopping after a storm leaked through the damaged roof and ruined much of my small wardrobe, but I still only owned three pairs of shoes. Ashleigh Eriksen would no doubt be horrified if she saw my closet.

A bright orange skateboard caught my eye as a young, dark-haired woman skated through the parking lot of the museum. The figure in the distance reminded me of Veronica, and the graceful movement on wheels made me think of a day earlier this year when I first realized I didn't hate all physical activities on wheels.

I've always hated riding a bike. I'm biased, because I first rode one shortly after they were invented, back when they were called velocipedes—and when they didn't have air-pressurized tires. "Bone shakers" were given their nickname for a reason. I stayed away from bicycles since then, and was never interested in testing a unicycle, skateboard, roller skates, or roller blades, when they came along.

Until Max.

When he learned I had never been roller skating, he insisted I go with him to a roller rink on '80s night. I recognized the music the DJ played. I could sing along and enjoyed doing so. But to Max, it was reliving his youth.

I hadn't expected what happened when I put on the rented bright white skates with fluorescent pink wheels and Max took my hand in his and led me to the rink. I came alive.

Skating was nothing like riding a bike. It was like driving a car—something I'd always loved, though I'd hated it when speed limits were imposed. Roller skating was even better. It was like flying.

Since I'm terrible at staying awake after dark, we'd gone to the roller rink as soon as it opened for the evening at five o'clock, thinking we'd go for an hour or two before dinner and an early night. But as soon as the wheels began to spin, I didn't want to stop. We ate pretzels from the snack bar for dinner and closed down the rink. The next day, Max bought me a pair of skates as a gift. I don't know how he'd found the perfect pair so quickly, but they were a deep forest green with lime green wheels. I hadn't used them since Max left for his grandfather's funeral. I didn't want to fly without Max.

I crossed the park and unlocked the door of my truck. The dark-haired girl in the distance flipped up her skateboard and disappeared behind the Cabots' house.

CHAPTER 42

"We need to get Ethan." Veronica slid her skateboard into her backpack. "We need to tell him what we learned about the pirate treasure."

Brixton swore. "He invited Harry to have dinner with us later, remember?"

"I don't think we need to worry about that." She hovered on the board but didn't push off. "Look."

The screen went dark, but Dorian could still hear the teenagers.

"Where's Harry?" Brixton asked.

"He and his mom are going to visit his dad at the hospital," said Ethan, "so we can't hang out tonight."

"It's for the best," Veronica said.

"You don't like Harry?" Ethan's voice was sharp.

"I like him. But forget about Harry for a second. Ethan, it's amazing." She paused, and Dorian could hear the excitement in her voice when she spoke once more. "We found out where the treasure map leads."

"Wicked, huh?" said Brixton.

"Seriously? How?"

"Veronica needs to tell you. Oh, crap. Dorian is still on the line, too."

They adjusted the phone for Dorian to see them, and Veronica told Ethan her discovery about the map being a closeup of the inlet near Astoria.

"We've got more than half of the weekend left," Brixton said. "We can leave this afternoon."

"That's a big area to search," Ethan said.

"Wait, you don't want to go anymore?" Brixton asked.

"It's just... You guys are way too excited about this. We don't even know where the painting came from, since Dorian bought it from a guy that lied."

"We never examined the frames more carefully," Veronica said. "Why didn't we look more carefully? My mom would kill me if she knew how bad my research skills have been on this project."

"Um, your mom would kill you if she knew you were about to go on a treasure hunt," Brixton pointed out.

"Dorian." Veronica took the phone in her hands and looked imploringly at him. Her face filled the screen, her black hair falling over part of the lens. "It's the middle of the day so I know we can't come over to the attic and have people know we're friends in real life. But maybe you could look—"

"*Mon dieu,*" Dorian murmured. He left the laptop on the table and scampered to the pile of paintings and broken frames he had cleaned up. The glass had been swept into a wastebasket, but the boards behind the paintings remained. Or rather, the board that was behind one of the paintings. The rest only had thin paper, not nearly sturdy enough to contain the doubloon...

Dorian ran back to the computer. "I am afraid I may have made a slight miscalculation, *mes amis.* The only painting which could have safely held the map, notes, and doubloon is the one Madame Flamel had left in my attic next to my own purchases."

"It's one of Zoe's stepmom's paintings?" Veronica said.

"No," said Dorian. "It was a seascape painted by the person blackmailing her."

Veronica was silent, yet her face expressed that she was processing this information.

Brixton snatched the phone from her hands. "A seascape? Could it be the Oregon coast?"

"Without seeing the coast itself, it is not possible to tell. We must travel there ourselves to see. I can be packed by the time you return—"

"You want to go *now*?" It was Ethan's voice that spoke from off camera.

"Are you not intrigued?" Dorian asked. "Simply because you already possess great wealth—"

"That's not what I meant," Ethan snapped. This was, Dorian suspected, a sore spot. Dorian knew from Brixton that when Ethan had moved to Portland two years before, many of their classmates tried to befriend Ethan once they learned of the mansion he lived in. Brixton and Veronica, lifelong friends since elementary school, had been unimpressed. Yet they came to realize they liked Ethan anyway, and he them. The three had become inseparable.

"I'm having second thoughts," Ethan continued as he took the phone from Brixton, "because of the first person who figured out the fictional treasure was based on a real one. This researcher who left this note." He paused, drawing his brows together. "What do you think *happened* to them?"

Nobody spoke. The boy, Dorian mused, was quite intelligent. Even the great Dorian Robert-Houdin had not considered this point. Ethan was someone to be respected. No, perhaps that was going a bit far. The boy did refer to him as Scooby, which would not do.

"Why was their discovery hidden?" Ethan continued. "Why did they feel the need to do that? *And what happened to this person who once hid the map and coin*? Nothing good, I bet."

"You don't want to find out?" Veronica asked.

"Hell yes. I'm in. I'm only pointing out it might not just be a treasure we find. It might be a pile of old bones from the adults who tried to find it before us."

Veronica stopped sliding back and forth. She flipped her garish skateboard into her arms. "Then we'll need to be smarter than them."

CHAPTER 43

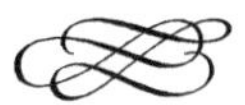

On my drive home from the museum, I played my eight-track tape of Tobias's song "Accidental Life." When the song was released in the 1950s, I immediately felt drawn to it. It was familiar in that way that some songs are, even when you've never heard them before. At least that's what I'd thought at the time. Now I knew that the reason it felt like home was because the musician who created it was Tobias Freeman, performing as The Philosopher. After we parted ways more than a century-and-a-half before, I hadn't known he'd found the Elixir of Life. I knew he had a strong singing voice, but he'd been a younger and less healthy man with a different voice when I first knew him.

With the comforting song playing on the tinny speakers, I tried to wrap my head around what I knew about the heist. It wasn't much. I'd already looked up what the police had released to the press, which wasn't much either. They might be close to an arrest, for all I knew, but nothing had been reported.

I pulled over to the side of the road as the tape ended. I lifted my phone into my hand, but hesitated before dialing. Since Max hadn't returned my calls, should I try him at the police station? I had an overwhelming amount of evidence he was back home, from Dorian's search of his house to what both Tobias and Heather had said. I expected that meant he was back at work as well.

I hesitated. Even if he could tell me more, would he? And what could I tell him about why I was asking?

I didn't even know what was real anymore. I had the strongest impression that what we'd all seen on the video wasn't real. Not that the video itself had been doctored, but that it wasn't the full picture.

I put the truck in gear and drove home, watching the juxtaposition of modern architecture and ancient nature living side by side. And above, blue sky in front of me and storm clouds behind. The world wasn't black and white. Neither were people. By the time I pulled into the driveway, I knew what was wrong.

I took a deep breath as I looked at the Craftsman house I'd been fixing up for the past year, the cherry trees in front, a flourishing garden in back, and a warm and welcoming home inside. I didn't want to leave Portland. I didn't want to be forced to leave my home. Exposure for Perenelle being an alchemist was sure to blow over, but being accused of a theft that left a man near death? That was another matter altogether.

I found Perenelle and Nicolas in the kitchen. Nicolas was drinking a cup of toasted rice green tea and Perenelle was eating an open-faced toasted sandwich. Half of the bread was burnt to a crisp. They hadn't gotten the hang of modern appliances yet.

"Did you learn anything new?" Perenelle left her burnt sandwich on the plate and stood.

"I have a theory," I said, "that the blackmailer could be the thief."

"What are you going on about? She's blackmailing me for the gold. Why would she do that if she had it already."

"Don't you see? We know the blackmailer is a *con artist*. That's how they stole the gold nugget you created, by getting into the house pretending to work with the window repairman. Before that, the event that started this whole mess, is when they saw you make the gold. They could be a serial blackmailer, or at least someone who likes to keep tabs on people to make sure they haven't been found out. That's why they set up a camera that caught you on tape—because they know how to spy on people. We might have been right from the start after all. If they saw enough to suspect you're truly an alchemist, they think they can scare you into making more gold for them." I pressed my eyes shut. "That would explain what's wrong with the video of the heist. Why it's too quick. *Because it was a con.*"

"Fascinating," Nicolas murmured.

"You don't believe the gold was stolen at all?" asked Perenelle.

"The theft caught on camera was staged," I explained. The pieces clicked into place as I spoke. "The gold was already gone, taken by our con artist blackmailer's partner. Someone with access to the museum at any time."

"Someone," Perenelle said softly, "who did not chase after the thief they had hired."

"Gin Cabot."

"She didn't tell her husband what she was doing, so he attacked the thief, who got the better of him."

"I think," I said, "it's time to get the police involved." I called the police station and asked to be connected to Max Liu.

"I'm sorry," the person on the line said. "Max Liu is no longer affiliated with Portland Police Department."

CHAPTER 44

"Hello?" the voice on the other end of the phone line prompted. "Are you still there? What's the nature of your problem? Is there someone else who can help you? If this is an emergency—"

"No. No, it's not an emergency," I stammered before hanging up.

"What's the matter?" Perenelle felt my forehead. "You look ill."

Max no longer worked for Portland PD?

And I truly had no way to reach him.

"He's not there," I said. There was one other person on the police force I knew. Detective Vega. The question was, could I trust her?

I knew I could trust that she wasn't in league with the blackmailer and thief. What I didn't know was how much I could reveal to her about my and Perenelle's situation. I'd saved Detective Vega's life earlier this year. She didn't know I was a centuries-old alchemist, and I wasn't going to risk explaining that part to her. Without letting her know how I was involved, would she give me any information?

Knuckles rapped at the front door.

"Our decision is saved by the bell, eh?" Nicolas said with a chuckle, which disappeared when neither Perenelle nor I joined him. "That's the correct expression, is it not?"

"I believe so, my dear," Perenelle said. "Zoe is distracted by the matter at hand."

The knock sounded again.

Brixton's mom, Heather, stood at the door. In shiny silver sandals, she rocked back and forth from her heels to the balls of her feet and held a gigantic bouquet of flowers in her hands. The stems weren't in a vase, but were tied with a braided piece of twine.

"A hand-picked gift," she said, thrusting the bouquet into my arms. "Since Brix is spending the rest of the weekend at Ethan's house, I spent the afternoon picking wildflowers from Blue's land. I ended up with way too many, even after dropping off most of them at Blue Sky Teas for her to use as decorations."

"What delicate blossoms on the *agremonia gryposepala*," said Nicolas, coming up behind me. "And the purple of the *symphyotrichum novae-angliae* is stunning."

Of course he would know the names of each of the obscure wildflowers in the bouquet. I agreed the purple of the aster was stunning. As Nicolas nodded approvingly at the mix, I wondered if the bouquet would disappear the next time he retreated to the basement alchemy lab.

"Thanks for bringing these by," I said. "I'd invite you in but we're a little busy right now—"

"Nonsense," Nicolas said. "One can never be too busy for friends. Friends can also help us see things most clearly—don't you agree, Zoe? Now let's find a vase, and will you join us for tea on the back patio, Heather?"

"I'd love to." Heather beamed and accepted Nicolas's gallant gesture of offering his arm.

With his free arm, Nicolas lifted the flowers from me, and the two of them went in search of a vase large enough for the arrangement.

"There is a method to his madness," Perenelle said softly. "He can see how much stress you are under. Remember your teachings. You will not be able to find the answer to this conundrum while under such stress. My husband is right. We need a cup of tea and the company of a carefree friend."

I fixed a pot of mint tea, my mind already feeling calmer from the familiar action, then joined the three of them on the back porch while they were discussing Heather's selection.

"*Atropa belladonna* is an unusual choice," Nicolas was saying.

"You mean the deadly nightshade?" she asked. "I knew Zoe didn't have pets, so I thought it was okay since nobody would be eating it. The purple flowers are so beautiful I couldn't resist. I hope you don't disapprove."

"Quite the contrary. Did you know Zoe had a poison garden when she was a youngster?"

The garden had been at his urging. He wanted me to learn to control the balance of nature's healing and dangerous properties.

"Like from an Agatha Christie novel?" said Heather. "I can't grow anything myself, but I love harvesting wildflowers."

"And painting them," Perenelle said. "Nicolas, you realize this is the young woman who created the faces in the woods painting hanging in Zoe's living room."

"You're quite talented," Nicolas said.

"One second," Heather said as her phone rang. "Let me just silence this. Oh. Wait, it's Veronica's mom. I'd better take it." Her face turned from a smile to horror as she listened. "No. Are you sure? But they—No, I see. I'll be right over."

"What's happened?" I asked.

"I thought Brixton knew he could trust me. I really thought... I'm sure it's nothing, but Veronica's mom is worried."

"What exactly is going on?" I asked again.

"Brixton and Veronica aren't at Ethan's house like they told us, and Ashleigh's car is missing."

CHAPTER 45

They were on the road by 4 p.m.

The weekend was nearly half over, and Brixton and his friends would need to return to school Monday morning. They did not have much time, so they had acted quickly. They each returned home to pack. Dorian, too, gathered important items together. First, he retrieved the painting of the seaside in which they deduced the map and coin had been hidden. Next, there was one more important thing to take: cooking implements. They would be gone for two nights before the trio of teens needed to return to school. During that time, they would need sustenance. Dorian would make sure it was of the highest caliber.

Ethan had borrowed his mother's car as planned, and they were now on the highway, with Dorian sitting on the floor of the spacious backseat and Veronica on the seat beside him.

From the road, while Ethan drove, Veronica sat at his side and booked a vacation rental from her phone, using Ethan's name and the credit card his parents had given him. They wished for something private, and this rental was described as a detached "tiny house."

One hour outside Portland, the blare of a loud, rhythmic noise sounded behind them. Dorian was crouched in the backseat, unable to see, yet he was certain the noise sounded like the siren of a police car.

The sound grew closer, louder. Yet it did not pass them and grew weak as the police car faded into the distance. In spite of his worry, Dorian congratulated himself on being such a keen observer of his surroundings. He was a fantastic detective. Zoe and Madame Flamel should not have kept secrets about the blackmailer from him.

Ethan swore. "Those sirens can't be for me."

Brixton looked back. "Um, it really looks like they are. But I don't get it. Even if our parents talked to each other and found out we lied about whose house we're at, it's not like we've been gone long enough for them to call the cops."

"But Ethan stole his mom's car," Veronica said.

"Borrowed," Ethan corrected. "And she'll just think my dad moved it to mess with her. Really."

"We're so dead," Brixton whispered.

"I suspect, Ethan," Dorian said, "it has more to do with the fact that our velocity is quite high. This is not the Grand Prix."

Ethan groaned. "Time to turn to stone, Scooby."

Dorian lifted himself from his crouched position on the floor of the backseat so he could address them all.

"What are you doing, Dorian?" Veronica shrieked. Or perhaps she was just speaking loudly enough to be heard above the sirens.

Dorian scowled at them. "Surely you do not plan on stopping."

"Omigod, we're not going on a chase, are we?" Veronica checked her seatbelt.

"I wish we could," Ethan said, "but I think we should stop. Don't worry. I have a plan."

"Please just turn to stone," Brixton said, "okay?"

"Very well." Dorian lay back down on the floor of the backseat. He nodded at Veronica, who placed the blanket over him. In the darkness, he focused his intent and felt his body stiffen into stone. His senses were not exactly heightened in this form, yet he was more aware of his surroundings when he knew he would not be able to move. The vibrations on the floor of this automobile were much less intense than those of Zoe's truck. He could easily hear the voices above him.

"You're putting on glasses?" Brixton said as the car slowed. "You mean you should have been wearing them this whole time?"

"They're plain glass," Ethan answered. "Gotta look studious for the officer."

"You just happened to have a pair of Giles the librarian glasses with you?"

"The round copper frames go with the Dark Academia vibe he's going for," Veronica answered for him.

They came to a stop. The sirens behind them kept wailing. A second later, the sound was deafening. After a moment, it faded into the distance.

"They weren't stopping you!" Veronica cried.

"The police," said Ethan, "don't hassle people who look like me."

"You were speeding," Veronica said. "He totally could have been coming for you. My heart won't stop racing. Is it normal for it to stay this high?"

"*Allo*?" Dorian whispered. "May I come out now?"

Ethan laughed. "Yeah, Scooby. He's gone."

Dorian stretched and peeked out of the blanket. "Your heart will return to normal once your adrenaline has worn off, Veronica."

"That was really close," Brixton said. "Maybe avoid speeding for the rest of this trip."

"It's fine." Ethan's voice was steady, yet his fingers gripped the steering wheel as he spoke. "I've never been stopped before."

"What would you have done if the cop asked to see your license?" Brixton's voice rose.

"He has a fake ID," Veronica said. "Show him, Ethan."

Ethan released his death grip on the steering wheel and grinned. "I'm 19-year-old Ethan Cumberbatch." He removed his unnecessary glasses, then took an identification card from his wallet and tossed it to Brixton.

Brixton laughed. "People seriously believe you're nineteen? And that you didn't just steal your name from that Sherlock Holmes actor Veronica drools over—*ouch*! It's true."

"Ethan Cumberbatch," said Ethan Eriksen, "has the youthful face of an actor. You know most of the actors in the shows we watch, who are supposed to be our age, are like 30 years old, right? That cop with the wrinkled face wouldn't know the difference. *Ow. What*, Veronica? Why'd you punch me too?"

"You two are such toads."

"What if he'd insisted on seeing your registration," Brixton said, "or if he'd run your plates?"

"I thought it was unlikely he'd do either. But I would have said it was my mom's car—lots of people have different last names than their moms. It's not like she's going to report the car missing. She and my dad are even busier than their usual work-all-the-time schedules now that they're getting divorced. They won't even know I'm gone."

"Still," Brixton said, "we should turn off our phones so they can't see where we are. Let's get back on the road."

"Yes," said Dorian. "If we hurry, we can make it before nightfall."

CHAPTER 46

After Heather failed to reach Brixton on his cell phone, she left to meet with Veronica's parents.

"I know it's age appropriate for fifteen-year-olds to borrow a parent's car without a license or permission," I said to Nicolas and Perenelle as I cleaned up our empty mugs, "but with everything going on, I don't like it."

"Don't look so glum," said Nicolas. "They are probably simply following the treasure map they found behind the painting."

My mug slipped from my hand. "What did you say?"

"When they were dining here with Dorian, they spoke of a map. They are the right age for an adventure, are they not? Why are both of you looking at me as if I have grown two heads?"

"They know about Dorian?" I gaped at him.

He blinked back at me. "Why would they not know Dorian? He lives here."

"He's a gargoyle, Nicolas. A gargoyle." I ran up the stairs. How could Dorian have let more people know of his existence?

"Brixton dined with us all," Nicolas called after me. "These were only his friends. It's not as if I threw a *fête* in your absence."

"Dorian," I began as I burst through the attic door. "Dorian?"

The room was empty.

But a sheet of paper with a few lines of text was sticking out of the Smith Corona typewriter. It caught my attention because it began with my name.

Dear Zoe,

I have gone on a brief holiday. Please give my apologies to Blue that there will not be home-baked pastries for her café tomorrow.

Yours truly,

Dorian Robert-Houdin

"Where's Dorian?" Perenelle asked from the attic doorway.

I held up the note. "He's gone with them."

"Following their treasure map," Nicolas said, then ran a hand over his wild hair. "Oh dear…" His face fell and his hand trembled.

Perenelle wrapped her arm around her husband's waist. "Were the steep attic stairs too much?"

"Oh dear, oh dear…"

I brought a chair closer to him. "Sit down. Catch your breath."

"Do you need one of Zoe's tinctures?" Perenelle asked. "Or a glass of water?"

He swatted away our concern and rejected the chair. "Physically, I am no worse. Yet I am a stupid, stupid man. Dorian had a painting with him when he came down the stairs. I recognized it, yet I did not inquire…"

"What painting?"

Nicolas pulled free of Perenelle's arm and stomped across the attic, tossing aside the antiques with abandon. "Yes, that must have been what he had with him."

My heart continued to pound more furiously at each passing moment. "Which. Painting. Nicolas?"

"I believe," he said slowly, looking up at me with frantic eyes, "it was the blackmailer's painting of the seaside."

"The seascape should be right over…" I trailed off when I saw the seaside painting was no longer in the corner where we'd put it with the paintings that had come with Dorian's typewriters. *Of course.* "That was the stack of paintings Dorian tripped over and broke. That's where he found the map. He told me as much, but I wasn't listening." *Because of Max.* Where *was* he?

"They've taken the painting along with their treasure map," Nicolas said.

"But why?" Perenelle knelt in front of what remained of the broken frames. "It wasn't old. And it wasn't particularly well done."

"But it showed a coastline," I said. I closed my eyes and thought back to the hand-drawn map Dorian had showed me. The faded sheet of paper he'd called a treasure map. "The map wasn't obviously a treasure map. It wasn't even obviously a map. It showed a clipper ship with flames coming out of it, and an X nearby, but I don't think there was a dotted line or symbols like a skull and crossbones." Not that I'd given it more than a brief examination. My breath caught.

Perenelle was immediately at my side. "What is it?"

"The painting," I murmured. "Did you notice the rippled reflection in the ocean water? I remember thinking it looked as if the artist was going to add something on the top of the water but abandoned the idea."

"Yes. It was as if they thought better of it, realizing sand, water, and rocks are one thing, but their skills weren't up for painting something more detailed... *a ship*?" Her eyes grew wide.

"What if it wasn't a reflection at all," I said, "but something *under the water.*"

"The painting," Perenelle said, "is a clue to supplement their treasure map."

I shook my head. "Except that it's not a real treasure map. It's fake. Just like our blackmailer, who we now know is a skilled con artist. Dorian and the kids must think they're on a fun treasure hunt adventure, following a map they found behind a random painting."

"But the painting was far from random," Perenelle said.

"No. They're going after a con artist who's willing to resort to violence."

CHAPTER 47

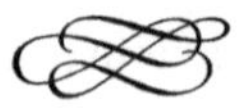

My tires screeched as I pulled into the Elements Art House parking lot.

Inside, Sameera sat at the front desk. In a khaki green T-shirt, her tattoo-covered arms were bare. She hadn't been hit with my paint bomb. A workshop was going on in the classroom to our left. I didn't sense my paint anywhere either.

"Hey, Zoe." Her smile faded. "Everything all right?"

"Perenelle forgot something in her studio. I'm here to get it."

I let myself into Perenelle's studio with her key and stood in the semi-darkness. The sun hadn't yet gone down, but the windows were still covered in paper. I jumped onto the chair and ripped off the paper.

Thin beams of sunlight forced their way into the art and alchemy lab through cracks in the butcher paper. I could sense that this wasn't my space, yet I also felt its energy. I only needed to stay a few moments longer. I'd needed to give Sameera a reason I was there, and this was the most plausible excuse since I couldn't exactly explain to Sameera that I was checking to see if she was a murderous blackmailing thief.

I paused in the doorway before letting myself out. The two Superman figurines rested on a corner shelf near the door. Kent

Clarkson had moved out of this studio just before Perenelle had moved in. That was about two weeks ago…

I pulled out my phone and looked up the date the gold had been stolen from the Oregon Gold History Museum. The night Harrison Cabot had been left for dead and ended up in a coma. Fifteen days ago.

Rushing back to the front desk, I skidded to a stop in front of a wide-eyed Sameera. "What was the date Kent Clarkson moved out of the studio?"

She blinked up at me and took the unlit cigar from her lips. "I can check. Why?"

I forced a smile. "Perenelle has accomplished so much in such a short time. I couldn't remember how long she's been here."

"You're an intense person, Zoe. I can appreciate that." Sameera pulled a laptop from a drawer and tapped a few keys. "Kent left exactly two weeks ago. Perenelle was approved three days later."

Kent had departed fourteen days ago. The robbery took place fifteen days ago. *He'd left the day after someone stole a huge amount of gold and nearly killed Harrison Cabot.*

"Did Kent give advance notice?"

"This isn't about Perenelle's progress, is it?"

"Can you just tell me?"

"He didn't. But he wasn't happy here, so we weren't surprised."

"Thank you," I said. "You've helped more than you could possibly know."

"I can help more if you told me—Zoe? Hey, Zoe?"

I was already out the door.

The date Kent Clarkson left Elements on short notice couldn't have been a coincidence, could it? Someone at Elements would have been best equipped to spy on Perenelle and leave the blackmail notes for her. But he was a man, and the person who'd conned their way into my house had been a woman. Hadn't they?

I groaned. He was a small man and I never saw the face of the person behind the window. I'd never spoken to him and I didn't know if he could make his voice sound like someone I'd assume would be a woman. His involvement would also explain why I couldn't find the person who had any evidence of my paint bomb on their skin.

I didn't have proof Kent was involved in the heist or blackmail any more than I had proof the blackmailer and thief were the same person. But I knew there was a connection. Something just below the surface I couldn't quite fit together. With Max gone from the police force, I needed more before I could go to someone who wouldn't automatically trust me.

I sped home and frantically searched the attic, breaking a teacup from an antique tea set and ripping a postcard of *le Cabaret de l'Enfer*—an early twentieth century Parisian nightclub that literally called itself the Nightclub from Hell. Which, as I sat in the middle of my self-ransacked attic, seemed appropriate.

Why would Dorian have enabled Brixton? He was impulsive, yes, but he must have had an even better reason for being so reckless.

My laptop balanced precariously on the edge of a shelf. That wasn't where I'd left it. It couldn't be as simple as that, could it? I eased open the computer and looked at my browser history. Or rather, Dorian's browser history.

They were heading to the coast, on their way to Astoria.

CHAPTER 48

"Ugh," said Veronica as they stepped onto the rickety porch.

"You sure this is the right place?" Brixton asked.

"This is more like a shack than a tiny house," Ethan added.

"I knew there must've been a reason the rental was available at the last minute," Veronica muttered as she punched a code into a keypad next to the door. The box popped open and she extracted a key.

Dorian agreed with her assessment. The decor was not what modern travelers preferred. The interior of the small shack was quite dark, due to its small windows—which was perfect for Dorian.

"How much did this serial killer shack cost us?" Brixton asked as they dumped their overnight bags onto the uneven floor.

"Doesn't matter," Ethan said. "It's far away from other houses. It's not like we'll be here long. We just need a home base for the next 24 hours."

"And somewhere to stay until it is dark," Dorian added.

"Aren't we going in search of the treasure now?" Veronica asked.

"We cannot explore," Dorian explained, "while it is light out."

"Then why were we rushing to get here?" Brixton asked.

"Do you not know me by now?" Dorian dumped out the contents of his bag, revealing an assortment of cooking implements and ingredients he had taken from the house. "I wish to cook us a hearty dinner, so our bodies and minds will be nourished for our nocturnal excursion to find the treasure."

Ethan grinned. "Brix, I can't believe you kept this guy from us for so long. You're the best, Scooby. Literally. The absolute best. What's on the menu?"

Dorian sorted through his provisions, then clicked his tongue. "I need a few more ingredients if I wish to make a full feast. I presume there is a market nearby?" He began scribbling ingredients on a scratch pad left on an entry table.

"Yeah," Ethan said. "We passed one only a minute or so—"

"If it is this close," Dorian said, "we should not risk using the car more than necessary. Brixton can walk."

Brixton glanced at Ethan and Veronica before scowling at Dorian. "Just me?"

Dorian extended a hand with the list. "You are most familiar with my standards. And we should not draw attention to ourselves. One boy alone is less memorable than the three of you together."

"I need a credit card then."

"Here." Ethan handed him a stack of twenty-dollar bills. "What? I went to the ATM before we left."

Brixton took the money from Ethan and snatched the list from Dorian. "Back in a few."

"Hang on," Ethan said. "I know our phones are off so our parents can't find us if they try tracking us. But we're going after something we don't understand. I don't like Brixton on his own without his phone."

"That's so sweet," Veronica said.

"And true. Whenever we split up, we turn on our phones. If we're together, we can turn them off, but right now Dorian can't go out, right? So we turn on our phones."

"It is true," Dorian murmured. "This is a fair point. Yet if it is true that your parents can track your location through these devices, you must only have your phones on for the shortest amount of time possible."

"Agreed."

Ten minutes later, Veronica jumped as her cell phone rang. "My dad is going to kill me… Oh! It's not him. Hey, Brix. Is everything okay? Yeah." She held out the phone to Dorian. "He wants to talk to you."

Dorian accepted the phone in time to hear Brixton's voice say, "I couldn't find a bunch of the stuff on your list."

"Which *stuff*?" Dorian asked.

Instead of a proper answer, Brixton swore.

"Really," Dorian said, "there is no call for—"

"Max is here."

"*Merde*. We have been reported? He is after you?"

Veronica gasped. "Someone is after Brixton?"

"That's weird." Brixton paused. "Max just smiled and waved at me, but… he looks kinda embarrassed—like I caught *him* doing something, you know? Why would he look like that?"

Dorian attempted to press the screen of the phone, but as usual the imbecilic *modern* screen would not respond to his fingertips. "Veronica, could you turn this device to speaker audio, *s'il vous plaît*?"

She took the phone and put it face-up on the table.

"Is Max walking over to you?" Dorian asked.

"Max is here?" Ethan asked, joining the others at the table.

"Yeah," Brixton answered. "I mean, yeah he's here, but no, he's not coming over to me. He saw that I was on the phone. He's shopping on the other side of the store. This is so weird. Isn't Max out of town at his grandfather's funeral? Is that why he looks guilty—he didn't want to go to China to hang out with his family? But I don't think he's after me. It's not like our parents know we're gone yet--"

"Max was indeed abroad, but has returned," Dorian said. "And he has broken up with Zoe." This was not strictly true, as far as he knew. Yet it was effectively the case. He had learned from Tobias that the rake had not contacted Zoe, and he could tell how much it pained her.

"What?" The anger in Brixton's voice came through clearly.

"That's awful!" Veronica cried. "But that explains why Max came home. He grew up in Astoria. That's why he loved *The Goonies*. Don't you remember—"

"Um, guys?" Brixton interrupted. "What should I do?"

Dorian wove his fingers together behind his back and began to pace.

"You cannot leave without speaking to him without it being suspicious. It is the weekend. You and your mother are here for the weekend, *n'est pas*?"

"Nest *what*?"

Dorian pinched the bridge of his snout. "Your story is that you are in Astoria for the weekend with your impulsive mother. You are on the phone with her now, telling you what to bring back from the market."

"My story?"

"*Oui*. You need a cover story. You cannot leave without speaking with Max. If you do, he will be suspicious."

"I wouldn't run," Brixton hissed. "I need to yell at him for breaking Zoe's heart. I'm muting you now."

"Wait—" Dorian heard the sound of shuffling.

"Yo, Max." The phone was in the boy's pocket.

"I never expected to see you here," the cad Max said to the boy. His voice held a hint of embarrassment. What *was* Zoe's former beau hiding?

"Yeah, my mom wanted to come up for the weekend. Something about good views of the ocean."

"It's a beautiful setting, for sure—"

"Why'd you break up with Zoe? I thought you two were solid."

Max cleared his throat, and Dorian imagined him glaring at the boy. "Did she tell you that?"

"Um, no. You just haven't been around."

"My grandfather passed away."

"I heard. I'm sorry. I thought you were still gone."

Another pause. "I grew up here in Astoria. My mom is still here."

"You didn't really answer my—"

"I'm sure your mom will worry if you don't get back to her soon. Being in a strange city and all. I'll let you get going. Good seeing you, Brix. Say hi to your mom for me."

Another pause on the phone.

"Can you hear anything?" Veronica whispered to Dorian.

"You don't have to whisper," Ethan said loudly. "Brix muted us."

"My young friends," Dorian said slowly, "That was strange, was it not?"

Ethan shrugged on his coat. "Yeah, I'm going over there."

"No!" Veronica tugged him back. "Brix told him he's here with his mom."

"We shouldn't have let him go on his own. Max could have kidnapped him."

Veronica's hand flew to her mouth. "No. Max wouldn't—"

"The man was acting strange," Dorian said. "We must do something."

The three of them jumped as a loud voice boomed from the phone on the table.

"He's gone."

Veronica snatched up the phone. "Brix, can you hear us?"

"You don't have to shout."

Veronica rolled her eyes and held the phone in her outstretched hand.

"Max didn't try to kidnap you?" Ethan asked.

"What? No, but it kinda seemed like someone had kidnapped *him*. Like someone was waiting for him that he didn't want us to know about. You think he's cheating on Zoe?"

"He wouldn't do that," Veronica insisted.

"How do we know what this guy would do?" Ethan asked. "I know you two have known him for a long time, but you can't trust adults."

"Just because your parents are having trouble—"

"Leave them out of it." Ethan glared at Veronica. "I'm the only one allowed to bash them."

Dorian had never seen Ethan look sharply at the girl before.

"We must not get distracted," Dorian said. "We can deal with Max's indiscretion later. We cannot keep up your ruse to your parents beyond this weekend. We do not have much time. Brixton, get whatever groceries you are able to, then return immediately so we can safely turn off your cell phones. We must stay focused if we are to find the treasure."

Veronica's cell phone beeped.

Dorian frowned. "What is this beeping? Has it disconnected?"

"Oh no…" Veronica bit her lip. "It's my dad. They've found us."

CHAPTER 49

Though it wasn't definitively conclusive, I had enough information now to feel I could ask for help. I turned to the one other police contact I had. Someone whose life I'd saved, but who was already skeptical of me. I hoped the former fact would mean she'd at least hear me out.

I called Detective Vega. After our previous experience together, I had her cell phone number, though I hadn't used it.

"Zoe Faust?"

"I'm sorry to bother you, but it's urgent."

She said she wasn't at the station but asked me to meet her at a café near her location. It was only a few minutes away from me.

I was confident she would believe my report that the kids had taken off on what they believed to be a treasure hunt—but would she believe my fear that they were walking into the trap of a con artist who could be dangerous? Would she believe me when I said that Kent Clarkson was someone they should look into for the museum heist, and that he might have been working with Ginessa Cabot?

In spite of the fact that it was after 5 p.m., Detective Vega was holding a mug of black coffee when I arrived. Her chestnut hair was tied back in a utilitarian ponytail, and a damp black jacket rested on the back of her chair. I didn't take time to remove my silver raincoat.

As I slid into the seat opposite hers, I noticed a cup of tea was waiting for me. A lid covered the cup, but the scent of chamomile and lavender escaped with a thin wisp of steam. The fact that Detective Vega was thoughtful enough to order me a cup of tea and had remembered my preference for herbal brews gave me hope that she'd give me the benefit of the doubt with the imperfect information I had.

"Their parents have reported them missing," she said as soon as I began to explain the urgent problem of finding Brixton and his friends. "They're minors, so we can look for them. But honestly, teenagers borrowing a parent's car for a joy ride isn't much of a priority."

"Unfortunately," I said, "there's much more to it than that."

I told her as much as I could: that the kids had found a treasure map that most likely pointed to Astoria, and that it wasn't a harmless game like they thought. That I believed the map was part of a con from someone currently targeting Perenelle. And that the suspicious timing of when Kent Clarkson left Elements Art House suggested he could be involved with the Oregon Gold History Museum heist that turned violent, as well as the threats against Perenelle.

"If you're right about this," she said, "the kids could be in danger."

"Agreed."

"You have a copy of this map? The Oregon coast and Astoria are a start, but still a big area."

I shook my head.

"Their parents already told us they've tried finding them through their phones."

"And?"

"They turned them off."

"Or somebody else did."

Detective Vega made some calls from her car before departing. I was relieved the situation was being taken seriously. But there was only so much she could do. I had to help.

I didn't care if Max didn't want to talk to me. If he could help find the kids, I had to try him. I was getting ready to call Max from the café parking lot when Detective Vega knocked on my window.

"You're right," she said. "Something's going on. Kent Clarkson was reported missing last week."

"Oh no…" I felt no satisfaction that I'd been right.

"We still don't know if it's connected to the kids' treasure map. A little earlier this year, we had a report filed by a man who was swindled out of money by someone with a supposed treasure map. They told him they needed the money to pay for diving equipment."

"There's your connection—"

"The swindler doesn't fit the description of Kent."

"They were caught?"

"Not yet. I can't tell you more. But people are looking into it now. Thank you, Zoe."

I watched her drive off, then called Max. His phone went straight to voicemail, just like Brixton's had.

"I know you don't want to hear from me," I said to his voicemail box, "but Brixton, Veronica, and Ethan are in trouble. They've taken off in Ethan's mom's car—I don't even want to think about whether any of them can drive safely—and turned off their cell phones, so Detective Vega and their parents haven't been able to trace them. They're looking for some sort of pirate treasure—"

A beep cut me off. I squeezed the phone with frustration.

Was I sure enough about where Brixton and his friends were to head there? I didn't have any other choice. I tried Brixton again, but his phone went directly to voicemail. Since Detective Vega had said their phones were off, I didn't expect otherwise, but I had to try.

Just like I had to try to find them in Astoria. The town was small compared to Portland, but over 10,000 people lived there. How did I think I could find them if the police couldn't?

I swung by my house to check on Nicolas and Perenelle before heading to the highway.

"I have faith in you, Zoe Faust," Nicolas said from the doorway. "We both do."

"We always have," Perenelle added. "Now go find your young friends."

A crash of thunder sounded above. The kids were in far more trouble than they knew. I donned my silver raincoat and set out to find them.

CHAPTER 50

Brixton burst through the door of the shack. "I knew turning on our phones was a bad idea." He dropped a small bag of groceries onto the rickety kitchen table. The bag tilted to its side as the table shifted.

"It would have been stupid for you to go out without any way to reach us," Ethan mumbled.

"It is done," Dorian said. "There is no sense in berating each other." None of them had answered their phones, but was it possible they had been tracked in the short time in which their phones were on? It was impossible to determine. They had to act as if they had even less time than they previously thought.

"You never cared about finding the treasure," Brixton said to Ethan.

Veronica stepped between the two boys. "Stop it. Dorian is right. The damage is done. Our story about being at each other's houses didn't work. They know we're gone. We don't know if they know *where* we are yet. We're close. If we can find the treasure tonight, I say we finish this."

"Now that we are all here," Dorian added quickly, before the boys could continue arguing, "I am certain the map and painting will illuminate our understanding. Would one of you be so kind as to remove the painting from the trunk of the car?"

"I'll go." Ethan spun the car key around his index finger.

"I'll help," Veronica added before pulling on her coat and following him out the door.

"It's not like it's heavy," Brixton mumbled.

Dorian peeked through the curtains. Ethan and Veronica stood at the open trunk of the car, conversing instead of removing the painting. Wind whipped around them, but no rain was falling at that moment. He could not hear their words, but Veronica nodded solemnly. A moment later, Ethan lifted the painting from the trunk and the pair returned to the shack.

A burst of wind caused the shack's door to slam against the wall as the pair entered. A storm was coming.

"Are we all in agreement," Dorian said, "that our next step is to search the coastline for a spot that has the same rock formations as this painting?"

Brixton tapped his finger on the seaside canvas, as if it was a screen he expected to move beneath his touch. "We have to look for this while there's still a little sunlight. Looks like there's maybe half an hour of daylight left. We'll never be able to see well enough in the dark."

"Speak for yourself," Dorian said. "I have perfect night vision." It was not strictly true, yet there was usually enough moonlight to make it factual.

"Whenever I think this can't get any weirder..." Ethan shook his head. "Brix is right. None of us will be able to see well enough later on, even with flashlights. I'll do a reconnaissance mission while there's still light and report back."

"I'm coming," Brixton said. "You in, V?"

"I'll stay here with Dorian. Not because of the expectation that I should be the one to help with the cooking, but I don't want to be a toad and ditch Dorian, since he can't go out until later. With each of us with someone, we can keep our phones off. Just in case they haven't tracked our location already."

"Look for the jagged rock that looks like flames rising from a hearth," Dorian said. "This is the most distinctive feature. If it truly exists, it is the spot we seek."

"On it," said Brixton. "Let's go, E."

The door banged shut on their way out.

"*Merci beaucoup,* Veronica," Dorian said as he carried the small bag of groceries to the kitchenette. "Yet if I may be so bold, you did not merely wish to keep me company so I am not lonely or so we are safe. Surely you realize how much time I am used to spending on my own, and that I am accustomed to taking care of myself. What is your real reason?"

"I thought you might be more willing to tell me about your origins if Ethan wasn't around. Especially since this might be the last time I'm out of my house in ages. I'm going to be grounded forever." In spite of her words, she was smiling. "I read more about Notre Dame."

"What, pray tell, did you learn?"

"Are there really alchemical symbols all over the cathedral?" Her dark brown eyes grew wide as she whispered her query.

"That is a question," Dorian replied. "Not an answer."

"I know you said those other gargoyles weren't trapped in stone, but with all the alchemy stuff connected to the cathedral, are you sure there aren't more living gargoyles out there?"

"The gargoyles you see on the Parisian cathedral are simply stone." He answered the girl truthfully. The fact that there was one other living gargoyle connected to the same dangerous alchemy that had given him life was not something he wished to discuss. Yet she was looking at him as if she detected his reticence. "You do not need to worry about them," he added.

"Now you're the one ignoring a question."

"I would not do you such a disservice. I am thinking what I may tell you about myself that does not betray the confidences of others. It is disrespectful to do so."

"The *secrets* of other people, you mean. I *hate* secrets." There was more to her statement, he knew. Something behind the words. Yet he also knew he should not press too hard.

"Sometimes, my young friend, they are necessary. You and Ethan, for example. You are keeping something from Brixton."

"That's not—" She stopped herself. "You're right. I can't tell you what it is without asking Ethan, though. But I'd still love to know more about your history."

"I will tell you more of my story, yet you cannot share it with your beau. He is not fully accepting of my existence."

"You mean *Ethan*? He's not my—" She broke off again. "I won't tell anyone. I promise. How much does Brixton know?"

"He knows as much as he has asked, which is quite a lot. I had no choice but to tell him more about myself before I wished to do so, because otherwise the consequences would have been far worse. In your case, I wish to tell you."

"You mentioned having a father."

"Jean Eugène Robert-Houdin is my father. He is the reason I learned how to cook. Ah! I should begin cooking." Dorian had not thought to bring his stepping stool with him, but luckily the counters of this shack were relatively low.

"Let me help." Veronica unloaded the bag Brixton had returned with.

"*Merde*." Dorian looked on in horror. These ingredients were all wrong! The boy had been flustered by the interruption, no doubt. Picking up a bag of potato chips and a can of mushroom soup, neither of which had been on his list, Dorian realized Brixton must have been at a convenience store, not a larger market.

"Forget about the grocery haul," Veronica said, though she, too, was frowning at the items. "The French magician is who you think of as your father? Not the people who carved you?"

He abandoned the dismal allotment and turned his attention to the studious young woman. "He is the one who raised me, at great sacrifice. Thus, I think of him as my true father. It is actions that create family, more than anything else."

"Like Zoe's stepparents, the Flamels?"

"Quite," Dorian murmured. "My own father could not tell his human family about me. They believed him to be working on his memoirs when he would disappear into his study and say he would not be disturbed. He requested food be brought to him at his door."

"Were you little when you were younger?"

Dorian chuckled and stood tall to his full three-and-a-half feet. "No. I was carved at this size. This form was not large enough for the Cathedral of Notre Dame, which is why Violet-le-Duc presented his friend—my father—with this gift. As a magician, my father loved all things mysterious. His friend knew he would take good care of his carving. Could you hand me the onion that has rolled too far back on the counter? I will make the best of our choices, as I always have."

Veronica handed him the onion. "The way you talk about being carved in stone feels really weird."

"I am simply describing a fact."

"Yeah, but it's like you're talking about someone else."

"It sounds, perhaps, like I am detached?"

"That's it."

"That is because my soul did not yet exist at that time. I was merely form, but it was my father who brought me to life and raised me. It is by his hand that I exist."

"But he wasn't an alchemist."

"No. Nor did he possess magic—such things do not exist. Alchemy transforms elements, but does not create from nothing. It is the intent and energy that is put into something. At least, intent should be present in true alchemy. In my case, it was energy from a backward alchemy book. My father only had the intent to read from the alchemy book as a dramatic gesture on the stage. He was planning to build an automaton that looked like me, to show a stone carving on the stage, have it examined by the audience, then read a few Latin phrases to bring the stone to life—but in reality, it was to be a magic trick using his automaton switched in my place."

"An automaton? That's like an old-time robot, right?"

"A figure that moves through mechanical means, yes."

"But that's not what happened."

"No. He never made his automaton. When he read those words of Latin, he got me instead. A son he needed to hide away."

Veronica smiled, yet it was a sad smile.

"Do not worry for me," Dorian continued. "I have had a full life, in spite of my solitude. It helped that I discovered gastronomy."

Veronica grinned. She watched as he chopped onions and potatoes, peppering him with more questions as she thought of them.

A crash of thunder sounded. Veronica jumped, splashing half her glass of fizzy water onto the linoleum floor. "How long do you think they'll be? It's nearly dark and a big storm is about to break."

Dorian had been trying to focus on cooking with rudimentary ingredients and answering the girl's questions, yet if he were honest with himself, he had failed. There was a ticking clock! It was much more fun to read about such things in the novels he read and the one he was writing. In real life, the stress was grating on him. He could not remember if he had already used a pinch of salt. He could taste, of course, but it was not like him to not remember.

"I do not know, Veronica," he said. "I do not know." Sometimes he thought of Brixton as an adult and sometimes a child. Should he have sent the boy and his friend to the coastline in the fading darkness as such a fierce storm broke?

Another clap of thunder sounded.

CHAPTER 51

My gearshift stuck as I halted in a mud puddle at a stop sign in Astoria.

I hadn't planned on a road trip, so I hadn't inspected the truck. It surprised people that I cared for my truck myself. As did the fact that I didn't upgrade my choice of vehicle.

After two tries, the transmission cooperated, and I was moving again. Not that there was anyone behind me to honk at me. And not that I knew where I was going from here.

The only place I knew in Astoria was Max's mom's house. Max brought me there for his mom's 64th birthday. I hadn't been driving, but I remembered the general directions, plus there was a distinctive inlet of trees I hoped I'd recognize when I spotted it.

Fifteen minutes later, I found the house. What was I doing here?

I knocked on the door, and a few seconds later Mary flung it open. "Zoe!" She enveloped me in a hug. "Come inside. This storm is picking up strength. Did I miss a message from Max that he was bringing you around to dinner? I wasn't planning on cooking, but I can throw something together or we can go out—"

"Is he here?" I wouldn't say that seeing Mary Jasper made everything all right, but hearing her familiar Texas accent and feeling the genuine warmth of her hug helped a lot. "I… I haven't seen him since he got back."

"You haven't?"

I could barely get out the word "no" as I felt my throat constrict.

She shook her head and grabbed a jacket from a coat rack. "That boy."

"You know where he is?"

"He really hasn't told you?"

"Told me what?"

She sighed and locked the door behind her. "I knew he didn't want to tell Mina what he was doing. But you? That 'rational' son of mine is more foolish than he likes to think. I'll drive slow so you can follow in your truck."

"We're going to see him? You could give me directions—"

"GPS doesn't work where we're going."

It began to rain harder as I followed Mary over a dirt road. We drove for about ten minutes, until we reached a small log cabin. Smoke billowed from the chimney.

She rolled down her window and motioned for me to pull forward.

"I'll leave you to it," she said with a wink. "If he doesn't answer right away, give him a few minutes." She backed out of the narrow road and was out of sight a few seconds later.

I tucked my collar up before stepping out into the rain. A gust of wind crept up on me, and I winced as the truck's door slammed harder than I meant it to.

As I approached the structure, the door creaked open. The person inside was already speaking before they could see who was outside. "I wasn't expecting you, Mom. I thought—" Max froze with his hand on the doorknob.

"I know you don't want to see me," I said. "But it's an emergency. It's—"

He'd started walking as soon as I began speaking. As he reached me, he cut me off with his lips. They tasted of fire. He pulled me tighter, with a loving urgency I hadn't ever expected to feel again. I didn't care that cold rain was bearing down on us.

I knew I shouldn't have let myself enjoy the moment, but I couldn't stop myself. I don't know how much time passed before I was able to pull myself away.

"I wasn't expecting you either," he said softly. "Sorry, I appear to have gotten you soaking wet. Come in by the fire—" He tugged my hand, but I stayed put.

"You should be sorry for a lot of things, Max. I wish I could ask you what's going on and why you've been lying to me, but we don't have time for me to be mad at you. First, I need your help finding Brixton, Ethan, and Veronica."

His brows drew together with concern as a wet lock of black hair fell onto his forehead. "What are you talking about? Brixton is here in Astoria for the weekend with his mom—"

"Heather? No, she's not here. You've seen Brixton?"

"Yeah." He wiped the wet hair out of his face, which still bore a confused expression. "Ran into him when I had to get something at the market."

"He's here with his friends. Not his mom. Haven't you checked your messages?" I asked.

"My phone? I haven't been on all day. I've needed to concentrate. I —" He ran back inside. This time I followed. His phone was in his hand by the time I closed the door. He was waiting for it to power on.

The one-room cabin was one of the coziest spaces I'd ever seen. No, that wasn't right. It wasn't cozy because of what I *saw* but what I *smelled*. The aroma of teas of all kinds mingled in the warm air. Dozens of glass jars of fresh and dried tea leaves, along with dried flowers and other herbs to make teas, lined nearly every surface. A cast iron Dutch oven rested in the coals of the warm hearth and his grandmother's teapot hung above it.

"What's going on, Max?"

But he wasn't looking at me. "They've gone after a pirate treasure?" he read from his phone. "There's only one spot where they could be."

CHAPTER 52

Two sopping wet boys burst through the door.

"We found the spot," Brixton said. "And it's dark enough now that we can go back. All of us."

"That dinner Dorian has been cooking smells way too good," Ethan said. "Five minutes. That's all I need to inhale that casserole."

"What did you discover?" Dorian asked as he served up plates of mushroom potato casserole with crispy potato chips on top.

"Not the treasure." Ethan grabbed a towel and wiped the rainwater from his face and hair, then tossed it to Brixton.

"The distinctive rock," Brixton said. "The jagged one that looks like flames rising from the water. We found it just a few miles from here."

Dorian was outvoted. There would be no civilized meal, even after Dorian had created a sumptuous one-pot meal out of the barest ingredients Brixton had brought him. The three teens dug into the crispy casserole while standing around the stove. They were done eating within five minutes, as promised.

Sighing, Dorian donned his hooded cape. In the stormy darkness, the four of them drove down the coast. Ethan proceeded far more slowly than he had before.

"Is the vehicle in need of attention?" Dorian asked.

Ethan pursed his lips but didn't remove his gaze from the road. "I've never driven in a storm like this. It's not easy."

Rain fell sideways against the windows. An especially vicious burst of wind rocked the car. Ethan veered off the road, but quickly righted the vehicle. Dorian was about to suggest another of the teenagers maneuver the large automobile, but Brixton spoke first.

"There." He pointed. "That rock that looks like flames rising from the sea. It has to be the only formation like it. It's in the painting."

From his seat next to Veronica, Dorian watched as the girl searched through a bag. He was unsure if it would be called a purse, but that was irrelevant. Veronica had the foresight to pack each of them a waterproof rain cape. She had a proper flashlight for each of them as well.

"From the camping box in our garage." She tossed bright yellow bundles to each of them.

"Fluorescent ponchos?" Brixton commented. "Aren't we trying to *avoid* attention?"

"It's for safety. But sure. Go ahead and get drenched if you'd like to freeze to death. You'll be soaked to the bone in less than a minute without one." She checked that each flashlight was working, then handed them around.

"I do not require either a rain cape or added light, young Veronica," Dorian said. "But thank you for your consideration." He pulled the hood of his own red cape over his head before venturing outside.

Exiting the car, they had to raise their voices as waves crashed loudly. There was no way to reach the rock off the coast they had identified. Instead, they sought partial shelter next to a large evergreen tree.

"Should we hire a boat to go out to that rock?" Ethan suggested.

Dorian's cape flapped wildly around his wings in the bursts of wind and rain. "Any ship would crash if it approached that rock." Where could the X on the map be meant to reference? Even without a storm, how could that rock in the ocean hide a treasure?

"This is the area of the coast where that rock looks like flames,"

Brixton said. "From further down the coast in either direction, it only looks like a slab."

"But there's nothing here," Veronica shouted into the gusts of wind and rain.

"The night is young," Dorian said. "We did not expect it to be an easy quest."

The children looked at each other.

"Yeah," Ethan said, his voice half drowned out by the storm. "I think I can speak for all of us when I say I think we kinda did. We figured out where the treasure map leads. That's supposed to be the end. Our solution. Right here. But it's not."

"I'm freezing," Veronica said through chattering teeth. "The sideways rain broke through my poncho. Let's go back to the shack. We can't see anything out here anyway."

Ethan swore. "Have you guys seen the car key?"

Brixton groaned. "Seriously? You lost it?"

"There's a small cottage we just passed," Ethan said. "It was dark. Looks like the type of place where the owners only visit in the summer. I bet it's empty."

"You want to *break in*?" Veronica gaped at him.

"You want to freeze out here or walk half an hour through this storm to get back to our rental?"

With weary, wet feet, they approached the dark cottage.

CHAPTER 53

Max's jeep bumped over the rough terrain as he drove us to the spot where he thought we'd find the kids.

"There's a distinctive rock shaped like flames," he said. "That's the spot where the Wizard of the West's ship was supposed to have sunk."

"Has anyone ever found anything?" I asked.

"Of course not. It's not real, Zoe. It's a local urban legend someone made up because there's a rock that looks like flames, but only from a certain angle. It's as good a spot for a pirate legend as any. You don't need to be as worried as you are. Brix and Veronica are going to be in serious trouble from their parents, but I don't think you have to worry about a criminal mastermind going after them."

"Not because of a pirate treasure. Because the person who faked it is the same person involved in stealing the gold nuggets from the Oregon Gold History Museum, the person who put Harrison Cabot in the hospital."

Max slammed on the brakes right before the dirt road gave way to a larger paved one. He put the jeep into park and turned to face me. "I think you'd better tell me more about what's going on."

"I will. Keep driving."

"That urgent?"

"I don't know. But I'd never forgive myself if we could have helped and were too late. How far are we from that rock?"

"Ten minutes. Maybe a little more in this storm." He put the car in gear. "How is this pirate treasure related to the Oregon Gold History Museum robbery?"

"I don't know exactly. But if I'm right, the same person is involved in both. A thief who's also a con artist. They're both blackmailing Perenelle—"

"What?" He didn't stop the car again, but his hands gripped the steering wheel more tightly. "We've been talking every day and you didn't think to—"

"And you didn't think to tell me you'd returned to this country. We're not doing this right now."

"Right. Back to this blackmailer thief." His jaw clenched so tightly I was concerned for his teeth.

"I told you how Perenelle got an artist studio at Elements Art House. Someone affiliated with the art house is the person blackmailing Perenelle for gold. Notes in paint said they have proof she's the museum thief—which she's not."

"Then why worry?"

"She's an artist. She created something that looks identical to the gold that was stolen. They have it on video."

"Let me guess," he said. "The gold is real. Because she's an alchemist."

I gasped. "That's the most explicit thing you've ever said to acknowledge what I've tried to tell you."

"A lot's happened in the last few weeks. I promise I'll tell you everything."

"As soon as we're sure the kids are safe. I know." I grabbed the dashboard as he hit an unexpected pothole. "There was an opening at Elements Art House Perenelle was able to fill because the previous occupant, Kent Clarkson, left unexpectedly—the day after the museum heist. He hasn't been heard from since."

"Please tell me you've already told this to the authorities."

"I met with Detective Vega and told her to look into him. She said people are looking for the kids, too. They'd turned their phones off, so their parents couldn't find them."

"You suspect foul play?"

"I hope they're simply trying to evade their parents while on a grand adventure. They borrowed Ethan's mom Ashleigh's car without asking and told their parents they were at each other's houses. That's how their parents figured out something was up."

"So you think Kent disappeared because his planned simple theft turned violent?"

"Exactly."

"Why does that make him your blackmailer?"

"Perenelle has worked with pigments so long that she's able to notice subtle differences in paints that have been mixed by hand. The person who wrote the blackmail notes disguised their writing by painting the notes in block letters with a paint brush. The same pigments were used in a painting left behind by someone at the art house. Perenelle brought the framed painting back to my house so we could examine it." I paused to collect my thoughts. Max knew I had a French friend named Dorian, but not that he was a gargoyle who lived in my attic.

"The frame broke," I continued vaguely, "and I'm pretty sure that Brixton and his friends found a treasure map behind it. They showed it to me when apologizing for breaking the frame. At the time I didn't realize that's where it came from—"

"But now you think if the blackmailer tried to convince Perenelle into thinking he'd frame her for the museum robbery, anything connected to them could be dangerous?"

"Detective Vega told me about a con artist swindling people with a treasure map, so I think it could be one of Kent's cons. I don't know for sure it's him, or if he's working with someone else. I don't have all the answers yet, but there are too many things coming back to Elements Art House and that painting to be a coincidence."

"We'll figure it out." He pulled off the coastal road and stopped the car. "We go on foot from here."

The rain was coming down hard. Max reached across me and grabbed two flashlights from the glove compartment. He handed one to me and we set out searching for the kids.

CHAPTER 54

Dorian used his claws to unlock the front door of the darkened cottage.

"Wicked," Brixton murmured behind him as Dorian used one of his bigger claws as a tension wrench and another as the pick to lift the lock's pins into their proper positions.

"I don't like this." Veronica's black hair whipped around her face as she looked from side to side.

"Relax." Ethan squeezed her hand. "This one is isolated from other houses. Besides, Dorian is breaking in without a set of lock picks, so even if the police come, it's not like there's any evidence we're breaking in."

Veronica groaned.

"*Bon*." The last pin of the lock clicked into place. Dorian turned the knob. The door swung inward. He took a hesitant step forward, listening to make sure the hut was truly empty.

"We're in?" Veronica gave a last glance behind them before following.

"*Zut*!" Dorian cried as he tripped over something blocking his path. A string? What an odd place for such a thing. He spread out his wings to steady himself.

The four of them dried off as best they could, but there was no electricity—and no heat. Ethan and Veronica huddled together for warmth, and Brixton stormed off to a corner and wrapped himself in a knitted blanket. They did not dare turn on their cell phones once more, even for light. Rummaging in the drawers of the kitchenette, Dorian found two candles and a box of matches.

The candles shrank as the storm stretched on. Dorian was glad he had insisted on cooking dinner before they left.

Peeking out the window, he was struck by a jarring sight. The view of the rock shaped like flames looked very much like it did in the painting, almost as if it was painted from this very room. There was only a narrow angle of the coast in which the rock took on this appearance, and from the cottage, the resemblance was even more striking. He gasped.

"What's up?" Brixton rushed to the window.

"Look at the rock and tell me what you see."

"Um, I see a whole lot of nothing. It's pitch black out there. How can you see anything at all?"

"*Zut*." The children's eyes were not equipped to see in the dark as his were. Yet fate, it appeared, was on their side that night. As he and Brixton looked out the window, a crash of thunder and lightning lit up the sky.

"No way," Brixton said. "That shape. It's the exact same shape as in the painting."

"You see it. It is not my imagination, no?"

Veronica stepped between them. "What are you two looking at?"

"You must wait for another strike of lightning, I fear," said Dorian.

"This cottage," said Brixton, "is where the artist sat when they painted that landscape painting with the rock. The strange shape of the rock looks the same from here."

"I can't see any rock," said Veronica. "But look. Someone is out there. I can see their flashlight."

In the distance, a beam of light appeared. Who would be foolish enough to go for a stroll tonight?

"They are coming this way," Dorian said.

"How did the police find us?" Ethan asked. "Wasn't that the whole point of turning off our phones?"

"This does not appear to be the police," Dorian said. "Quickly, extinguish the candles."

"Are you sure they're coming this way?"

"Quickly!"

Veronica pinched out both candles.

Less than a minute later, a key turned in the door. A figure stood in the doorway.

"I know you're in here," a woman's voice said. "You activated my security system two hours ago, but I saw your light a minute ago. I won't press charges. I just need to make sure you're not going to take anything that isn't yours."

Though the voice was that of a woman, she was covered in a thin ski suit, including high gloves on her hands and a ski mask covering her head over a nylon stocking that obscured her eyes. This was a person who did not wish to be observed.

Dorian gasped as he saw a glimmer of light on the object in her right hand.

The disguised woman held a gun.

The children were defenseless. In the instant that followed seeing the metallic gleam of the deadly weapon, Dorian knew what he must do. And he must do it before the intruder illuminated the room with the flashlight in her other hand that she was surely about to switch on to blind them. Here in the dark, he was the one with the advantage.

Without giving himself time to think, or to consider that this might be his last moment on earth, Dorian acted on instinct. He leapt forward and crashed into the figure.

A deafening sound rang out.

"Dorian!" Ethan cried. He'd finally called the gargoyle by his true name, instead of the name of a childish talking canine, now that he saw Dorian was dying.

Dorian blinked, but all he saw was a burst of white stars. He had heard the expression before, but never experienced it. It was not stars, exactly... No, it was more like fireworks. Bright white fireworks bursting through his head.

Then everything went dark.

CHAPTER 55

Max swore. "That was a gunshot."

We ran toward the sound. I was soaked to the bone and shivering, but my shaking legs kept up with Max's pace.

We were alone on the coast. This wasn't a resort or beach town, and we were a distance from central Astoria. Houses and other structures were nestled between trees, even along the water. Where had the sound come from?

"We didn't imagine it, did we?" I asked.

Max stopped running. "It wasn't a backfire. It was a gunshot." He swung his flashlight around. His chest heaved as he looked around for a few more seconds, before calling in the suspected gunshot. Someone else had already reported it.

The rain crashed down harder around us, which didn't matter much since we were already soaked through.

Max gave me a concerned look and stroked my cheek. I pushed his hand away.

"It's hardly the time—"

"You're bleeding. Pretty badly. A branch must've got you."

I touched my cheek. When I looked at my fingers, they were coated in blood.

"Let's get back to the car and get you cleaned up."

"You're giving up?"

"I'm regrouping. Running on empty when freezing cold and bleeding, without knowing what we're looking for and where? That's when you're going to fail."

He was right. I followed him back to the jeep. He pulled a bag of dry clothes and a large first aid kit from the back. Five minutes later I was dressed in gray sweatpants and a black sweatshirt, and my cheek was stinging but clean and covered with a bandage.

Max leaned back from his handwork on the gash on my face and held my gaze. "I know it's real, Zoe."

"You're not talking about the Wizard of the West's pirate treasure."

"No."

"Alchemy?"

He nodded. "My grandfather left me a small trunk of items my grandmother wanted me to have. The things I'd convinced myself were the overactive imagination of a kid… I know now. I know it's real."

"You were practicing alchemy in that log cabin." I thought back on all of the glass jars of tea leaves. Of course. Alchemy is so personal. That was his personal alchemy. Just like plants were for me, cooking was for Dorian, and pigments were to Perenelle.

"I don't know if I'd call it alchemy—not yet—but he left me a box of my grandmother's apothecary wares. And he left me a beautiful letter that reminded me of how he'd helped my grandmother with her tea plants in our backyard. I'd forgotten I was the one who planted them. Under her direction, but it was my energy as a toddler that went into it."

"The tea plants are still there." I'd noticed them when I saw his mom.

"I'm the person who made them grow into what they are today. The microclimate here works for tea plants if they're planted with enough shelter and shade. Our soil wasn't acidic enough, so we had to add elemental sulfur."

"Sulfur. One of the elements of alchemy's *tria prima*."

"I'd forgotten all about that until I began reading more about alchemy. After what you told me."

"You've got an alchemical furnace going in that cabin as well."

"I'm using the same teas that my grandmother used when she was an apothecary. She used a lot more than just tea, but that's what I was most drawn to. Even as a small child, that's what I helped her with. Harvesting and drying the ingredients for teas. Technically tisanes. Tea only refers to *camellia sinensis*, the tea plant itself. As soon as Mina and I landed, I drove straight to my mom's house to see our tea plants. I walked through the shaded rows of the tea plants before I went inside to see my mom. She saw me there. She brought me a cup of tea. Not made from those plants—she's a store-bought kind of woman. I hadn't done that in so many years, but I knew… I knew it was something personal that I had to do on my own."

"In your own space. I understand. That's why you came out here. You took your teapot with you."

"You noticed it with everything else in there?"

I reddened. I'd forgotten it was when Dorian broke into his house that we saw his teapot was missing.

"I knew," Max continued, "that if I saw you after I got back from the funeral, I wouldn't have the resolve to see this through. That I'd ask you for guidance, but that instead of guidance we'd end up distracting each other with other things… There's such a fire between us. I needed to keep that fire for my transformations. At least until I got a bit further."

"You even quit your job."

"Granddad's inheritance isn't much, but it's enough for me to figure out what I want to do next. As soon as I read Granddad's letter, I knew I was no longer the person I used to be. The job wasn't what it used to be either. I know I did some good, which is what I always wanted, but now… this is what I feel is right."

"You could have told me."

"I know. I liked being able to talk to you each day without it hanging over me, though. I'm sorry. I love—"

A scream pierced the air.

CHAPTER 56

"Dorian?"

Someone was shaking his arm.

Dorian opened one eye. Cautiously. Since discovering true alchemy, he had never had the opportunity to bleed. He was unsure how his body would react, thus he was quite hesitant to find where the bullet had punctured his body. He was not sure if his blood would be red, gray, or perhaps black. The only fact he was certain of was that true alchemists could die violently, just as anyone else could.

He opened his other eye. He was in the same room in which he'd been in before. His head ached terribly, especially the top of his skull near his left horn. The three children stood over him, smiling. Smiling?

"You have staunched my bleeding," he croaked. "Miraculous!"

Brixton shook his head. "You weren't shot. She missed. You got a bump on your head when you dove forward to protect us. You'll be fine. But Lucy's painting will never be the same."

"Lucy?" Dorian sat up.

"*Mhmphf!*"

His gaze fell to the person making the strange, muffled screams. A woman with duct tape across her mouth, wrists, and ankles. A bandana was tied over her eyes.

"*Mhmphfffff!*"

"She's one of the women at the art studio my and Ethan's moms go to. I could never remember her name, and she doesn't have ID on her, but then she kicked me."

"So hard that he screamed for like a full minute," Ethan added.

Brixton shrugged. "I'm going to have the biggest bump ever on my shin. I thought she was devilish, which reminded me what her name was."

"Lucy," Dorian muttered, still getting his bearings. "Ah. For Lucifer. You have called the police?"

"Our phones are soaking wet," Veronica said. "We have them in a bowl of rice to try to dry them out, but we can't call out yet."

"One of us will go for help in a minute," Ethan said. "As soon as the storm lets up a little."

Lightning lit up the sky and an ear-shattering crash of thunder sounded less than a second later.

"Um, maybe we better tie her up better," Brixton said. "Looks like we could be here a little while."

The boy was mistaken, for another surprise was only moments away. The beams of two flashlights shone through the window. Seconds later, Zoe and Max burst through the door.

CHAPTER 57

"Astoria PD will be here soon," Max said as he hung up his phone. He made sure Lucy was tied securely. Veronica's knots were skillfully done, but Max added an extra binding with zip ties from his car.

I could hardly believe it. I'd been so sure Kent Clarkson was the person we were after. Everything fit. Well, *nearly* everything.

I pulled off Lucy's gag. "How did you not get my paint bomb all over you?" I don't know why that was the first thing I said, but it's what came out.

"This is kidnapping," she spat out. "I own this house. These kids broke into my property, and you're holding *me* hostage?"

"You fired a gun at them." Max had taken the bullets out of the gun.

"I was protecting myself from intruders. I didn't know they were kids. I would have felt terrible if I'd hurt anyone. I thank God I missed. But why did they throw a statue at me?"

Dorian stood watching us from the corner, in stone form.

"I think she broke my leg," Brixton said, rubbing his swollen shin.

Lucy burst out into tears. "I'm so sorry. So, so sorry. I was frightened. I couldn't see that you were kids."

Veronica stepped in front of Lucy with her hands on her hips.

"Gag her again. It's an act. She started crying when we first tied her up. When we thought she'd shot Do—"

"Me," Ethan cut in. "They thought she'd shot me. It was a frightening couple of minutes."

The three of them exchanged a look and I knew they were covering for Dorian.

"She stopped crying when she saw it wasn't working on us," Veronica said. "Just like a light switch. I didn't think anyone was that good an actor."

"My fiancé Gerald is in the hospital," Lucy said through hiccupping sobs. "It's been a trying time. My emotions are all over the place."

"How did you find her hideout?" I asked Brixton, trying not to let my guard down.

"This isn't a hideout," Lucy said. "I own this little home. I know it doesn't look like much, but it's all I have." She sniffled.

"This cottage has a view of that rock from the angle where it looks exactly like the flames," Brixton said. "We didn't know this place had the same view at first, but we were right in front of it when we saw the rock looking like it does in the painting and treasure map."

"You used the local urban legend about the Wizard of the West for a con," said Max.

Lucy looked sharply at Max. All pretense of being a grieving fiancé was gone. The shift only lasted a second, but I saw it. So did Max.

"She's smart," I said. "I bet she's the con artist Detective Vega mentioned who swindled a man out of money, saying it would go toward finding a pirate treasure. It sounds like he was only one of many."

Lucy's face tightened. She didn't speak, but I knew now that I was right. "Did you convince older wealthy men—the type of guys who fancy themselves explorers because they've visited a non-Western country or two on a cruise—that you had come across evidence of a long-lost pirate treasure? A real map that everybody else thought was fictional, which was another way to play to their egos. Making them feel superior. You created just enough tantalizing details, like a real doubloon, to whet their appetites, but then you could tell them you needed funding to find the full treasure. They gave you money, then you disappeared."

"Hold on," Brixton said. "The treasure map isn't real?"

"I knew it," Ethan muttered.

Veronica groaned. "My parents are going to kill me, and it wasn't even a real treasure hunt."

Lucy remained silent.

I couldn't read her expression, so I continued. "Men who lost money wouldn't be likely to report you, out of embarrassment. Were you sure to never ask for more than you knew they could comfortably lose? You could save the doubloon and treasure map to reuse on future marks. The 'research notes' were a nice touch. You tucked everything away behind a painting. Were you lying low trying to make money with blackmail because one of the men you swindled *did* report you? You shouldn't have tried to extort my friend. That was your biggest mistake."

"I don't know what you're talking about," she said calmly.

Max stepped closer to me. "I need to make one more call," he whispered. "I'll be in the back room if you need me."

I nodded but kept my eyes on Lucy. She looked so different from the timid woman I'd met earlier that week. A woman who purposefully made herself appear mousy so she wouldn't be memorable, and so she could be close to people and spy on them. That's why she'd been in the way for Perenelle to bump into on more than one occasion.

"What did you mean about a paint bomb?" Veronica asked.

"She was threatening Perenelle," I explained. "She said if we didn't give her money, she'd harm us."

Veronica gasped. "That's terrible. Even worse than blackmail to expose a secret."

"I made a DIY version of those dye packs banks use inside stacks of bank notes to catch robbers. I knew I'd see it on the skin of whoever set it off..." I stared at Lucy. She was dressed in all black. Not just black, but a sweater with long sleeves and a turtleneck that reached her chin. Next to her on the floor were both a single nylon stocking and a ski cap. I stepped behind the chair she was tied to.

"What are you doing?" She twisted but was unable to move. "Get away from me."

"Gloves. You're wearing gloves. You were covered head to toe in fabric when you picked up the fool's gold." She'd been wearing an outfit that covered her whole body, including nylon covering her face beneath a ski mask. She never got any of the paint on her skin. "Just like you were tonight when you came in and tried to hurt my friends. I don't think it's as easy to claim self-defense when you arrive dressed in a disguise."

Anger flashed in her eyes.

"Is that what you were wearing when you robbed the museum and nearly killed Harrison Cabot?" I asked.

"That wasn't me!" she shrieked. "He betrayed—" She stopped herself.

Max stepped back into the main room. "Don't stop on account of me. Actually, it's fine if you want to. Because regardless of what you say, you're about to be found out." He turned to me. "She's currently living in Portland in the penthouse suite of a man who lives half the year in Europe. I don't know how she convinced him, but she's good. Maybe he's even one of the people she blackmailed into it. He gave Portland PD permission to search his penthouse."

Lucy groaned. She was still swearing and kicking when the Astoria officers took her away a few minutes later.

CHAPTER 58

The police in Astoria were happy to let Portland PD take custody of Lucy. The epicenter of her crimes was Portland. I went to the station to answer questions, and the kids' parents picked them up, leaving Ethan's mom's car in Astoria for the moment. Max had been in the middle of an important transformation, so once he was sure everyone was safe, he went back to the cabin he was renting in Astoria, promising he'd be back in Portland by dawn.

The storm broke just as I was crawling into bed at 4 a.m. I got couple of hours sleep before waking up at dawn on Sunday morning.

Max had driven back to Portland as well. He arrived ten minutes after I called him, eager to apologize for his missteps in how he handled keeping his alchemy from me and to fill in the rest of the blanks. Because he was no longer on the force, he wasn't kept informed about the evidence unfolding against Lucy. Since I was involved and had answered so many questions that night before going home, I'd also learned more about Lucy's story. Max and I were now seated on my back porch, sipping tea made from the tea leaves he'd brought over. It might have been the most exquisite tea I'd ever tasted.

"It's okay if you'd rather appreciate the sunrise and fill me in later about the rest of last night's events," Max said.

"Really?"

His lips ticked up into a smile as a gust of wind blew a lock of black hair onto his forehead, above tired yet contented eyes. "Maybe not."

I wrapped my wool sweater more tightly around me before picking up my mug of Max's jasmine green tea. "Harrison Cabot II was someone she had explored as a previous mark. *That's* the connection between the crimes. But she didn't initially try her con with him. Once she dug into his life, she learned that he'd already squandered his inherited wealth. He still put on a good show of being wealthy, which is why she looked into him in the first place. So she wrote him off—until she saw that his son had discovered a real historical hoard of gold from Oregon's Gold Rush.

"Then she approached Harrison with what she believed to be an offer he would not refuse. She proposed that she would help him steal the loot from his own museum, since it was insured. By working with her, he could be assured he wouldn't be implicated. She knew he was in dire financial need and could only bounce around loans from one place to another for so long before his financial charade fell apart. If he refused, she would tell his wife he'd done some shady things and lost their wealth. He agreed—but then fate intervened. Three days before she was due to stage a museum robbery, *another thief couldn't pass up the temptation*. She didn't know how they did it."

"How *did* they do it?" Max asked. "Who is the thief who was able to rob the Oregon Gold History Museum?"

"Harrison Cabot II himself."

"He's in a coma," Max pointed out. "I think you mean he hired someone to steal his gold, but that doesn't make sense, because we all saw that video of the thief trying to kill him."

"I don't think that level of violence was part of his plan. I think Kent Clarkson got scared."

Perenelle gasped as she stepped through the back door and joined us on the porch. "Kent? The man whose art studio I moved into? He was involved after all?"

"Kent was picked up last night," I said, "soon after Detective Vega's alert. I was right that the timing of his disappearance and his description fit. He's the one who's talking. I believe him that he didn't mean to harm Harrison. But things got out of control. Harrison planned to double-cross Lucy. He's not a man who likes being manipulated. He looked into Lucy after she tried to extort him, and he found out he wasn't the only person she'd been spying on. Kent Clarkson was another of the people she had dirt on, though just for something minor he would have been embarrassed about."

"Harrison and Kent were working together." Perenelle pursed her lips and sat down on a chair next to us on the back porch.

"That's why it was so difficult to figure out what was going on," I said. "There were *multiple* thieves, each betraying each other. Harrison went to Kent with an offer. A white-collar crime, very low risk. All Kent had to do was sneak up to the museum in the middle of the night, take the pouch of two gold nuggets Harrison had left for him, and smash the window. No violence. No entering the museum at all. Harrison had already removed the gold earlier that night. For Kent's part of the charade, he needed to be covered up to avoid being recognized by any external security cameras."

"He was a small man," Perenelle said. "That's why Lucy thought it could have been me in that security video. It was a good plan to have someone who could have been any gender."

"It was. But when the alarm from the smashed window woke up Gin Cabot, she told her husband she was going after the thief. She couldn't bear to have a thief steal their son Harry's discovery. Harrison couldn't have his wife actually catch the thief he'd hired, so he had to say he'd chase the thief in her place. He must have thought Kent would see it was him and play along. But desperate people do desperate things. Kent, quite reasonably, assumed Harrison was double-crossing him, so he lashed out to get away. I expect he didn't mean to hit Harrison quite so hard, but he did what he had to do to get away. Harrison's son, Harry, suspected something was going on, but since his dad was in a coma, he didn't come forward. Harrison is showing signs of waking up from his coma, so we'll know even more soon."

"If Lucy hadn't threatened you and Nicolas, and then pointed a gun at your young friends, I would be sympathetic," Perenelle said.

"Her fiancé is recovering from a terrible stroke that left him unable to speak."

"Actually," I said, "he's not."

"Oh no... He died?"

"He's not her fiancé."

Both Max and Perenelle gasped.

"The supposed fiancé she's been visiting," I said, "is just a single man in the same wing of the hospital as Harrison Cabot. He'd suffered a stroke so bad he can't speak and tell anyone she's not really his fiancé. Lucy wanted to get close to Gin Cabot to learn more about the robbery that had left her double-crossed, so she wanted to ingratiate herself to Gin at the hospital."

"The rat," Perenelle huffed.

"A very adaptable rat. She looked for opportunities everywhere. Like the hidden camera she used to see Perenelle with a piece of gold. Gold that was supposed to be hers. We misunderstood when she sent Perenelle a first blackmail note. We should have realized that people see what they already believe. Even though Lucy *saw* Perenelle making gold, she assumed the gold was simply in the studio where Perenelle was turning pigments into paint for her artwork."

Max squeezed my hand. "It's a natural reaction. One I'm guilty of. It took me so long to believe you. I'm sorry."

"Lucy never suspected I was an alchemist." Perenelle stood and walked into the garden, giving Max and me a modicum of privacy as Max brought my hand to his lips. She stooped and stroked the leaves of the flowering yarrow that would soon make a vibrant yellow pigment.

"She was far too rational for that," I agreed. "But she did believe that an eccentric woman, new in town with no previous records of her existence, was a con artist and thief herself. Lucy thought she could blackmail Perenelle into giving her half the gold from the spoils of her heist, because it was the path of least resistance. When Perenelle didn't cooperate, she snuck into our house via her ruse of being an assistant to the window repairman—for the window she herself had broken. She didn't find the whole stash of gold from the museum, because of course it wasn't there."

"I'm so sorry I wasn't here for you for all of this," said Max.

"You can apologize properly later."

"I think you turned Perenelle's ears red." He kissed my cheek.

"My head is spinning from lack of sleep," I said. "What else haven't I explained?"

"I know the map and painting led you to Astoria," Max said, "and that Lucy had heard of the Wizard of the West pirate legend—which the kid in me is still disappointed to learn isn't real—but why on earth did she keep all of the evidence that proved she had conned so many people through elaborate schemes?"

"Ego," Perenelle said, twirling a yellow bud between her fingers. "Her ego did her in in the end. She didn't want to get rid of her previous successful exploits. I'm certain that's why she kept things at that spot where she'd set up one of her most successful confidence games. She'd gotten away with things for so long that she never truly believed anyone would catch her."

"She did have the trip-wire set up," I pointed out, "which Do—" I coughed. "Which Brixton tripped over. After her security alert went off she drove the two hours to Astoria. She swears she never planned on using the gun."

"That's one last thing I don't get," Max said. "When you and I arrived, she said the kids hit her with that gargoyle statue of yours. Why would they have brought it in the first place?"

"Don't you know?" Perenelle asked with a twinkle in her eye. "That gargoyle is a good luck charm."

CHAPTER 59

Dorian may have been a good luck charm, but even he couldn't change the horrific fact that stared up at me the following week.

"The museum sold the painting." The words barely escaped my lips. My throat was so constricted I could barely sleep. "Perenelle's painting of me with my brother."

We'd been celebrating a successful resolution to the blackmail ordeal and Dorian and Perenelle finally getting along, and Perenelle insisted I use her solitary gold nugget to finance a trip to France to visit the small museum with the painting of my brother.

Before I booked my ticket, I looked up the museum, making sure it was open all seasons of the year, only to find a notice that the painting would no longer be on display, having been sold to a private buyer.

"Blackberry tart?" Dorian asked hesitantly. "I have always found a good tart to enhance one's mood." He gingerly shut the screen of my laptop and said quietly, "I had wished to find the Wizard of the West's treasure so I could buy the painting for you myself. I am sorry I failed you."

"It's not your fault, Dorian. You haven't failed me. You're the one who made me feel truly at home in my new home."

"I am?" Dorian flapped his wings, avoiding clipping the edge of one of his newly restored typewriters. "Yes, of course I am. I am experimenting with yet another set of new recipes this week. I shall cook you a feast tonight so you will forget all about—"

A rapping at the attic door sounded behind us. Nicolas and Perenelle stood in the doorway, the former carrying a tray of four small mason jars filled with beer. "I have perfected this wondrous alchemical brew," he declared. "I brought samples for all."

Nicolas was looking the heartiest I'd seen him. He passed around the small jars of dark beer. "*Salut*."

I raised my glass, but my heart wasn't in it.

"Whatever is the matter, my dear Zoe?" Nicolas asked.

"Perenelle's painting of me and my brother has been sold."

Perenelle gasped, but the words that followed weren't what I was expecting. She looked sharply at her husband. "You didn't tell her?"

"I thought you were going to."

I set down my glass, not trusting the steadiness of my hand. "Tell me what?"

"The portrait of you and your brother is on its way, via courier, from France."

"But how—?"

"You did not think I was so exhausted from our excursion to downtown Portland last week," Nicolas said, "did you?"

"What really exhausted him," Perenelle explained, "was that he's been making gold. He was afraid he'd forget his previous knowledge if he didn't dive in right away, and also afraid of failure if he told us what he was attempting. He didn't even tell *me* what he was doing."

"You made enough gold to buy the painting of Thomas?" I heard myself speak the words, but it sounded to my ears as if someone else had spoken. I couldn't dare hope.

"Far more than that." Nicolas grinned. "You've been terribly generous letting us stay with you, and I'm so proud to see the woman you've grown into. But we all need our own space." He eyed the crowded attic. "You already have a roommate and run a business out of this home. I found a house a few streets away that we plan to purchase and move into."

"It has two fireplaces," Perenelle added. "One for each of us, so we'll have our own alchemy labs."

"And it's all thanks to Dorian," Nicolas said, grinning at the gargoyle.

Dorian blinked back at him. "I am not generally one to shy away from accepting deserved accolades, but I must confess you have me at a disadvantage. I have had no hand in arranging for your new home. *Alors*, I am not certain what assistance you are referring to."

Nicolas chuckled. "It was your cooking that nourished both my body and spirit, bringing me back to my former self, the Nicolas Flamel who is able to transform enough gold to buy a painting and a house."

"And who is eager to have some privacy with his wife," Perenelle added. "I can hardly wait to show you the new house we plan to make a home. The backyard isn't much yet, but Brixton has already offered to help me plant my own pigment garden."

"You've seen Brixton?" Brixton, Ethan, and Veronica had all been grounded because of lying to their parents and borrowing Ethan's mom's car.

"Heather let him come over to weed your garden, since it's the day he was scheduled to do so. He was just arriving when I went into the kitchen to find this silver tray."

"I wanted to invite him inside to join us for a beer," Nicolas said, "but Perenelle reminded me that it was inappropriate in this day and age."

Perenelle kissed his cheek before turning to me. "I told Brixton you'd be down after we sampled Nicolas's beer."

My hands no longer shaking, I picked up the small mason jar and sipped. It really was a delicious alchemical brew.

I found Brixton next to my backyard potting table, searching for gloves. "I don't know why you won't let me pull out those prickly nettles."

"They're worth the effort."

"That was such a *mom* answer. You mean it to apply to life, not just that plant that stung the back of my hand."

"You got stung?" I ran inside and brought him a salve that would help soothe it.

I observed him as he applied the salve. "You look surprisingly happy for someone who's going to be grounded for the rest of the semester and who was just attacked by my stinging nettle."

"Veronica and Ethan aren't a couple."

"You thought they were?"

He scratched the back of his neck. "They'd grown so close this year. They were leaving me out of stuff. A lot. They were keeping secrets from me… But after everything that happened, nearly getting shot and everything, Ethan decided to tell me. To come out to me. He'd told V already. I still feel kinda bad that he couldn't trust me with it. Who cares if he's gay? Why does that even matter? I'm glad he finally told me."

"Is it okay for me to know?"

"Oh. Yeah. He's done with secrets. Ethan is the only one of the three of us who isn't grounded. His parents felt like they drove him to steal their car because they've been so awful to each other from the divorce. So now they're being overly nice to him. He's been spending all his free time after school with Harry Cabot. Harry invited me and V over too. We'll go as soon as we're not grounded anymore. Harry's dad is still in the hospital, but if he wakes up he'll be in trouble for insurance fraud for stealing the gold Harry found."

"I heard they haven't yet found the gold nuggets," I said.

"They've got his accomplice's portion back, but you're right, they haven't found his dad's share yet. Once they find it, Harry's mom is going to sell part of the gold to larger museums to pay off her husband's debts she didn't know about, but hopefully there will still be a small exhibit at their family museum to show Harry's discovery."

"I wish the Wizard of the West's treasure had been real," I said, "so his mom wouldn't have to sell part of the gold Harry found."

"Um, yeah, about that…"

"About *what*?"

Brixton grinned. "Harry has a theory. He's wicked good at

research, and when Ethan showed him the photo of that awful woman's painting of the rock that looks like flames, he noticed a reflection in the water."

"I remember that."

"There's really a sunken ship there."

I stared at Brixton. Had he and Dorian found a treasure after all?

"We don't know what's down there," Brixton said, "and I learned there are tons of sunken ships and boats near coastlines that have lots of rocks. But who knows... you know? Maybe there's a pirate treasure there after all."

CHAPTER 60

After leaving Brixton to finish weeding the garden, I took the familiar walk to Blue Sky Teas. Only this time, I wasn't stopping at Blue's. I was heading for the storefront next to it. The one that would be opening to the public sometime later this fall.

Max wasn't yet a full alchemist, but he'd succeeded in his alchemical transformations to create the most splendid tea. Blue had never been interested in selling tea leaves or tea bags out of her own teashop, but with an empty storefront opening next to hers, Max would be opening his own store, a narrow little shop where people could purchase Max's tea blends or mix their own to create the perfect mix for themselves or as a gift. Customers would also be able to order cups of select teas from Max's shop at Blue Sky Teas. It was perfect that the shop and café would be next to each other.

I knocked on the locked glass door and caught Max's eye. He unlocked the door for me and gave me a kiss.

"The store-opening gift Dorian promised you," I said, handing him the heavy satchel in my hand.

Max still didn't know Dorian was a gargoyle, but he knew Dorian was the French chef who baked pastries for Blue Sky Teas.

"It's perfect," he said, lifting up the red Valentine typewriter in the front window. "I'll write my tea labels with this, and I'll leave the typewriter in the window in a display with my grandmother's poetry she wrote about tea. I'd love to thank Dorian properly. Should I invite him over to dinner at my place? We could make a dinner party of it, with Mina and Tobias, and Perenelle and Nicolas."

"You can invite him," I said. "My guess is that he'll decline—unless you entice him by offering to let him cook."

"We should probably invite a few more people, so it's not just alchemists and people who know about them. Does Dorian know?"

"You could say that."

"Zoe Faust, you never cease surprising me." He pulled me close, and I was sure he was about to kiss me, but he stopped abruptly before his lips reached mine. "Is that your real name?"

Zoe Faust has been my name for longer than Max had been alive, but somehow I didn't think that was the best answer. I didn't want to ruin the moment. Though I knew, now, that there would be many, many more of them.

"I take back the question," Max said. "Because I know your true name. To me, you're the alchemist of fire and good fortune."

I thought the same about him. He kissed me, and my world did burn as bright as alchemical fire and I felt like the most fortunate woman in the world.

THE END

Never miss a new release in the Accidental Alchemist series: Sign up for Gigi's email newsletter at www.gigipandian.com.

Don't miss Gigi's next novel, *Under Lock & Skeleton Key,* the first Secret Staircase Mystery, now available for pre-order. Learn more about it after the recipes!

RECIPES

CHOCOLATE HAZELNUT SPREAD (VEGAN)

Total cooking time: 30 minutes. Active cooking time: 10 minutes. Makes approx. 3 cups.

Ingredients:

- 2 cups hazelnuts
- 3/4 cup Medjool dates (or substitute another type of date)
- 3/4 cup almond milk (or other nut milk of choice)
- 3 Tbsp cacao powder
- 1 Tbsp maple syrup
- Dash (approx. 1/8 tsp) salt

Directions:

Preheat oven to 350° F and soak the dates in 1/4 cup boiling water. Spread the hazelnuts on a baking sheet and cook for 10 minutes. Once cooled for a few minutes, scoop them onto a clean kitchen towel to brush off any loose skins. (If you're using a high-speed blender, you can skip this step.)

Place all ingredients, including the boiling water used to soak the dates, into a blender and blend until smooth. If you're using a high-speed blender, you can use the dip setting and it will take under 1 minute. If using another type of blender or a food processor, it will take a few minutes and you'll probably need to scrape down the sides.

Keeps in a jar in a fridge for about a week, though it never lasts that long at my house!

WHITE BEAN DIP (VEGAN)

Want a spread that's savory instead of sweet?

Total cooking time: 10 minutes.
Makes approx. 2 cups.

Ingredients:

- 1 15oz. can of white beans, such as cannellini beans or butter beans, rinsed and drained
- 1/4 cup sundried tomatoes
- 1/4 cup tahini
- 2 Tbsp freshly squeezed lemon juice
- 1 Tbsp nutritional yeast
- 1 tsp smoked paprika
- 1/4 tsp cumin
- 1/4 tsp salt
- Dash (approx. 1/8 tsp) pepper

Directions:

Soak the sundried tomatoes in 1/4 cup boiling water while assembling the other ingredients. Combine all ingredients in a blender or food processor. Blend until smooth, stopping to scrape the sides as needed.

KALE AND BASIL PESTO (VEGAN)

Total cooking time: 15 minutes.

Volume varies, depending on density of your greens, but this always packs a flavorful punch.

Ingredients:

- 2 cups kale, stems removed and ripped up
- 2 cups basil leaves, thick stems removed
- 2 garlic cloves (or more if you love garlic)
- 2 Tbsp freshly squeezed lemon juice
- 1/2 cup walnuts (or 1/3 cup pine nuts if you prefer the standard pesto nut)
- 1 tsp salt
- Between 1/3 and 1/2 cup olive oil

Directions:

Add all the ingredients except for the olive oil into a blender or food processor. Blend until the ingredients begin to come together, then drizzle in the oil through the top opening. Start with 1/3 cup of oil. Depending on how thick your kale is, it may take a few minutes to become smooth and creamy, and you might need up to 1/2 cup of olive oil to reach your desired consistency. Once blended, taste to see if more salt is needed.

Store in the fridge for up to a week, or pour into an ice cube tray and store for up to six months in the freezer.

Looking for alternatives to pasta for your pesto? Dorian served this dish with farro and chickpeas. Farro and spelt are hearty grains that works well with this rich pesto.

Note: It's worth it to use high quality extra virgin olive oil here.

An impossible crime. A family legacy. The intrigue of hidden rooms and secret staircases.

Multiple award-winning author Gigi Pandian introduces her newest heroine in this heartfelt series debut. *Under Lock & Skeleton Key* layers stunning architecture with mouthwatering food in an ode to classic locked-room mysteries that will leave readers enchanted.

Advance Praise for *Under Lock & Skeleton Key*

"With dazzling sleight of hand, Gigi Pandian launches an enchanting new series . . . **a must-read**." —Deanna Raybourn

"An absolute sparkling gem of a book!" —Jenn McKinlay

"**A stand out mystery**. The fast-reading, suspenseful tale delights, with dashes of international spice and a powerful new heroine." —Sujata Massey

"**A perfect blend** of adventure and mystery." —Paige Shelton

"**A love letter to golden age mysteries** . . . will keep readers guessing whodunit until the very end." —Ellie Alexander

"Pandian is **this generation's queen of the locked-room mystery**! A whimsical confection." —Naomi Hirahara

"Gigi Pandian does it again! A wonderful new series full of twists and witty insights." —Aaron Elkins

Learn more about Gigi's next novel, *Under Lock & Skeleton Key,* at: www.gigipandian.com. Available for pre-order at book stores everywhere!

BOOKS BY GIGI PANDIAN

Jaya Jones Treasure Hunt Mysteries

In this *USA Today* bestselling series that reviewers compare to Elizabeth Peters novels and Indiana Jones movies, historian Jaya Jones solves present-day crimes linked to treasures from India's colonial history. Each book takes Jaya from San Francisco to a different foreign destination—so far Scotland, India, France, Italy, Japan, and Cambodia.

Artifact (Book 1)

Pirate Vishnu (Book 2)

Quicksand (Book 3)

Michelangelo's Ghost (Book 4)

The Ninja's Illusion (Book 5)

The Glass Thief (Book 6)

The Cambodian Curse & Other Stories (Locked Room Mystery Short Story Collection)

The Accidental Alchemist Mysteries

This paranormal mystery series set in Portland, Oregon, features a centuries-old female alchemist a gargoyle who was once stone before being accidentally brought to life through alchemy.

The Accidental Alchemist (Book 1)

The Masquerading Magician (Book 2)

The Elusive Elixir (Book 3)

The Alchemist's Illusion (Book 4)

The Lost Gargoyle of Paris (Book 4.5, a novella)

The Alchemist of Fire and Fortune (Book 5)

The Secret Staircase Mysteries

Meet Tempest Raj in this new gothic cozy mystery series. These locked-room mysteries pay homage to the deliciously devious mysteries from the Golden Age of detective fiction.

Under Lock & Skeleton Key (coming March 22, 2022)

ACKNOWLEDGMENTS

I'm grateful to so many people who helped this book come together. Thanks to Ellen Byron, Lisa Q. Mathews, and Diane Vallere for our wonderful brainstorm sessions; Mysti Berry, Lynn Coddington, and Lisa Hughey our virtual writing meet-ups; and my artist mom Sue Parman for encouragement on so many levels, including sending me sketches of gargoyles. Big thanks to my editorial team of Nancy Adams, Terri Bischoff, Amy Glaser, and Carmen King, and my agent Jill Marsal. Sisters in Crime, Crime Writers of Color, and Mystery Writers of America NorCal provided a much-needed sense of community during this challenging year, as did all of you who reached out to let me know my lighthearted escapist books were helping you get through a tough time. I so appreciate it! I had to learn to write from home (I'm normally a café writer) but I'm lucky to share a house with the most amazing and supportive guy. Thank you, James.

—August 2021

ABOUT THE AUTHOR

Gigi Pandian is a *USA Today* bestselling and award-winning mystery author, breast cancer survivor, and accidental almost-vegan. The child of cultural anthropologists from New Mexico and the southern tip of India, she spent her childhood traveling around the world on their research trips. She now lives in the San Francisco Bay Area with her husband and a gargoyle who watches over the backyard vegetable garden. A cancer diagnosis in her thirties taught her that life's too short to waste a single moment, so she's having fun writing quirky novels and cooking recipes from around the world. Her debut novel, *Artifact,* was awarded the Malice Domestic Grant, and she's won Anthony, Agatha, Lefty, and Derringer awards. Her books include the Accidental Alchemist Mysteries, the Jaya Jones Treasure Hunt Mysteries, and the Secret Staircase Mysteries (*Under Lock & Skeleton Key* comes out in March 2022). Read more and sign up for Gigi's email newsletter at www.gigipandian.com.

BB bookbub.com/profile/gigi-pandian
f facebook.com/GigiPandian
instagram.com/GigiPandian

CPSIA information can be obtained
at www.ICGtesting.com
Printed in the USA
LVHW081506051021
699577LV00016B/641